THE TULIP SHIRT MURDERS

A DELANIE FITZGERALD MYSTERY

HEATHER WEIDNER

SUMMARY

Private investigator Delanie Fitzgerald, and her computer hacker partner, Duncan Reynolds, are back for more sleuthing in The Tulip Shirt Murders.

When a local music producer hires the duo to find out who is boot-legging his artists' CDs, Delanie uncovers more than just copyright thieves. And if chasing bootleggers isn't bad enough, local strip club owner and resident sleaze, Chaz Smith, pops back into Delanie's life with more requests. The police have their man in a gruesome murder, but the loud-mouthed strip club owner thinks there is more to the open and shut case. Delanie and Duncan link a series of killings with no common threads. And they must put the rest of the missing pieces together before someone else is murdered.

The Tulip Shirt Murders is a fast-paced mystery that appeals to readers who like a strong female sleuth with a knack for getting herself in and out of humorous situations such as larping and trading elbow jabs with roller derby queens.

PRAISE FOR THE TULIP SHIRT MURDERS

"Smart, sassy Delanie is back for more murder and mayhem, and readers will enjoy every twist of Weidner's cleverly plotted mystery."

— LYNDEE WALKER, AGATHA AWARD-NOMINATED AUTHOR
OF LETHAL LIFESTYLES

~

"Weidner's latest Delanie Fitzgerald mystery delivers everything her fans have come to expect—a spunky P.I., a fast-paced plot, and a supporting cast of deliciously sleazy characters."

— MARY MILEY, AUTHOR OF THE IMPERSONATOR

~

"The intrepid Delanie Fitzgerald once again teams up with a computer geek and an English bulldog named Margaret for a hair-raising adventure in *The Tulip Shirt Murders*. You'll be hooked from page one."

— MAGGIE KING, AUTHOR OF THE HAZEL ROSE BOOK
GROUP MYSTERIES

~

"In Heather Weidner's latest mystery, *The Tulip Shirt Murders*, feisty private investigator Delanie Fitzgerald proves yet again that she can handle everything from bootleggers to murderers to strip club owners. Never shying away from dangerous situations, Delanie doggedly chases down clues until she flushes out the bad guys and solves the crime. *The Tulip Shirt Murders* is a fun read that will keep you laughing...and guessing...until the very end."

— FRANCES AYLOR, AUTHOR OF MONEY GRAB, A ROBBIE
BRADFORD NOVEL

~

"Stakeouts, disguises, and surveys lead PI Delanie Fitzgerald on the road to catch the Tulip Shirt Murderer."

— TERESA INGE, VIRGINIA IS FOR MYSTERIES & 50 SHADES OF
CABERNET AUTHOR

PRAISE FOR SECRET LIVES AND PRIVATE EYES

"Move over Kinsey, there's a new sassy PI in town – Delanie Fitzgerald. *Secret Lives and Private Eyes* is an impressive debut for Heather Weidner."

— DEBRA H. GOLDSTEIN, AUTHOR OF SHOULD HAVE PLAYED POKER

~

"If you like spunky sleuths and mysteries brimming with local color, then you'll love Heather Weidner's fun debut set in Richmond, Virginia!"

— MEREDITH COLE, AWARD-WINNING AUTHOR OF POSED FOR MURDER AND DEAD IN THE WATER

~

"Delanie is masterfully written. She's the strong woman readers cheer for."

DEDICATION

To Stan,
thanks for all the love and encouragement!

PROLOGUE

DELANIE FITZGERALD HOPPED ON THE STOOL AT LUCILLE'S LOUNGE TO get a better view of the guy she tailed. He leaned forward, inching closer to a raven-haired woman at the end of the bar. Delanie ordered a ginger ale and straightened her Lycra dress. The glances from the other male patrons let her know that it was the perfect outfit for this evening.

The man looked past his companion and stared at Delanie, who smiled and tossed her red curls over her shoulder. She sipped her drink and waited. The dark-haired woman moved on to talk to two guys at the pool table. The man picked up his drink and slid into the empty seat next to Delanie. That didn't take long, she thought.

"Hey, there," he said, moving in closer and brushing her shoulder with his.

"Hi," she said as she pressed her lips together in a half-smile.

"I haven't seen you in here before."

"I'm new in town. And this looked like a fun place to spend a Saturday night. I didn't want to stay home by myself."

"It's a friendly place," he said, signaling the bartender for a refill.

"I'll be back in just a minute. Don't go anywhere, and save my seat," she said, winking at the forty-ish man next to her.

"Hurry back," he said, leaning toward her.

A few minutes later, she pulled her barstool back. "Did you miss me?" A full drink greeted her on her return.

"Most certainly," he said, scooting his barstool closer to hers.

"Thanks for the refill. I didn't catch your name."

"It's Joey."

"Well, hello, Joey. I'm Misti," she said, sticking two fingers into her glass. When she pulled her hand back, the pearly white nail polish turned purple. She smiled and pretended to take a sip. "So, Joey, what do folks do for excitement around here in Mechanicsville? I've only been here a month or so. And I need some ideas for fun."

He leaned toward her again. Any closer, and he'd be sitting in her lap. "I like to have a good time. We could go somewhere quiet and have our own party. And we could talk about other things we could do next weekend."

"We could, but we just met," she said, batting her false eyelashes.

"Ask anything you want. I'm an open book."

Noticing the indent on his ring finger, Delanie/Misti smiled, "No wife or girlfriend waiting for you?"

"No. It's just me. Any misters in your life?"

"Nope," she said, licking her lips.

"What do you do?"

"I'm a counselor," he said, looking over his shoulder.

Before he could ask about her job, Delanie grabbed her drink and let it slide out of her hand. Most of it landed in Joey's lap. He jumped up, sopping up the liquid with several cocktail napkins.

"Oh, Joey. I'm so sorry," she said with her pouty lips. "It was damp, and it just slipped." When he didn't say anything, she continued, "Let's get out of here. We'll go somewhere where you can get out of those wet clothes."

He dropped a twenty and the balled-up napkins on the bar and rushed her to the front door.

He pushed the glass door open, and she said, "I'm over there." She pointed to the black Mustang. "How about I follow you to your favorite spot?"

"Okay. I'm in that white Accent."

Delanie slid in her car and locked the doors. She put her purse with its hidden camera on the dash. She followed Joey to a roach motel and made sure the camera caught him going in to register with that huge wet spot on his jeans. When he was engrossed in a conversation with the desk clerk, she backed out of the parking lot and floored it toward the interstate.

She would gladly turn over all the goods on the Rev. Joseph Milton, especially after he slipped something in her drink. Her first task tomorrow would be to complete her report for her client, the Southern Oak Avenue Church council. They suspected their assistant pastor had a secret life, and Delanie had the proof for them. Case closed on another Saturday night of pretend dating.

1

DELANIE HIP-CHECKED THE DOOR TO HER CAR AND SMILED AS SHE glanced back. The fortune cookie she'd had with yesterday's lunch predicted an exciting future. Maybe today?

She grabbed the mail from Saturday and headed inside the dark office suite. "Dunc, hey, Duncan," she yelled as she locked the front door behind her.

A muffled, "We're back here," came a voice from somewhere inside.

She followed the voice to the kitchenette, part of the two-office suite and conference room she shared with her partner, Duncan Reynolds, and his English bulldog, Margaret. Duncan supplemented his PI income with computer work. He referred to himself as a computer geek, his euphemism for a hacker. Delanie looked the other way and never asked about his sources because he was a wizard at getting computers to cough up information.

"Hey, what's up?" she asked.

"Breakfast. Want some?" he asked as he closed the microwave door and pressed several buttons.

"It's almost lunch time. What is it?"

"A bagel sandwich made with jalapenos, some leftover fish sticks, and bacon. Oh, and some cheese."

"No thanks," she said, hoping Duncan didn't see her wrinkle her nose. Fast approaching forty, Delanie and Duncan still had teenage junk food habits. But sometimes, Duncan's food concoctions surprised Delanie.

"I'm trying to add more protein to my morning diet," he said as he joined her at the table. Margaret, the brown and white log with legs, positioned herself under his chair to ensure she got any scraps that hit the floor.

She smiled. "I finished the swinging reverend case on Saturday night, and I emailed my report to the church council yesterday. What's new with you? I haven't seen you in a couple of days."

"I've been working on a website for a deli. Oh, we got a call this morning from a music producer about a job. He wants to avail himself of our investigative talents. He thinks he's being bootlegged."

"Interesting. Did he hear about us?"

"Our fabulous website," he said, winking.

She smiled again. "I'm going to check email. We'll call him when you're done eating," Delanie said.

"I'm done," he said, handing the last bite to Margaret and wiping his hands on his jeans. The computer whiz and his four-legged side-kick followed Delanie down the hall to her office. Duncan plopped down in her guest chair and flipped open his laptop. He jotted a phone number on a Post-it. "Here. Ask for Ian Barnes. He's the head honcho of marketing." Duncan's voice trailed off as Delanie pushed the speakerphone button and punched in the number.

After three rings, a female voice said, "It's a good day at RVA Recordings. How may I help you?"

"I'm returning Ian Barnes' call," Delanie said. After a "one moment please," a montage of on-hold music blared through the speaker.

"Barnes here."

"Mr. Barnes, this is Delanie Fitzgerald and Duncan Reynolds from Falcon Investigations. You called earlier about our services."

"Yes. I'd like you all to come out and talk with us about some issues we're having with our CDs from some of our artists. Can we meet tomorrow around three? We're on Broad Street across from the Science Museum." After a pause, she heard, "I look forward to talking with you."

"And we look forward to meeting you. Tomorrow at three works," Delanie said.

"Sounds good," he said before the line went dead.

"Are you available tomorrow?" Delanie asked Duncan.

"I'm working on a website for my client who owns a deli and wine shop. I'd rather focus my attention there if you don't mind. Do you really need me?"

"I always need you, but I can meet with them and take notes. Fill me in on what you know about Mr. Barnes' company."

"RVA Recordings is a small company based here in Richmond. Its bread and butter is bluegrass, country, and gospel, but they've recently created an R&B and rap offshoot. They rent studio time if you want to record your own music or create radio ads. And they have a pretty nice website."

"Anybody famous come out of their operation?"

"I'm sure they're probably popular and maybe even famous in bluegrass and gospel circles, but I don't recognize any of them. The website touts Doc Sutton, Hazel Crowe, and Sam Hartland as part of their operation. Hey look, on some Friday nights, they have jam sessions. Guests can bring instruments and play or hang out and listen."

"I'll check it out and let you know what I find. I forgot to tell you. I saw a banged up Honda Civic on Craigslist for fifteen hundred. I'm going to go look at it. After that idiot vandalized my car last summer, I was thinking about getting a beater for stakeouts."

"You sure it's worth what he's asking?"

"I think so. I looked at the CarFax and called my brother, Robbie, last night. The car doesn't look great, but it's old and gray. It would blend in when I want to spy. And it wouldn't be too conspicuous in most neighborhoods. I need something other than the Mustang some days."

"If you want a second car, that'd probably work. It's nondescript."

"Uh, Dunc. If I buy it, I'll need a ride. Would you be able to take a break and drive me over this afternoon to look at it?"

"Give me about an hour to finish some things," he said as he stepped into the hallway. Margaret waddled out after her best friend.

"Thanks," she said to her empty office.

AN HOUR LATER, DUNCAN PULLED HIS CAMARO INTO THE WALMART parking lot in Chester.

"The guy said to meet him in the row closest to the main road," she said.

"I don't see a gray car, but we can wait here a bit," he said, pulling out his laptop. Margaret snored loudly from the backseat. Delanie got out of the car to watch for the seller.

A Honda Civic with the radio blaring, followed by a blue minivan, eventually pulled in beside Duncan's Tweetie-bird-colored Camaro. A thin guy jumped out of the car. The woman in the driver's seat of the van sat ramrod straight with both hands on the wheel and kept the engine running. Delanie thought it odd that she stared forward and never turned her head.

The man said, "Delanie? I'm Dan Taylor."

"Thanks for meeting me, Dan. This is Duncan, my partner." Dan nodded and Delanie continued, "And that is?"

"My wife, Sandy."

After a long pause, Delanie asked, "Do you mind if I drive it around the lot?" She looked the car over, but refrained from kicking the tires. It looked okay for an older car. She'd have to see how it rides.

"Uh, okay. The window on the passenger side sticks a little bit, but if you pull on it when you push the button, it eventually goes up," he said.

"Not a problem," she said, sliding into the driver's seat. She adjusted the rearview mirror and the seat. After a quick lap around the parking lot, she stopped beside the minivan. The woman looked at her phone and paid no attention to anything around her. "Is your wife okay?" she asked.

"Yep," Dan Taylor said. "She's not too happy about me selling the car to get a motorcycle."

Delanie climbed out and looked under the car. She opened both doors, the hood, and the trunk. "It looks good to me. Will you take twelve hundred for it?"

"How about thirteen? And you can drive away with it today."

"Let's split it at twelve-fifty, and I'll take it off your hands."

"Deal," he said, shaking her hand.

After he passed her the signed title, Delanie waved to Dan Taylor as he clambered into the minivan that his wife had already started backing out of the space. Duncan rolled down the window, and Margaret climbed onto Duncan's lap and stuck her ample head out the window. Delanie didn't lean in too closely. Margaret was the slobber queen with a three-foot tongue.

"Well, it's all mine. And if you're nice, I'll let you borrow it."

"Lucky me," he said. "Do you want me to follow you back to the office?"

"Might not be a bad idea in case it's jinxed. I think I'll leave this in the alley. You can use it if you need to."

"See you back at the ranch," he said, rolling up the window.

THE NEXT DAY, DELANIE CROSSED THE POWHITE PARKWAY BRIDGE. SHE admired the river and the clear autumn sky, punctuated with puffy clouds. A freight train inched along on another bridge on its way to the Acca train yard. She switched lanes and exited the highway, where she found the recording studio across the street from the Science Museum.

A small bell tinkled when she pulled open the glass door, triggering the receptionist's wave. The receptionist twanged, "Thanks for calling. I'll let him know." She hung up the phone and smiled.

"I'm Delanie Fitzgerald. I'm here to see Ian Barnes."

"Hi. He's expecting you. Have a seat, and I'll let him know you're here," said the woman behind the desk who resembled a Disney pixie.

"Thanks," Delanie said, sinking down in the modern blob of a chair in the small reception area. Before she could get comfortable, the receptionist returned. "He's in the conference room. If you'll follow me." Delanie trailed her down a long hallway lined with framed photos of musicians and bands. She didn't recognize any of the names or faces.

The receptionist pulled open the glass door and ushered her in. Two men lounged in leather chairs, watching a rap video on the big screen that spanned the back wall. The rest of the room boasted a lot of glass and chrome, accented with swirls of light blues and browns.

The man in jeans and a khaki shirt stood, muting the sound. "Hi, Delanie. I'm Ian Barnes. This is Tim Peters, my attorney." He pointed to the other man in a tailored suit and expensive looking shoes. "Thanks for coming down. Have a seat. Would you like something to drink?" he asked.

"No, I'm fine, Mr. Barnes," Delanie said as the receptionist backed out and pulled the door closed. Sliding her chair to the teak conference table, Delanie opened her portfolio and readied herself to take notes.

"Call me Ian. I'm not sure how much you know about us," he said. "We're a boutique studio that my dad and uncle started about fifty years ago. Since then, we've added other genres and do some voiceovers for local radio and TV commercials."

"And how can Falcon Investigations help you?"

The attorney cleared his throat and shifted in his seat. "Ms. Fitzgerald, we have it on good authority that some of our recordings have been turning up in area flea markets and other locations. The only problem is there are more CDs and DVDs on the streets than what RVA Recordings licensed. We would like your firm to investigate this for us, so Ian can protect his investment."

"I'm sure we can help you. This is Falcon Investigations' fee structure, and this is our standard contract," she said, pushing the papers across the table. "After we take care of the administrative items, my partner and I can begin our research. Where have the CDs turned up?"

"Local flea markets and at a couple of music festivals," Ian said. "One of our bands reported seeing a guy selling them out of a truck at Cousin Billy's Bluegrass Jamboree last month."

"Do you have a phone number for the witness?"

"I do. And I think one of the guys in the band got a photo of the truck. I'll check."

The lawyer scanned Delanie's documents and then slid the contract in his briefcase. "I'll have this faxed to you."

"My partner, Duncan, and I will get started as soon as we have a ratified contract. Any ideas or guesses about the bootlegging?"

"No, not really. It's definitely not our downloads. It's only happening with the physical media. It seems to be across our entire portfolio and not just with our A-list artists. Please copy Tim on everything," Ian said, picking up his phone and tapping a message. Tim Peters pushed a business card toward Delanie.

"Will do," she said.

"Would you like a quick tour of our place before you go?" Ian asked, rising.

Delanie nodded, and the lawyer said, "I'm going to head back to the office. We'll talk next week." The record producer rose and shook hands with his lawyer.

Ian led Delanie down another hallway lined with more headshots and several gold records. At the end of the narrow walkway, he pushed open a door. A technician with headphones watched a bank of dials on his laptop. On the other side of the large picture window, a bluegrass trio played in a room covered with white acoustic tiles. A variety of instruments and microphone stands lined the perimeter of the room. It was more nondescript and utilitarian than what Delanie imagined for a recording studio.

"Jordan here makes sure everything is right in our recording studios. All the rooms are soundproofed, but he can see and hear everything. He's got one eye on the performers and the other on his computer." The other man nodded, but kept looking forward at the trio. Another young woman stepped in and handed the music producer a folder.

"Thanks, Kelli. Here are our marketing materials and contact information for you," he said, handing the packet to Delanie. Through the glass, they watched the trio warm up and launch into a song.

After two takes of a song, Ian said, "Let me know what you uncover. I want to get these jerks. They're ripping off the musicians and my company."

"I'll be in touch in a few days," she said. "My partner and I will do an in-depth investigation and send you a report of our findings."

On the ride back to the office, Delanie called Duncan. After his quirky voicemail message, she said, "Hey, Dunc. I met with Ian Barnes and his attorney. We should have a ratified contract later this week, but we can go ahead and get started with the research on the counterfeit CDs. And when I see you next, could you look at the Honda with me? I drove it around last night, and I heard a kerthunking sound coming from the back."

2

Delanie flipped on the coffeemaker and escaped to her office to make a call. Three rings later, she heard, "Thanks for calling Butterfly Blue."

"Hi, Robin. I need to ask you a favor. Can I bribe you with lunch in a trade for some information? I need to tap into your flea market knowledge." Delanie and Robin Kirby had been friends since economics class at Virginia Commonwealth University.

"Sure. I'm knee deep in some refinishing projects for a client, but if you don't mind eating in the workroom, you could bring lunch today or tomorrow. We need to catch up. It's been too long."

"Okay. I'll bring food. Is one-thirty today okay?"

"That works. I should be at a good stopping point. See you then."

Before she could move on to her email, Delanie heard the back door slam. Moments later, Duncan wandered in with Margaret at his heels. "What's up?"

"You would have liked the tour of the recording studio. They had all kinds of gadgets and computers. I watched a bluegrass band record some tracks, and I met Ian Barnes and his lawyer. They believe the company's CDs are being bootlegged and sold at flea markets. He also gave me the contact information for the band who spotted the hot items at a festival."

"Interesting," he said. "We'll figure out who's copying their stuff. I'm surprised that they're still selling CDs. It must be to an older audience."

"I'm going to talk to my friend, Robin, at lunch. She used to sell her furniture at local flea markets, and I was hoping she could give me an insider's view of what goes on."

"Give me what you have from the studio, and I'll do some research. What's wrong with your new car?"

"Oh, right. When I drove it back to the office, there was a weird noise in the back. It drove okay. And before you ask, there were no warning lights. It sounded like something rolling around. I checked the trunk, but didn't see anything."

"Let's go take a look."

Duncan drove Margaret around the parking lot several times in the Civic. He parked, climbed out, and crawled under the back of the car. Delanie sat down on the back steps, and Margaret plopped down on her feet to await the verdict.

He slid out and popped the trunk. He poked and prodded and pulled up the flooring. "I think I found it," he said, moving the jack.

"What?" she asked, jumping up to see what was inside. Margaret glared at her for disturbing her resting spot.

"There's a vase back here in the wheel well."

"Uh, oh," Delanie said. "That's not a vase. That's an urn."

"What's the difference?"

"The lid. Vases usually don't have sealed tops."

"Looks like you got something extra with your used car. You've been driving around with someone's Aunt Clara or Uncle Clem."

"Who would leave that in a car? Or who would carry an urn around in the trunk? That's a little creepy."

"People leave all kinds of things in their cars. Look, there's a funeral home plaque with a serial number on the base. You call the previous owner, and if it's not his, I'll see what I can find from this," he said, closing the trunk.

Delanie dialed the seller. Duncan took the urn inside, and Margaret followed close behind her guy.

"Hi, Dan. This is Delanie Fitzgerald. I bought the Honda Civic from you this week. I found something curious in the trunk, and I wanted to see if it was yours."

"If it's not legal, it's not mine."

"No, nothing like that. I heard a thunking noise and found an urn in the wheel well. I wanted to return it to the family."

"Did you say urn? Like with ashes?"

"I guess there are ashes. I didn't open it."

"It's not ours," he said, hanging up.

"Well, that was weird," Delanie muttered. Dan Taylor's behavior was as odd as his wife's had been during the test drive.

She found Duncan with his feet propped up on his desk. The urn, with a baseball cap perched on top, rested on the credenza.

"What's that all about?" she asked, pointing to the newly decorated urn.

"I'm calling him Bruce. He seemed like a Nationals fan. I thought he needed some personality. Any luck with the previous owner?"

"Nope. The car guy asked if what I found was illegal. Then he said the urn wasn't theirs and hung up."

"Well, leave Bruce here. I'll do some research. He has to belong to someone. Margaret and I are on the case."

Delanie rolled her eyes and left for her meeting with Robin.

After a quick stop for salads, Delanie parked in front of her friend's shop, which was bookended by a cell phone store and a smoothie shop in an older strip mall.

Filled with all kinds of brightly painted furniture and accessories, Robin's store reminded Delanie of the tropics. A tuxedo cat, curled up on a tasseled pillow in an orange side chair, guarded the front lobby. His eyes followed her as she moved across the room.

"Robin. Hey, Robin. It's Delanie," she called.

"Be up in a minute," came from the back area. The cat raised its head, yawned, and returned to its napping spot.

Robin came through the swinging doors, wiping her hands on a rag. "Hey, girl. It's good to see you. My sister's at a doctor's appointment. She usually works the front counter. Thanks for bringing lunch." Robin had her long brown hair pulled up in a twist – though several tendrils had escaped and curled around her oval face. Pastel colored paint splatters covered her sweatshirt and jeans.

"Your store is lovely. And your friend here is a good greeter," Delanie said, scratching the cat's head.

"That's Penguin, my guard cat. I got custody of him after the divorce. Come on back, and I'll show you what I'm working on. I love that I now have a work area back here. I don't have to tear down furniture in my dining room anymore."

"Wow. You've got all kinds of things going on," said Delanie. She handed her friend a bag.

"I'm painting a children's bedroom set for a little princess. Pink and purple with lots of polka dots are the order of the day. I love doing kid projects."

"How fun. Thanks for letting me pick your brain. Here's the deal. I have a client who thinks some of his merchandise is being counterfeited and sold at flea markets. What can you tell me about the flea markets in the area? Any rules or expectations I need to be aware of?"

Robin cleared an area on her desk and drug a guest chair over for Delanie. The two women dug into their salads.

After finishing a bite, Robin said, "Well, when you get a booth, you sign something stating that you're not selling any illegal or stolen items, but no one really does a lot of checking. I don't ever remember anyone asking about my wares. Anyway, you'll see all kinds of stuff. I wondered sometimes if some of the merchandise fell off a truck somewhere." After pausing for another bite, she continued, "There are a few fleas close to us. The old drive-in on Jefferson Davis Highway is an outdoor one called the Big Flea. Some of the sellers are private individuals, but most are pros who are there every weekend. Then there's another indoor one up Jeff Davis on the Chesterfield County side called Bev's Collectibles. Oh, and then there's one on the way to Amelia County. It's in a field next to a truck stop. The owner's wife rents spots by the day on Saturdays. I'm not sure if that one has a name. It's next to CJ's Truck Stop. There is one in Hanover too. And there's a really big one off I-95 near Fredericksburg."

"So what do the ones on this side of town sell?"

"They have anything you can imagine. When I had a booth, I was usually in the back with the other furniture vendors. But they have everything from clothes and appliances to sports memorabilia. You'd be surprised at what you find there."

"Do all of them cater to the same level of clientele?" asked Delanie.

"Sort of. Bev's tries to be more upscale. It's billed as antiques and collectibles. It's a lot of booths in an old department store. The drive-in one is outside and filled mostly with dealers trying to make a living. If you're looking for bargain basement prices, you won't find them at the ones on Jeff Davis. And if you hang around long enough, you'll start to recognize the regular vendors. The one out in Amelia County is more like a yard sale."

"Any words of warning before I go and visit?" Delanie asked as she wadded up her napkin.

"If you're buying, be aware of what you're getting and what you're paying. You could get soaked on the memorabilia stuff. There is also a lot of junk passed off as antiques. And if it's a collectible, make sure it has provenance with it. Sometimes, there are autographs that don't have any documentation. Lots of fake autographs are out there floating around at sales and on the Internet."

"You sold at that one?"

"At the Big Flea and sometimes at the one in Amelia. I used to have a booth at another one on Hull Street, but it closed a few years back. I get most of my stuff at yard sales and auctions. The prices are better. Hey, I'm going to a storage auction in a few weeks. Wanna go?"

"That sounds like fun. I like to see what people save and pack away. And it will be fun to hang out with you."

"Good. I'll text you the information. Enough about work stuff. So, what's new with you? Dating anyone interesting? Details. I want details!"

"Sadly, there's not much to tell. I dated this guy from Amelia

County last summer, but he turned out to be a less than sterling prince charming with a huge fear of commitment. C'est la vie. He's out of the picture. It's been all work lately. What about you?"

"The store and my projects keep me busy. Right now, Penguin is the only man in my life, and I like it that way."

"I love what you've done here. Thanks so much for letting me drop in. I appreciate all the insight on the flea market world. I think I'm going to visit some this week."

"Good luck with your investigation," Robin said as she moved her drop cloth and picked up a wooden paintbrush. "I'll text you about the auction." Delanie hugged her friend.

Outside, Delanie fired up the Mustang and checked her phone. Finding a "call me as soon as you can" message from Duncan, she told the car to call his cell.

"Hey, I think I solved your problem," he said.

"Which one?" she asked, making a right turn.

Ignoring her comment, he replied, "I called a guy I know at Barlow's Funeral Home. My buddy, Harold, traced the serial number on Owen's urn. He located what's left of the family."

"Okay, but who's Owen?"

"Harold said the ashes are a Mr. Owen Boseman's. There are some distant relatives in Lynchburg. I looked up the history on the car. It was owned by a Sharon Boseman Todd about ten years ago. I guess she put the urn in the trunk and forgot about it when the car sold."

"That's really sad," she said. "It's also unusual that the last owner didn't notice the sound coming from the trunk."

"Yep. He probably had the radio cranked up all the time. But at least we know who the urn belongs to. And we solved the mystery of the noise in the trunk. Be grateful that it wasn't the car acting up already. Margaret and I are going out for a late lunch. We'll drop the urn off at Harold's place. He'll make sure Owen gets back to Lynchburg."

Glad that she didn't have to worry about the noise in the trunk or the urn anymore, Delanie poked around on the Internet looking for used CDs on Craigslist and other local for sale sites. Not having much luck, she switched her search to area flea markets which turned into perusing Facebook.

Hours later, she closed the laptop and decided a visit to the Big Flea would be her best chance to find a lead on the RVA Recordings' bootlegged CDs.

3

THE NEXT SATURDAY, DELANIE CLOSED DUNCAN'S CAR DOOR AND adjusted her black ballcap with the hidden video camera while he pulled out Margaret's pet stroller from the car's trunk. Smaller than one for a baby, the pet model had a black mesh covering. Duncan clicked her leash to the handle and got her settled in for another midmorning nap. Walking the length of the flea market would have been more exercise than Margaret did in a month.

Delanie paid their admission, and they wandered up and down the rows of tables and temporary displays. Sports memorabilia and "as seen on TV" items seemed to be everywhere.

At a table covered with sports jerseys and hats, a large man with a bushy beard asked, "Who's your favorite baseball team?"

"The Nats. Hey, you've got quite a collection here," Delanie said as she picked up a red ballcap and pretended to look at the price. "Actually, I was looking for CDs and DVDs. I was hoping to find some old stuff. Do you have anything like that?" She put the cap down in front of a stack that sported logos for the New York Yankees.

"Nope. But you might want to try a couple of aisles over. The tech-nomedia stuff is over there," he said, pointing over his shoulder. "But

I've got jerseys and hats if you change your mind. Plus, I'm more fun than the guys over there." She smiled.

Delanie jogged to catch up with Duncan and Margaret who were already halfway down the next row. On Aisle D, they struck gold when they found electronics, speakers, and cellphones lining each booth. Midway down on the left, Delanie spotted a display with boxes of CDs. She reached up and pushed the button on her cap to start recording.

At the first table, she spotted used CDs of songs from the seventies and eighties. Moving on, she zeroed in on another booth across the aisle. Stacked boxes and bins outlined the perimeter of the booth and made a short wall around the tables. Turning her head slightly to pan the entire area, Delanie pointed the brim at the two men dressed in jeans and camo t-shirts. They hadn't shaved in days. Differing only in height, they shared the same square jaw and receding hairline.

The larger of the two asked, "Can we help you find anything?"

"Hi," said Delanie as Duncan and Margaret strolled ahead. "I'm looking for CDs and DVDs. You have a good selection. Do you mind if I have a look?"

"Nah," said the shorter one who sounded like he had a wad of something in his mouth. "Help yourself."

"Any Elvis or Johnny Cash?" she asked.

"I don't think so," said the other guy who could have been a linebacker. "We might have some country in this box."

Delanie browsed through several bins and recorded the inventory with her hidden camera. Bingo! She recognized some of the bands from the material Ian Barnes provided. None of the CDs had any branding for RVA Recordings on them. When she explored further, it looked like the covers were printed on low quality paper by an inkjet printer. "How much for these?" she asked, fingering the paper insert. The ink rubbed off on her hands.

"Seven a piece or two for ten."

"I'll take these four," she said, handing the short guy with sideburns a twenty.

He pushed the four CDs across the table.

"Do you have a bag?"

"Uh, nah," said the bigger guy. "But thanks for your business." She dropped the CDs in her purse.

"Oh, by the way, I have a website where I sell stuff. Do you have a card or number where I could contact you in case I wanted to buy more? Do you guys ever sell in bulk?"

"Maybe," said the big guy. "We don't have a website, but here's my cellphone number. We might be able to work something out." He jotted his number on the back of a crumpled receipt he pulled from his pocket.

"Thanks," she said, taking the slip of paper. Flipping over the fast food receipt, she saw handwritten, "Frank" and his cell number. "Hi, Frank. I'm Christy."

The tall one nodded and the men returned to their conversation. Delanie left and caught up to Duncan and Margaret at a nearby booth with a display of laptops and computer gadgets.

"Uh, hey," Duncan said. "He's got routers and blades."

Delanie didn't see any knives, so she guessed he was interested in something geeky. "Okay good. I bought some CDs. I'm going to walk down this way. Are you getting hungry? We can stop by the snack bar or grab something on the way back."

"Let's keep looking to see what else we can find. We can do lunch later," he said.

They strolled through the former drive-in movie theatre for about an hour without seeing any more CDs. Back on the housewares aisle, a large mirror caught Delanie's eye. It would be perfect in her living room.

"How much for the oval mirror?" she asked a lady with long blond hair styled like Marcia Brady.

"Two hundred."

"Would you take eighty?"

"One fifty is as low as I could go," said the woman, swatting at a fly buzzing in front of her.

"Hmmm." Before Delanie could decide, she heard a guttural growl from Margaret's stroller. Looking around, she spotted a fat tabby curled up in a nearby chair. Margaret barked and jumped around in the dog stroller. It lurched forward and tipped, dumping the dog on the asphalt. The cat screeched and darted through the booth. Margaret woofed several times. Before Duncan could react, she took off after the cat, dragging her tipped stroller behind her.

Duncan raced after the menagerie. Delanie had never seen Margaret, or Duncan for that matter, move so fast. People screamed and swatted at the cat, dog, and the black stroller.

Duncan caught up with Margaret two aisles over. After some mild scolding and lots of babying, he put Margaret back in the stroller. Delanie paid for a few broken items, and they walked purposefully to the front gate. The cat disappeared into the crowd.

After closing the car door, Duncan asked, "Did you get that recorded?"

Delanie nodded and turned the hat camera off. "I forgot to turn it off after the CD booth. It should be fun to watch you all in action."

"Margaret wasn't playing with that cat. The chase was on. Let's head back to the office to see what you captured on the recording."

After a quick stop at Taco Bell, they settled in the conference room to watch the chase video. Duncan skipped ahead to Margaret's romp after the cat. After watching it twice, Delanie suppressed a fit of giggles and asked, "Okay, what did we get on the two Bubbas at the CD booth?"

"Wait a second. I'm posting the Margaret clip on YouTube. Don't worry; no one will be able to trace it back to us. I deleted the GPS and routed it through several different IP addresses. It'll go viral."

Delanie shrugged at his geek speak. "I'm surprised there wasn't major damage from the cat chase. The broken vase and lamp totaled about twenty bucks. And I'm glad none of that happened near the CD vendors. I may have to go back for another visit. I'm pretty sure we're interested in those two guys. I recognized some of the bands from Ian's marketing stuff."

"Thanks for covering the cost of the broken stuff while I was tending to Margaret. I'll buy you lunch this week."

"No problem," she said.

"Give me the guy's cell phone number. I'll see what I can find on him," Duncan said.

"What do we know from all of your secret sources?" Delanie asked impatiently after Duncan had been clicking for only seconds.

"Hold your horses. The Internet may move that fast, but I don't." He clicked several keys and started a search on one of his dark web sites. "Here, the cell phone's registered to a Frank Emerson. He's thirty-three and lives on Branders Bridge Road in Chester. Let me see what I can find on the address." After a pause, he continued, "The address is under the name of Muriel Emerson."

"Wife?"

"Hang on. Let me see if I can find the tax assessment. There it is. She's his mother. Frank Jr. has a white Dodge pickup truck from 2005, a double-wide, and a small boat on a trailer, according to tax records. The property is on ten acres with a main house that's a little over twenty-one hundred square feet with two outbuildings. It was originally purchased by a Frank and Muriel Emerson." Duncan opened another browser window.

"Flip to Google Maps. I want to see it in street view."

The surrounding woods obscured the street view, so Duncan clicked on the satellite view. A long driveway and a farmhouse appeared on the screen. "I see several sheds, a trailer, and a barn," he said.

"It's pretty isolated," she said, leaning over his shoulder. "Duncan, you always amaze me with what you can find."

"Hey, give me twenty-four hours, and I'll be able to tell you what kind of toothpaste they use."

"So what did you find out about RVA Recordings and the bands that Ian Barnes mentioned?" she asked.

"The company made about one and a half million last year based on what I could find. Most of the talent is local to Virginia and the

Mid-Atlantic region. They've had one Grammy winner and a few gold and silver records over the years."

"What about the guys dealing CDs at the campground's music festival?"

"Oh yeah. I talked to one of the pickers in that band. He and his buddies spotted the hot CDs at Bill's Camp Emporium and Resort near Lanexa, Virginia. It's been home to Cousin Billy's Bluegrass Jamboree for the last twenty-eight years."

"Where's Lanexa?"

"It's down near Williamsburg. It's a big campground. The festival is huge with visitors from all over the country. It's a four or five-day thing, really big in bluegrass and gospel circles. There's lots of Internet buzz about it. Anyway, Lizard Coleburn...."

"Lizard?"

"Yep. He plays banjo and mandolin. He's an older musician. You'd probably like him."

Delanie was sure that was a jab about her last boyfriend and former rock musician, John Bailey, but she let it go. She smirked, but Duncan didn't seem to notice.

Duncan continued, "He plays with the Good Time Band. At this festival, they were checking out the vendor tents, and two guys in a pickup had t-shirts and CDs. Lizard spotted one of theirs at a marked down price, and he sent me this picture of the guys' booth. The CDs didn't have any RVA Recordings markings."

"The CDs that I bought didn't have any RVA Recordings' branding either, and the insert was done on a cheap printer. Let me guess. Those are our flea market boys."

"One has a ball cap on, and you can't see all of his face. But the other one was the guy you talked to today. Let me do some more research on Mr. Frank Emerson and his buddy. I should have something for you by tomorrow."

"Okay, thanks," she said, wandering back to her office.

Not wanting to hang out by herself, Delanie texted her friends Paisley, Robin, and her brother, Robbie, but they all had plans for the evening. She didn't call her other brother, Steve, a Chesterfield

County police officer who always seemed to be at work or en route to a crime scene.

It was too early for dinner. On a whim, she decided to do a drive-by of the Emerson address in Chester. She took the Mustang, punched the address in her GPS, and headed south.

A half-hour later, she found the matching numbers on a metal mailbox with the door hanging askew. Thick trees and a field separated the property from its nearest neighbor. The other side of the property butted up to more woods, and it looked like the backyard did too.

From the road, Delanie could see a farmhouse that was probably once white. The aluminum gutter on the front almost touched the ground. The long, gravel driveway led to a clearing between the barn and several outbuildings. Delanie resisted the urge to get out and snoop.

She did one more pass in front of the house and then pulled into the driveway. The turnaround, which she hoped made her look like a lost driver, gave her a minute to capture some quick video. Delanie switched off the camera and headed home, hoping Duncan had uncovered something more about Frank Emerson from his Deep Web sources.

4

DELANIE LET HERSELF INTO HER BUNGALOW, ORIGINALLY A MAIL-ORDER house from a 1939 Sears catalog. She loved the house's character and the boards inside that had part numbers inscribed on them. The house was smallish by today's standards, but it served Delanie well. And she had room to spread out later when she decided what to do with the empty upstairs rooms.

Closing the side door, she dropped her laptop, purse, and take-out on the round kitchen table that doubled as her home office and settled in for some research. Or perusing Pinterest for new recipes or art projects she'd probably never get around to trying.

On a whim, she fished out Frank Emerson's number from her purse. After four or five rings, she got a gruff voicemail message. Clearing her throat, she said, "Mr. Emerson, this is Christy Forbes. I met you last weekend at the flea market in Richmond. I really like the CDs I bought from you, and I was wondering if I could work out a deal to get more. Please give me a call."

Hours later, a buzzing sound woke Delanie from a dream. It took a second to realize she was on the couch in a room illuminated only by the TV. Her burner phone vibrated across the coffee table and the DVR clock said it was eleven forty-five.

She grabbed it before it went to voicemail. "Hello," she said.

"Uh, Christy, this is Frank. You called me about the CDs from the flea market."

"Oh yes. Thanks for getting back to me. I bought some of your CDs, and I really like the music and the quality of the recordings. I have an online store, and I was wondering if I could get more from you. You seem to have more than any of the other dealers I've looked at," she said, stretching the truth.

"Why do you want so many?"

"I'm trying to expand my business. You know old people still buy CDs. And they like traditional and gospel music. I thought maybe I could market them if I could get a bunch at a good price. I mean, I know you have to make money, but maybe we could work something out that benefits both of us. You know, something like wholesale."

"I dunno. Maybe we could get you a batch. Let me talk to my brother, and I'll call you back. We could probably do something for you."

"Okay," Delanie said. She clicked off, hoping she didn't spook him. Her cover story sounded a little thin even to her own ears. Seriously, who sells CDs to the elderly online as a basis for a business? The flea market guys were definitely up to something fishy. It was time for another visit to the flea market.

THE NEXT SATURDAY, DELANIE BOUGHT AN ICED VANILLA COFFEE FROM a drive-thru and headed back to the Big Flea. Stopping at a strip mall a few blocks away to get ready for today's spying, she slid on a long blond wig and tucked in her curls. She topped it off with her ball cap with the video camera. She tried to change her look today by adding an oversized blouse and a pair of baggy sweatpants. She overdid the makeup with blue sparkle eyeshadow and thick Cleopatra eyeliner.

Delanie hoped the Emerson boys wouldn't recognize her as the same shopper from last weekend.

Wandering up and down the rows of household goods, she leaned in and pretended to look at some wind chimes and suncatchers in a booth across the row from the counterfeiting guys. She spied on Frank Emerson, dressed in jeans and a camouflage tank top. He was talking to the shorter man from her last visit who was probably his brother.

Strolling over to Frank's booth, she pretended to adjust her cap as she clicked the button to record. The two men stopped their conversation when she approached the table covered in CDs. More boxes filled every inch of the booth. The smaller man asked, "Can I help you?"

Delanie smiled sweetly and turned her head slowly to capture the entire booth on camera. "Hi, there. I see you all have lots of CDs. Any pop stuff?" she asked, disguising her voice.

"Sorry, not today. You like hip-hop? We have lots of good music for sale in that box with the red label on it. The one closest to your feet."

Delanie nodded, and he continued, "When you're done, look through that box over there. You may be surprised at what you find in addition to the old stuff. We have a lot of new artists." Delanie stepped around two tables filled with DVDs, video games, and a few cell phones to get closer to one of the boxes the guy pointed at.

"Oh, okay. Thanks," she said, flashing her best smile. The men returned to their conversation about fishing gear, and Delanie slowly browsed through each box on the table to get an inventory of their latest wares. She picked out several and set them to the side. Other customers strolled by, but she was the only one interested in CDs.

After she'd thumbed through every box and plastic bin, Delanie said, "Well, you do have some good stuff. And so many new artists. How about these four? How much are they?"

The shorter of the two men said, "Normally, they're ten each, but I can do two for fifteen."

Delanie nodded and pulled two twenties from her wallet. The

taller guy handed her two fives from his front pocket. "Jesse, get her a bag."

"Thanks." She smiled at the brothers' famous outlaw names. Delanie did one more sweep of the booth and pointed the bill of her cap at the two men before she moved on to the next vendor. The brothers jacked the prices up this time. It must have been because of the addition of the Walmart bags.

Around one o'clock, she wandered over to the drive-in's concession stand for a bottle of water. Sitting at a plastic picnic table that had faded to a rosy pink, she checked her phone and enjoyed the sun on what was probably one of the final warm days of the season. She texted Duncan that she was going to hang around to see where the Emerson boys went after they closed shop.

DELANIE KILLED TIME BY STROLLING THROUGH THE ENTIRE FLEA MARKET twice. She bought a red leather clutch purse and an old copy of *The Maltese Falcon* by Dashiell Hammett. When she noticed vendors packing boxes and dismantling their booths, she strolled over to the row in front of Frank and Jesse's spot. Jesse loaded boxes of CDs on a hand truck, while the taller brother leaned on the table.

As the crowds thinned, Delanie lost some of her cover for spying. She slipped out to get her gray Honda while the brothers were busy tearing down for the day. Driving around the road that bordered the old drive-in's outer fence, she spotted a parking lot full of trucks and trailers that she could use for cover. She turned her car around and parked off to the side next to a large panel truck where someone had painted large black rectangles over the previous company's name. It looked like a document that had been redacted.

Vendors came and went with crates and tables. About the time she was ready to give up, she spotted Jesse pushing a dolly full of boxes to a well worn minivan. He stuffed them in the back and retreated to the area behind the fence.

Frank and Jesse returned about fifteen minutes later with more cartons. The younger man put the remaining boxes in the back of the white pickup truck. After a brief conversation with his brother, Frank climbed in the cab of his truck. He saluted with two fingers, and Jesse followed him out of the lot in the beat-up van.

Waiting a few moments to let a few cars get between her and the Emerson brothers, Delanie crept down the asphalt road that had seen better days. At the stoplight, she watched Frank turn right toward the interstate and Jesse veered left on Jefferson Davis Highway.

She made a snap decision to follow the younger brother toward Chesterfield County. The road used to be a part of Route 1, a central artery on the east coast until the interstate highways came through and choked the life out of it. She passed what was left of crumbling old diners and roadside motels that dotted the landscape between strip malls and fast food joints, many of which sported signs in Spanish.

Delanie tailed Jesse from several car lengths behind. She assumed he was heading to Chester until he made a quick left turn into a storage facility. Circling the lot, she parked near the building marked "office." Delanie ditched the blond wig and ran her fingers through her flattened red curls. Her real hair was hopeless, so she put on the ball cap to cover the disaster.

Walking behind several cars and around the first corner of storage units, she caught sight of Jesse unloading boxes into one of the larger units at the end of the row. Turning on the cap's camera, she recorded the number on the outside of the unit. From where she was standing, she could see boxes stacked four and five high. She counted fifteen gray plastic barrels behind the boxes, but she couldn't get a clear shot without the chance of him noticing her.

Giving up on peeping, Delanie returned to the car. By the time she edged closer to the curb, Jesse barreled out and headed south. She had to run a red light to keep him in sight. Now that he had unloaded his stuff, he was in a hurry to get somewhere. He zigged and zagged across several lanes and did about sixty through thirty-five mph zones on old Route 1.

Delanie almost lost him when he turned without signaling into a convenience store lot. She parked at the Hardees next door and watched. Jesse came out a few minutes later with a bag of chips and a case of beer.

Pulling out of the lot, he gunned the engine in the old van. It sputtered and backfired before it gained enough speed to keep up with traffic. Delanie lingered at a safe distance. Then she raced through the back roads of Chesterfield County, trying to keep Jesse Emerson's blue van in sight.

Kicking up rocks and gravel, the van plowed down the driveway toward the farmhouse. Parking on the other side of the woods on the road's shoulder, she grabbed her keys and phone and trekked along the tree line paralleling the Emerson property. Nothing was going on in the front yard, so she walked farther back in the woods to where she could see what was behind the farmhouse. Delanie spotted the van parked between two outbuildings and a small green sedan. Four or five chickens scratched around the yard.

Hearing the rumble of an approaching vehicle, she ducked behind a tree and watched the chickens scatter. When the truck pulled next to the car and van, she stepped out and used her phone to record Frank climbing out of his vehicle. She counted a barn, double-wide, and five sheds on the property. Frank Emerson unlocked the shed closest to his truck and carried in two boxes. He kicked the shed door, and it stayed open long enough for him to enter.

Jesse exited the barn and joined his brother in the shed. Before Delanie could get situated for her stakeout, they stepped back into the daylight. Frank stopped to padlock the door, and the brothers disappeared through the house's back door.

After the slam of the screen door, all she heard were a few birds chirping and a generator's hum in the distance. Delanie waited. She heard a dog bark and another one answered. This was the part of the job that she liked the least. Her mind tended to wander when stakeouts became boring. To keep from zoning out, she counted trees, outbuildings, and vats stacked next to the outside of the barn. The chickens returned to the yard, accompanied by several guinea hens.

She didn't see the brothers reappear, but several trucks sped down the driveway and stopped near the barn. Their owners knocked on the back door of the house and then disappeared inside. The new arrivals didn't stay long. They all left toting gallon jugs. She hoped the camera on her phone was high res enough to record the license plates from her hiding place.

At about the time Delanie's legs began to stiffen, she spotted Frank and Jesse following a man to his car. They talked for a while. Frank leaned into the car. He stepped back when the guy handed him something and waved as he backed down the driveway. She pocketed her phone and headed back to her Civic.

Her pants snagged on a branch, causing Delanie to face plant on the ground in the leaves and sticks. A scuffed knee peeked out of the tear in her pants. Before she could tend to her injury, the brothers' heads turned toward her hiding place, and her heartbeat raced. Delanie didn't wait to see if they ventured toward the noise in the woods. She got up and ran as fast as she could in baggy pants to her car.

She sped off, leaving a cloud of dust and gravel in her wake. No one followed her. She'd have time to will her heart rate back to normal after she made it to the highway.

5

THE NEXT DAY, DELANIE GRABBED THE TRAY OF ICED COFFEES AND SLID into the truck's cab next to her friend, Paisley Ford, perched in the middle of the truck's bench seat. She bumped Paisley's hip, and the blond scooted over to make room.

"Here," she said as she passed a coffee to Paisley and her friend, Robin Kirby, who sat behind the wheel.

Delanie pulled her sunglasses out of her hair and clicked the seatbelt in place. The three hadn't hung out together in a while, and they planned to catch up during their ride.

"Ready?" Robin asked as she found first gear and coaxed the truck and its white trailer toward the highway.

"Road trip," Paisley said. Her long curls bobbed in time to a Katy Perry song on the radio. "This is going to be fun. Thanks for asking me to come along. I've never been to an auction before."

Robin signaled and changed lanes. "I appreciate you both helping me. I'm hoping to find things cheap there for the new store. And you haven't seen the storage units yet, so don't thank me until we're on our way home."

"So exactly what are we doing today?" Paisley asked, as she ran her fingers through her hair and checked her lipstick in the rearview mirror.

"We're looking for sturdy furniture and accessories I can clean up and refurbish. We're going for higher end stuff. I don't want boxes of household goods or other people's old clothes. No old TVs, dirty underwear, or broken down mattresses."

"Eww. Gross. Now I can't get the thought of creepy crawlies and bed bugs out of my head. Let's talk about something else. Expecting any cute guys to be at the auction?" Paisley asked as she leaned forward and changed the radio station when a commercial blathered on about refinancing mortgages.

"Well," Robin said, "It's usually an older crowd at these auctions. Most of the people own thrift or antique stores. Unfortunately, there aren't too many guys there our age. Also, the buyers don't socialize much. Most people bid, get their winnings packed in their trailers, and head home. It's not a sociable group. They're quite competitive. So what's new with you guys?"

Delanie shrugged, and Paisley smiled and said, "I met a new guy."

"Hey, what about Kyle?" Delanie asked. "I thought he was the love of your life."

"Except that it turned out that he wasn't," Paisley replied. "I've been going out with Geoffrey for a few weeks now. He works at an insurance firm downtown. We've gone on two dates, and it's been fun so far. He's more sophisticated than his predecessor."

"No more Kyle?" Delanie asked as she scrolled through email on her phone.

"Oh, that was months ago. Also, he was a little bit younger than I was." Delanie glared at her over her sunglasses. "Okay," Paisley continued. "He was quite a bit younger than I am, and we didn't have much in common after all. I'm so over the frathouse lifestyle. Geoffrey likes the theatre and the ballet. And he doesn't ask me to split the dinner tab all the time. What's with it with the guys in the dating pool lately?" Paisley continued before her friends could reply. "I'm tired of being the only adult in the relationship."

"I wouldn't know," Robin replied. "After Joseph and I called it quits, my projects have been my focus. I haven't been on a date in a long time. I wouldn't know how to act on one."

"So, Delanie. What about you? When do we get to meet the new guy you've been seeing?" Paisley asked.

"Past tense. It didn't work out," she said, looking up from her phone. Last summer, a tell-all writer had hired Delanie's firm to research a tip that a John Bailey from rural Virginia was really Johnny Velvet, lead singer of the eighties band, The Vibes. When Delanie got too close to John Bailey, he developed cold feet and hightailed it out of town. Her heart had been bruised, and Delanie had sworn off romance for the foreseeable future. She'd learned a hard lesson – never date people you're investigating.

Robin slammed on the brakes, and Delanie caught herself before crashing into the dash. Paisley made a huffing sound and checked her lipstick and hair again in the rearview mirror.

"Sorry about that. I'm glad the trailer has good brakes," Robin said, taking a deep breath. "I'm not sure why we have this sudden backup in the middle of nowhere on a country road. We won't see civilization again until we get to Farmville."

"It must be an accident," Paisley said, leaning forward to peer out the truck's front window. "I don't see anything."

The traffic crawled for miles in the westbound lane while the eastbound side hummed along. Twenty minutes and two radio stations later, Robin rolled up next to two men in fluorescent traffic vests and white hardhats. The older of the two, in an orange golf shirt, leaned toward the window with a blue piece of paper. "Sorry for the inconvenience," he said. "We're conducting a traffic survey as part of the road improvement work along 460 West between Amelia County and Farmville. The information about the survey is on this sheet. We're asking one person from each vehicle to either mail in the form or go online and complete it. This will help us with the final proposal for the Department of Transportation for improvements to this stretch of the highway," he said as the other man with the Goth look marked something on his clipboard.

"Thanks," Robin said as she gritted her teeth and started rolling forward. The men moved on to the beige car behind her. She closed the window and accelerated to make up some time.

"Well," Paisley said. "What year is this? You'd think they'd have a better way of doing a survey than creating traffic jams in the middle of nowhere. And why are they talking to one car at a time? This is stupid."

Robin shrugged. "Hopefully, we'll be okay for time. It's not that far from here. But you're right. Whose brilliant idea was it to collect data this way? Could you put this over there somewhere? I'll get to it when we get back home. And maybe, I'll comment on the way they blocked traffic," she said as she passed the blue sheet to Paisley, who handed it to Delanie.

Delanie read the survey information and a brief synopsis of the multimillion dollar plan to widen the road and to add a rest stop. She dropped the flyer on the dashboard as Robin pulled into the storage facility's packed parking lot. Whoever designed the traffic stop should be drawn and quartered.

AFTER SOME FINAGLING, ROBIN MANAGED TO GET HER TRUCK AND trailer maneuvered in the small, L-shaped parking lot. Locking the cab, she said, "I need to go and register to bid at the office. I'll be right back." Delanie and Paisley found a place to stand by the facility's metal gates. Rows of low buildings with corrugated doors stretched across the property like abandoned trains on parallel tracks. Pairs and singles of older men congregated around the outer perimeter of the parking lot. They drank coffee and chatted with each other. None offered any kind of greeting to the women – only sideways glances.

Robin returned with a list of units for sale and the bidding rules. The women merged into the small crowd milling about with cell phones and insulated coffee cups. Robin flipped through the pages, folded them, and stuck them in her back pocket. "Let's wait here," she said, directing Paisley and Delanie to a spot in front of a rusty metal door.

Delanie felt overdressed in jeans and a sequined t-shirt. Most of the men sported ballcaps and t-shirts advertising everything from trucks to chainsaws. Other than a few stares, the other bidders seemed to ignore Delanie and her friends.

"What's the matter?" whispered Paisley to Robin.

"We're definitely the outsiders. Lay low and don't stare at anybody. And don't act too interested in any of the storage lockers. Follow my lead. Sometimes the good ole' boys jack the prices up to drop an overpriced unit on an unsuspecting bidder. The locals often make it clear they don't like strangers muscling in on their territory. They're not always a friendly bunch." Paisley wrinkled her nose in disapproval.

Delanie and Paisley stood on the outskirts when the viewing began on the four units. A guy in an auction company t-shirt cut the locks off the doors while the crowd formed an impromptu line and filed by the open storage areas. The auctioneer's staff hovered like hawks ready to jump on anyone who moved too close to the merchandise.

Robin landed in a bidding war with two men old enough to be her father for the first storage locker, but she lost when the price went above three thousand dollars. She ignored the second unit, filled with stuffed animals, housewares, and two mattresses. An older man with a white Santa beard won that one for a bid of six hundred and fifty dollars.

Robin didn't bid on the third option either. It was filled with over-stuffed garbage bags, old TVs, and several more mattresses. The Santa look-alike won this one for a hundred and twenty dollars.

Bidding on the last unit started at fifty dollars, and the same two men from the first unit kicked off the frenzy. It was up to four hundred dollars before Delanie had time to blink. She watched as Robin stood on the sidelines. She had her arms crossed and her feet planted. The bidding jumped to six and then eight hundred in a matter of seconds.

Robin raised her finger and said, "One thousand."

Someone in the crowd coughed and another mumbled as the

heavier of the two older guys said, "Eleven." Someone in the back snickered.

He and the other guy volleyed back and forth, and the price jumped to sixteen hundred.

The bidding stalled for a moment until Robin said, "Eighteen."

Delanie smiled. It looked like Robin would win. Then the two men started again, upping the bid in ten dollar increments.

Finally, Robin, said, "Twenty-three hundred." All was quiet except for the auctioneer who tried to prod the other two back into the action. Both men shook their heads, and the auctioneer replied, "Sold to the little lady, bidder one-o-six."

"Whooo hooo," Paisley yelled. "You go girl!"

Robin glared at her and then said, "You guys start going through the boxes while I settle up at the office. I'll be back in a minute with the truck, and we can get packed up." The crowd dispersed as the winners followed the auctioneer to the office.

Paisley rummaged through boxes and bins while she waited for Robin to return. "This one is full of Beanie Babies, and that one contains a box of coins. This looks like a score!"

"Better than what I found – three suitcases filled with dirty clothes from twenty years ago, and not the cool or vintage kind – just stinky. I hope Robin can make a profit on this stuff."

"I'm really after the furniture," Robin said, rounding the corner and stepping into the small room, lit only by a light bulb on a chain. "If there's anything of value, I can sell that in the store. The collectibles will go fast online. Let's get this trailer loaded, and we'll be on our way."

It took the three of them two and a half hours to load all of the heavy furniture and boxes. After they wedged the last box in, Robin flipped the metal latch and locked the trailer door to secure it for the ride home.

"Oh, pooh," Paisley said. "That's the third nail I've broken today. I thought this would be more like shopping. I had no idea about all the sweat and dust and funky smells. And the people around here aren't all that nice with their sneers and dirty looks."

"Hey, I warned you," Robin said as she checked the trailer hitch. "I think we're about ready. You all want to grab lunch on the road?"

"I'm a mess," Delanie said. "We passed a McDonald's on the way in. Are you all okay with eating in the truck? I don't want to get close to people."

"Hey, we're people," Paisley snorted.

"But, you're as dusty as I am," Delanie said with a wink. Paisley smirked and slid back in her seat.

"Mickey D's it is," said Robin.

"This definitely makes me appreciate my day job. I'm going to be sore tomorrow from all the lifting and repacking. If you do this a lot, you're going to need a crew," Delanie said.

"I appreciate you two helping me. It's usually just me," Robin said. "It's a lot of work, but it's usually worth it. Buy low, refurbish, and sell high."

"I'm glad we didn't find anything creepy in the locker like a dead body," said Paisley.

"I've heard stories about drugs and snakes, but thankfully, I haven't seen any corpses. But, we're prepared if it happens. We've got Delanie, girl PI," said Robin.

Delanie smiled, but hoped there wouldn't be any more dead bodies in her near future. She had had enough with the mayor's murder last summer.

6

DELANIE DROVE THE CIVIC SLOWLY PAST THE EMERSON COMPOUND AT dusk the next day. She cruised along until she found a pull off that looked like a fire road leading into the woods. She grabbed her camera bag and hiked through the forest near the spot where she tore her pants earlier in the week. Delanie found a tree big enough to lean on and pulled out her camera and zoom lens.

Satisfied no one was looking toward the woods, she poked her head out and used her lens to spy. Today, somebody had propped the barn doors open. Three trucks and a car pulled up while she stood watching. All of the drivers made a beeline for the barn. She snapped pictures of the newcomers and their license plates. Like the last time, these people didn't stay long on the property.

She shifted her weight and leaned back against the tree. A generator rumbled and a bird cawed in the distance. Delanie hadn't seen the Emerson brothers today, but their truck and van were parked in front of the barn that could use a fresh coat of paint.

At about the time when she straightened up and stretched to ward off the kink in her back, she spotted Frank's large frame slip out of the barn. He hiked to the nearest shed and unlocked the door.

After stooping to pick up something, he propped the aluminum door open.

The taller brother disappeared into the barn again and returned seconds later with two boxes. It was the same routine as before. He trekked back to the shed. When he exited, he relocked the door. She snapped a couple of pictures as he retreated to the barn.

After a long period of inactivity, she picked her way carefully through the dark woods back to her car. She couldn't chance someone seeing her phone's flashlight bobbling along the tree line.

Twilight had faded by the time she climbed in and locked the door of the Civic. She missed the ambient light of civilization. And the night sounds, a cacophony of tree frogs and an occasional owl, gave her the willies. She started the car and drove about a quarter of a mile before she put her headlights on. She let out a breath she didn't realize she was holding. The flea market brothers were guilty of more than bootlegging music. She hoped Duncan could find out more about the brothers' visitors. A lot of traffic frequented that property on a lonely country road. And bootlegged CDs couldn't be the main attraction at the Emerson farm.

On the way home, Delanie gripped the steering wheel and sat straight in her seat when the piercing lights of a large vehicle lit up the inside of her car. The other vehicle backed off slightly, and she sped up and changed lanes to increase the distance between them. The dark SUV followed her onto Route 288 and kept about a car's length behind her.

With her heart pounding and echoing in her ears, she swerved and exited at Hull Street Road. On a whim, she did a U-turn and drove to the police station near the Swift Creek Reservoir.

Under the street lights, Delanie could tell it was a black or navy blue Chevy Suburban. She pulled in front of the police station in a small strip mall and parked. She left the engine running. The driver of the SUV sped off. The bent back license plate didn't lend a clear view of the number.

While Delanie waited to see if the SUV would reappear, she took several deep breaths. She needed a clear head to figure out her next steps. The dark SUV that had tailed her from Chester dredged up memories of the guy who stalked her and fractured her ankle last summer. She had learned her lesson about antagonizing stalkers. But she wished she'd had a chance to get the plate numbers off the dark colored Suburban.

~

THE NEXT MORNING, THE PHONE VIBRATED ACROSS DELANIE'S nightstand. It took her a moment to realize what the noise was. She rolled over and said, "Hello."

"What are you doing?" Duncan asked.

"Sleeping."

"At ten-thirty in the morning? Late date night?"

"No. I was in the woods next to the Emerson house until about nine o'clock last night. And then I got spooked on the way home. An SUV followed me for several miles. I detoured to the police station and stayed there until I was sure no one was tailing me."

"Did you get the license number?"

"No, it was bent or something, and he drove off too quickly. Before you say anything, it wasn't my imagination. It was definitely a tail. It followed me all the way from Courthouse Road to the police substation on Hull Street."

"Sorry for waking you then. I looked at all the video and pictures you sent. I'm working on getting names for all the visitors from their license plates. That shouldn't take too long. But until we know more, it's just a list of names. I did notice two of the vehicles were on the property on multiple days. It'll give us something to start with. Soon we'll know their friends, clients, or poker buddies. You coming into the office today?"

"Probably after lunch. Why?"

"Nothing. I thought we could brainstorm what we know about the flea market brothers for RVA Recordings. Have you sent them an update yet?"

"Nope. I was going to work on it today."

"Sounds like a plan. See you later."

Delanie rolled over and pulled the pillow over her head. The phone buzzed again.

"What? Did you forget something?" she asked without looking at the screen.

"Uh, no. I was calling to talk to you about a job. This is Chaz."

"I'm sorry, Chaz. I thought it was my partner calling again. How are you? I haven't heard from you in a while." Chaz Smith, a local strip club owner, had hired Falcon Investigations to find some dirt on the former mayor. When the politician was murdered, Chaz became the number one suspect. Delanie spent most of last summer helping Chaz clear his name and capturing the murderer who turned out to be her stalker.

"I'm just dandy. It's been busy, but that's always good in my business. You worry when it's slow and quiet. Anyway, I need your help again on something. Do you have some time to meet me today? Lunch? Dinner?"

Delanie wasn't sure she wanted to get involved with Chaz again, but he always paid in cash, so it couldn't hurt to meet him to see what he wanted. "Lunch is good. Where do you want to meet?"

"How about the Jumping Bean Cantina in Carytown? Does twelve-thirty work for you?"

She glanced at the clock on her nightstand and replied, "That's fine. I'll see you then."

"Good. I have a friend, and she really needs your help. Bye."

Delanie texted Duncan that she'd be in after she met with Chaz. His quick response was a dollar sign and a smiley face.

Duncan interrupted her thoughts when he texted back, *Him again? The man, the myth, and the legend in his own mind?*

She sent him a smiley emoticon and dragged herself out of bed. After a quick shower, Delanie dressed and drove downtown to see what the owner of the Treasure Chest, Richmond's Finest Gentleman's Club, wanted. With Chaz, it could be anything.

Surprised that she'd found an on-street parking spot at lunch time, Delanie left the Mustang about a block from the Jumping Bean Cantina. Teal and yellow umbrellas twisted in the breeze in front of the restaurant, which was wedged between a flag store and a Celtic gift shop in the eclectic part of town.

Stepping into the dimly lit alcove, Delanie said, "Hi. I'm meeting a client for lunch." It took her eyes a minute to adjust to the dark interior.

The hostess in the off-the-shoulder blouse said, "Two then? Follow me."

Delanie finished her iced tea and responded to most of her emails before she spotted Chaz walking her way. Wearing a shiny shark-gray suit with a red dress shirt, unbuttoned at the collar, the strip club owner hadn't changed at all since Delanie last saw him. His highlighted hair hung in a trendy style, carefully cut to look unkempt.

"It's good to see you," he said, putting keys, smartphone, and designer sunglasses on the table. He shook her hand before he slid into the booth. "It's been a while. Things have calmed down since the mayor's murder, so it's pretty much back to normal for my world. How about you?"

"Hi, Chaz. It's good to see you too. Did you ever open your second club?" She first met Chaz when he hired her to look into suspicious delays in getting permits to open his second establishment near the Museum District. That led to checking into the mayor's personal life and eventually, working to find the truth when the mayor was murdered. Delanie shook off the bad memory of the mayor's killer, whom she injured when he took her hostage. She hoped this new case wouldn't be like the last one.

"Uh, no," he said. "I sold that property to a guy in the neighborhood who's gonna turn it into an art gallery. The neighbors weren't thrilled with me moving in. I thought it would be better if I looked for property elsewhere. They were opposed to my establishment from the get go. Lesson learned – I'll try something different next time. You doing okay?"

She nodded, and he continued, "I need your help again. There's a girl I know who was murdered back in April. The roommate found her body when she returned from an out of town trip. They arrested her boyfriend, but the girl's family is convinced he didn't do it."

Chaz was anything but predictable. Some of his marketing stunts stretched community standards beyond the limits, and he often ran afoul of the law. But Chaz Smith had a softer, caring side that he didn't show very often. Even with his eccentricities, he grew on Delanie after a while.

"How did you know her?" she asked, wondering if this girl was one of his exotic dancers. She racked her brain to remember the details of the murder.

"Her name was Emily Menendez. She was the granddaughter of the woman who was our live-in housekeeper, Alma Sanchez. Alma cooked and cleaned for my parents for years. And she stayed with me when my parents were out of town, which was all the time. Alma was part of our family until she retired after I went to college. We kept in touch over the years. Emily had an apartment with a friend near the Poe Museum. I still remember her with pigtails. She was a sweet kid. It's hard to believe she's gone."

"Why did the police focus on the boyfriend?"

"He didn't have an alibi. His name is Justin Martin. He admits meeting Emily at her place the night of the murder. They hooked up and watched a movie. He said he had to go to work, so he headed out about six the next morning. Her roommate returned to find a bloody mess in the apartment and Emily was dead. His DNA was all over the place. And so the cops zeroed in on the boyfriend."

The waiter interrupted to take Chaz's drink order. When he left, Chaz continued, "The damning part is there were a whole bunch of witnesses on the day before who watched a loud fight between Emily and Justin at a party over another guy Justin thought she was seeing on the side. When he was arrested, he swore they had made up after the party. The police are convinced an amateur tried to make Emily's murder look like a break-in."

The waiter refreshed Delanie's tea and brought Chaz a Corona with chips and dip. Chaz ordered the lunch platter, which sounded huge when compared to Delanie's taco salad.

Dunking a chip into the ranch dip, Delanie asked, "Why do you want me to help Justin when the police are convinced they have their guy?"

"For Alma. She was so upset over Emily's death. She liked Justin and hoped they would eventually marry. Alma called me a few weeks after the murder. I hadn't heard from her in months. She wanted my advice about what to do for Justin."

"Why is she so sure of his innocence?"

He leaned forward and dipped a chip in the dip. Licking the white dip off the chip, he dunked again and shoveled the rest of it in his mouth. Losing her appetite, Delanie pushed the chip basket closer to Chaz.

"Alma said she talked with Justin, and she knows he's telling the truth. The fight was all a misunderstanding. Some girl started a rumor about Emily, and Justin blew up when the guy in question showed up at the party. Alma believes Justin loved Emily and would never hurt her."

"Why did the police think the burglary was faked?" she asked.

"Emily was stabbed multiple times. Her room was trashed, but the roommate couldn't find anything missing. If she surprised a burglar, why would there be so much destruction and violence when nothing was taken? There was blood everywhere in her room. But only her belongings were ransacked. The other girl had valuables in her room too. Get this – none of the neighbors heard a thing."

A waiter put their lunches on the table. Chaz crammed half of his burrito in his mouth. After a couple of chews, he continued with a full mouth, "I hired my attorney, Rick Dixon, to represent Justin. You remember Rick, don't you? Give him a call. He'll let you have copies of the files."

"If you believe the boyfriend's innocent, my partner and I will look into it for you." She took a Falcon Investigations' contract out and pushed it across the table.

Chaz pulled out an expensive pen and signed it without reading it. "Here," he said, pushing the papers toward her and a Treasure Chest envelope stuffed with a stack of twenties. "Here's a deposit. Let me know when you need more," he said, returning to the rest of his burrito.

"Thanks for the new assignment. I'll call Mr. Dixon this afternoon."

A blast of autumn heat greeted her when she left the restaurant. Carytown was alive with trendy people and shops, and the weather was perfect. Chaz's Hummer, wrapped in bikini-clad women, advertised his downtown club. There was nothing subtle about Chaz Smith.

During the ride back to the office, she arranged a meeting with Chaz's attorney and called to break the news to Duncan that the strip club owner was back in their lives. The money in the Treasure Chest envelope would make Chaz's quirky habits and bad table manners more palatable.

7

TWO DAYS AFTER HER MEETING WITH CHAZ, DELANIE PUT FOUR BOXES of copies from the attorney's office in the back of the Mustang and one in the passenger's seat. She had spent the better part of the morning getting the scoop on Emily Menendez's boyfriend from attorney Rick Dixon and his paralegal. Their angle was that everything was circumstantial. No physical evidence linked Justin to the stabbing death of the young woman.

Delanie pushed the button and told the car to call Duncan. "Where are you? Chaz's lawyer sent me home with boxes of documents about Emily's murder for us to wade through."

"I'm giving Margaret a bath, and I'm heading in to the office as soon as I dry off. What are you doing? Hold still and quit wiggling."

Stifling a laugh, she said, "I'm heading in, too. We've got enough work here to last us a week. Do you want me to bring lunch?"

"This is for your own good," he said. "Uh, yeah. Lunch is good. Bring something for Margaret too. After this wrestling match, we'll both need a treat and probably a nap."

On the way to the interstate, Delanie spotted a black SUV in her rearview mirror. When she changed lanes, it pulled up on her passenger side. She couldn't see the driver through the tinted windows.

Gunning the engine when the light changed, Delanie zipped to the ramp for the Downtown Expressway. When she turned, the SUV sped past her, but she didn't get a good look at the vehicle's bent license plate.

Taking a deep breath, Delanie tried to calm the butterflies in her stomach. There were hundreds of black SUVs in the metro Richmond area. Memories of last summer and her stalker came flooding back. She shook off the uneasy feeling and turned up the radio. She felt sheepish for being so jumpy, but she did check her rearview mirror every few minutes to see if anyone else seemed to be following her.

After doing a quick drive-thru for lunch in a bag, Delanie parked in the alley behind the office next to the gray Civic. Letting herself in the back door, she relocked it and flipped on the lights.

About twenty minutes later, she heard, "So what's for lunch?"

"Burgers and fries. I hope it's not too cold. I got a plain cheeseburger for Miss M. Did she survive the bath?"

"Barely. Margaret soaked both of us. She was determined not to go in the tub. She's a lot of deadweight when she refuses to move," he said, setting pieces of the burger on the wrapper down on the floor next to the table. Margaret wolfed down the food, and Duncan grabbed the yellow paper before she ate that too.

"Well, Margaret, you smell better and look fabulous," Delanie said, patting her on the head. "So what's new with the Emerson brothers? The boxes I got at Rick Dixon's office for Chaz's case are in the car. I figured we'd do the report for RVA Recordings first before we jump into the lawyer's files."

"Well, I have names and license plates for all the people who dropped in at the Emerson place. I haven't been able to connect any of them to the bootlegging operation. But many of them have previous arrests for drugs, DUIs, and petty theft. I started a matrix in case they pop up later."

"Good start."

"But, wait, there's more," he said with a smile. "Frank Emerson has done time for assault and battery. It was some sort of bar fight. And both brothers have been in and out of trouble for fencing stolen goods. Neither of them has held a full-time job in the last three or four years. Frank used to do construction. Jesse's last job was at a convenience store."

"Duncan, you always come up with great stuff," she said, clearing the table of food wrappers.

"The Deep Web and Holiday Road."

"Huh? The only 'Holiday Road' I know is Lindsey Buckingham's song from *National Lampoon's Vacation.*"

"No, it's on the dark side of the web. You can find anything on the underground Internet where normal people fear to go."

"Do I want to know?"

"Nope. Let's just say I have my connections – friends in all kinds of places. And none of it would be admissible in a court of law. Let me get my laptop, and I'll meet you in the conference room," he said. Noticing that the food was gone, Margaret waddled down the hall after Duncan.

He plopped down in a chair and propped his feet on a nearby box. Margaret curled up under the table. Delanie typed what he dictated, and an hour later, they finished the summary on their findings for RVA Recordings.

"Can you put all the video clips on a DVD? I'll drop off the package at Ian Barnes' studio."

Duncan nodded, and Delanie dialed the music producer. After the chirpy receptionist's greeting and several minutes of on-hold music, Delanie connected with the music producer.

"I have a report and a DVD of some video clips for you. Are you around this afternoon if I swing by?"

"Sure. I can make time for you. Hey, if you're free, there's a party this evening. A private concert for one of our bands. We could grab some dinner afterwards."

"That sounds wonderful," she said. "But I have to work tonight." Duncan looked up and frowned.

"Maybe some other time then. I'll be at the office this afternoon if you want to drop off the information."

"Will do," she said, clicking off.

Delanie sighed. After the relationship with John Bailey ended abruptly last summer, she promised herself she'd never date anyone connected with work again. But she would like to see more of the recording studio. Maybe she could score a second tour when she dropped off the report.

WHEN DELANIE RETURNED TO THE OFFICE LATER THAT AFTERNOON, SHE found Duncan lying on the floor in the conference room, surrounded by piles of manila file folders. Margaret had made herself comfortable on some of the discards under the table.

"I dropped off our findings," she said. "Ian Barnes was pleased at what we uncovered. And I squeezed in a few minutes to watch another bluegrass band lay down some tracks. The guitarist was amazing. Find anything good here?"

"Rick Dixon definitely has the circumstantial angle going for him with this case. All the stuff they have on Justin can be explained. Yes, his DNA and prints were all over the apartment, especially in Emily's room, but he visited a lot and often stayed over. No murder weapon ever turned up, and the roommate said no knives or sharp objects were missing from the kitchen," Duncan said.

"That just means the murderer brought his own and left with it."

"That's premeditated. The cops are working the angle that it was a crime of passion – a boyfriend's reaction in the heat of the moment."

"That doesn't add up," she said.

Duncan shrugged and rose, leaving the piles of papers on the floor. He slid into a chair next to his laptop and continued, "There were plenty of witnesses at the party who could vouch that Justin and Emily fought. Nobody saw him arrive at Emily's apartment or leave in the morning. I think you should talk to the roommate. You might get more than what's in her interview with the police. You have a knack for worming info out of people. I want to do some more online research. Something about this case sounds familiar to me."

"So the police think they have their guy."

"Looks like it. It was an up-close knife attack, driven by rage – very personal. Plus, they knew of the fight that the two had at the party. It looked like he murdered her and tried to conceal it by making it look like a break-in. But the cover up was very sloppy. They thought he faked the robbery to hide his tracks. The roommate had an alibi, and she and Emily had a good relationship. It looks like the cops zeroed in on the boyfriend."

"Females can be murderers, you know."

"Yes, but they tend to choose other methods of killing. This was messy and full of anger. I think the police settled on their man and didn't look any further. A good lawyer could make the evidence look flimsy."

"Plausible. Are these piles in any order?" she asked, pointing at the stacks of manila folders.

"By interview subject. The ones under the table are copies of things the law firm has billed for. Nothing jumped out at me in those."

Several hours and piles of folders later, Delanie stood and stretched. "I'm getting hungry. Do you want me to order something?"

"Pizza. There's a new place – Gotham Pizza, where the mattress store used to be. You know, down there by the pet store. Call it in, and Margaret and I will go and get it."

Duncan and Margaret returned a little while later with New York style pizza and a pile of napkins.

"Okay, so what jumped out at you from the files?" Delanie asked, folding the slice of pizza and taking a bite.

"The case against Justin is tenuous at best. All Rick Dixon's team has to do is create the question in the jurors' minds that it could have been someone else. As long as the doubt is strong enough, they shouldn't convict."

"It's our job to keep finding things that create uncertainty. I'll call the roommate to see if she can meet soon. I'd like to talk to her," she said.

"I think the District Attorney is going to focus on the fact the murderer tried to make the crime scene look like a burglary. They noted it was an amateurish attempt. And Zoey Thomas, the roommate, states emphatically that nothing was missing from the apartment. That makes it look like Justin was trying to throw suspicion off himself after he killed his girlfriend. A burglar would have taken the valuables."

Delanie shook her head and got lost in the legal files.

Hours later, a snoring duet from Duncan and Margaret interrupted her reading. She glanced at her phone, and saw it was after two in the morning. She nudged Duncan with her toe. "Dunc, Dunc. We need to call it a night and head out."

"Huh? I was resting my eyes," he said as he sat up.

"Sure. You and Margaret were snoring to beat the band. Next time, I'm going to record it and post it to YouTube. I need some sleep. Are you and Margaret leaving?"

"In a little while. I've got a couple of things I need to do. Lock the door on your way out. We're not going to stay long."

Delanie hoped she would be able to find something to help Chaz and Justin. But right now, she needed her own bed and not an uncomfortable office chair.

THE NEXT MORNING, A SHARP BUZZING WOKE DELANIE. WHEN SHE picked up her cell phone to stop the noise, she noticed it was ten o'clock. The sun left streaks across her bedroom carpet.

"Hello," she said, trying to sound perky before coffee.

"Ms. Fitzgerald, this is Special Agent Eric Ellington with the FBI's

Richmond office. Ian Barnes gave me your video, and I would like to set up some time to talk with you."

"How about this afternoon or tomorrow?"

"How about tomorrow at your office around three?"

"That's fine."

"I'll see you then," he said before he clicked off. Succinct. He didn't waste time on chitchat or to ask for directions.

After an extra-long shower and a double espresso, Delanie checked her emails and decided to call Emily's roommate, Zoey Thomas, to see if she had time to meet.

DELANIE PARKED IN THE DECK NEAR MONROE PARK AND HIKED ACROSS the urban campus of Virginia Commonwealth University to the tiny coffee shop, Sacred Grounds, where Emily Menendez's roommate had agreed to meet after her two o'clock class.

She took a seat with her back to the wall where she had a clear view of the front door and waited with her iced mocha. She had flashbacks to her college days. Odd-sized paintings in brightly colored frames covered the walls. The shop seemed to be a gallery for VCU art students.

A twenty-something woman with a black messenger bag cautiously approached Delanie's table. Wisps of brown hair that escaped from her hair clip curled around her heart-shaped face.

"Miz Fitzgerald? Hi, I'm Zoey Thomas." Delanie nodded, and the younger woman dropped her bag in the rickety lime green chair on the other side of the table.

"Call me Delanie. Thank you so much for taking time to meet me. I'm sorry for your loss."

"It's been a few months, but it's still tough. I miss Emily so much. I moved out of the apartment after it happened. I couldn't stay there even after the mess was cleaned up. I still have nightmares about the whole thing. I had to find a new place with different memories. And they haven't caught the demon-worshipper who did it."

"Demon-worshipper?"

"He left 666 and those funky pentagrams on the wall in blood –
her blood. Who would do that except a crazed demonic type? And
Emily's stuff was totally ransacked. It looked like a tornado hit her
room." Memories of the photos from Rick Dixon's files flashed in
Delanie's head.

"How well did you know Justin Martin?"

"Pretty well. He had been her boyfriend for almost four years. We
all met when we were undergrads. He always seemed to be around. It
was one of those 'love at first sight' things for them. They were going
to get married when they saved up enough money."

"How was their relationship generally? Did they argue a lot?"

"They had their moments. Emily exploded about some stupid
things he did, but then she calmed down. They'd argue, but it wasn't
serious. They broke up once after our sophomore year. Justin went
home to Norfolk. But by the fall semester, they were back together."

"Any other guys in Emily's life?" Delanie asked.

"No. I mean guys noticed her with her long black hair and big,
dark eyes. She was cute and petite. She flirted some, but she never
cheated on Justin."

"What about Justin? Any other girlfriends?"

"It sounds cheesy, but Emily was the one for him. He was always
talking about saving money and where they would go on their honey-
moon. They had big plans."

"What does he do?"

"He started working as a teller for a credit union on Broad Street a
few months ago. He was a waiter in college. He still waits tables, or
did, before he got arrested. He worked at Bambino's off Cary Street."

"What else can you tell me about Emily? Any enemies?"

"I don't think so. She was friendly. You know, the kind with eight
hundred Facebook friends. She made everyone feel like they were
special. Emily was a good listener. If someone needed help, she was
there. She was big on spending time with her grandmother, too.
Emily was the only relative she had in the area."

"Did she ever have problems at work?"

"Emily liked her job. She worked here in the Richmond office at an accounting firm. She traveled some during the week to their other locations in Norfolk and Farmville. She used to complain the traveling was a pain, but she got a raise recently, and that made her happy."

"Did she get along with her co-workers?"

"I guess so. She only ever mentioned a couple of people. She didn't really hang out with anyone from work. She was the youngest in her office, and I don't think they had a lot in common with Emily. We still have a bunch of friends from college who live in town. Most of the time, she was working, visiting her grandmother, or hanging out with Justin."

"So what did she do for fun?"

"Emily liked to ride her bike and take pictures of things she was doing. She was really big into posting her photos. This is the fun part of town. There's a party somewhere every weekend."

Making a mental note to comb through Emily's online pictures, she asked, "You were gone that weekend?"

"I went to see a friend in Northern Virginia. I didn't get back until Monday morning. It was terrible. I had no idea what I was walking in on," Zoey said, wiping her eyes with the back of her hands. "It was like a scene out of a horror movie. It didn't seem real."

"I'm sorry to dredge up such awful memories. Is there anything else you can think of that might help me as I look into Emily's murder?"

"I don't think Justin did it. He couldn't have," she said, sinking further down in her chair.

"Why?"

"He was crazy about her. It doesn't make sense. It had to be some psycho who followed her home, or somebody she was nice to, and he got the wrong idea."

"Had that happened before with Emily?"

"Hmmm. You know. Guys on the street or in bars always noticed her. A lot of men hit on her. I don't think she ever had any stalkers. But there was a guy named Douglas in one of her classes and study groups. He made her uncomfortable, so she dropped the group."

"What's Douglas' last name?"

"Uh, Black. He was a little creepy."

"Did she confront Douglas or make any kind of complaint?"

"I don't think so. She avoided him and found another study group. Plus, Emily didn't mention him after that."

"Do you know if she had any contact with him since college?"

"That was a few years ago. He was this really nerdy guy who had no social skills. I don't know what ever happened to him. I don't remember seeing him around."

"Thank you for talking to me, Zoey. If you can think of anything else, here's my card. Text me any time," Delanie said.

"I'm glad you're looking into this. The police have decided it's Justin. But I don't think they have the right guy. It freaks me out that the real killer is still out there." She sighed. "I've got to take off now. I have a date with my latest research project at the library." The straight-back chair creaked when she scooted it under the table. Delanie watched the graduate student move through the maze of chairs and tables to the front door.

Delanie strolled through Monroe Park, a green space the VCU students shared with the residents of downtown Richmond. She noticed a few people over thirty, but most looked like college students with beach towels, Frisbees, and soccer balls. Delanie wished she had time to lie in the grass and read a good book. Every once in a while, she missed being in college. The campus had expanded since she graduated. It was nothing at all like she remembered it. She felt a twinge of sadness that Zoey and Justin's memories of college would be tainted by Emily's murder.

8

RETRIEVING HER CAR FROM THE VCU PARKING DECK, DELANIE POINTED it toward the office and drove on autopilot. Zoey Thomas didn't suspect that the boyfriend killed Emily Menendez. Her reasons sounded viable. Could the police have the wrong guy? When she got to Chippenham Parkway, she took a quick left. Delanie didn't have any new leads on Emily's murder, so she decided to do one last drive-by of the Emerson property before she talked to the FBI agent. It troubled her that there was so much traffic around the farmhouse compound. Men came and went like it was a convenience store.

Parking on the old fire road again near the dilapidated farmhouse, she found a hiding place for snooping. She snapped pictures with her phone of the truck, Jesse's van, and a maroon car parked outside the barn. The car would be a new entry in Duncan's license plate inventory.

Frank, Jesse, and a third man came out of one of the sheds. They talked for a minute and then jumped in the blue van and sped down the gravel driveway.

When the dust had settled and Delanie was certain there was no other sign of life at the house, she trekked along the edge of the property. She darted behind the shed closest to the woods. When she didn't hear anything, she stole a look around the corner.

Spotting a small window, she tried shoving it open. The window didn't budge, so she slipped around the corner to check out the front of the shed. The padlock hung open in the door latch. Delanie took advantage of the moment and squeezed inside the door into the darkened shed.

Pulling the door shut behind her, she caught her breath and waited for her eyes to adjust. The only sound was her heart pounding in her ears. Her nose twitched from the industrial smells that reminded her of ammonia. She knew she had to get out of the shed and away from that smell, but she couldn't resist poking around for a few moments to see what she could find.

She flipped on the flashlight app on her phone. She scooted past a wooden workbench covered with hand tools, tarps, pipes, and hoses. In the back, rows of plastic vats stood like toy soldiers guarding the shed's secrets. Gallon milk jugs filled with a clear liquid encircled the vats. They looked like the ones she had seen at Jesse's storage unit. Delanie snapped a couple of pictures. She counted twenty-eight jugs and thirty-two vats of liquid. The Emerson boys were definitely bootlegging more than CDs. She paused when she thought she heard a car nearby. After a couple of seconds and no other sounds, she continued to snoop around the shed.

She heard voices and froze. When the voices got louder, she ducked under the bench and yanked a stool in front of her. Grabbing a nearby tarp, she pulled it over her. She hoped with all the mess, no one would notice a few things out of place.

Two men entered the shed. Delanie peeked around the edge of the tarp that reeked of gasoline. The beams from their flashlights crisscrossed.

"Grab those three," Frank yelled. Even in the shadows, she recognized the taller Emerson brother.

"Okay. But I need the handcart."

"I'll get it. Wait here," Frank said.

Jesse stepped through the open door and lit a cigarette. Delanie smelled the burning tobacco. He hummed while he waited.

"What are you doing? Trying to blow us to kingdom come? How many times do I have to tell you not to smoke out here?" bellowed Frank.

"Sorry," Jesse said, stomping his unfinished cigarette. "I forgot."

"Don't be a freakin' moron. Grab those containers and let's get out of here before you create a giant crater in Mom's backyard."

Jesse loaded two of the vats on the handcart, and the men left. Delanie's heart skipped a beat when she heard the door slam and the lock rattle.

Not good, she thought. Now she was trapped in a shed with some kind of flammable material. An engine started, and then the vehicle drove away. She exhaled and crawled out from under the tarp. She pushed on the door, trying not to make too much noise in case someone remained nearby. Switching on her flashlight app, she swept it slowly across the shed. There were no shovels or hoes – nothing with a sturdy handle to pry the door open.

She had no idea when the brothers would return, and she didn't want to spend any more time exposed to god-only-knows what chemicals the Emersons had stored here. She cleared part of the workbench and used the stool to crawl up on top. With a lot of pushing and prying, she was able to get the filthy window to budge slightly. She listened for a moment. Not hearing anything outside, she continued to push. With a loud cracking sound, the window slid up about ten inches. Pocketing her phone, she slid out feet first and landed with a thud in the grass.

The window side of the shed faced the other shed. She hoped it blocked the view of anyone who might be looking in this direction from the farmhouse.

She tried to close the window from the outside and managed to get it almost shut. Maybe no one would notice the small gap. She rubbed the glass with her palm to smear any handprints. Checking around the corner, Delanie took a deep breath and ran for the woods and the safety of her car.

No sooner had she backed out and reached the road, she noticed a black SUV about two hundred yards behind her. Speeding up, she drove through the town of Chester, changing lanes frequently. On impulse, she made a quick right and headed for Route 288. Exhaling loudly, she was pleased when she lost the SUV, but she wanted to kick herself for not getting the license plate number. She'd been too wrapped up in dodging him.

Before she could relax completely, there he was again, bearing down on her. She ducked off the exit and headed to the office. Zig-zagging among three lanes of traffic, Delanie finally ditched the tail and pulled into the lot in the back of her office.

She slammed the door, locked it, and willed her heart to stop pounding. She flipped on all the lights. When her phone buzzed in her pocket, she jumped. It was Special Agent Ellington.

"I need to talk with you. It's important," he said.

"I thought we were scheduled to meet tomorrow."

"Circumstances have changed."

"Where are you?"

"At the front door of your office."

A tall man in jeans and a dark blazer tapped on the glass with a gold badge. She inspected his credentials through the window and noticed the black Chevy Suburban parked in front of her building.

When she opened the door, he said, "Ms. Fitzgerald. I need to talk to you about what you gave to Ian Barnes at RVA Recordings."

She relocked the door and said, "There are chairs and a table in the kitchen." She pointed down the hallway.

"Why were you at the Emerson farm this evening?" he asked, walking toward the kitchen.

"Why do you keep following me?"

"There's a multi-jurisdictional task force watching the Emerson property, and you keep turning up in our surveillance. We thought you were done when you turned in your report to Mr. Barnes," he said, choosing the chair with the wall behind it. Delanie sat across from him in front of the doorway.

"They're bootlegging more than CDs," she said. She handed her phone to the agent. He flipped through the pictures as she continued, "That's what I took today. I only looked inside of one of the sheds. I think they've got a still somewhere on the property. I saw vats like that at their storage unit off Jeff Davis Highway too. Oh, and Frank told Jesse to put out his cigarette. So there's something flammable around."

"I need you to stay away from their property. The Emersons have criminal records and lots of weapons." He stopped talking to jot something down in a small notebook. "Send me your pictures." He pushed a business card toward her across the table. "We're continuing our investigation of the compound. We got a tip about drug distribution, and we've got a joint task force going with DEA and others. It's taken a long time to set up this kind of surveillance and collect evidence."

"The CD counterfeiting seems to be a small deal. I looked through their inventory twice at the flea market, and there wasn't anything mass market with the music," she said.

"The Emersons have a history of small-time hustles. There's a lot of traffic in and out of the property. We got a tip that there could be meth, and they've been known to grow pot from time to time," he said.

"I did notice a chemical smell in the shed," she said. "It was a heavy odor like ammonia."

"Hmmm. If you think of anything else, you have my card. Call me. And stay away from the property. I can't have you interfering with an active investigation," he said as he stood.

Delanie nodded but didn't reply. She followed Agent Ellington to the lobby and unlocked the door for him.

"Goodbye." After she shut and locked the door, she whispered, "And thanks for scaring the crap out of me by following me all around Central Virginia."

Delanie turned off the lights and returned to her office to text Duncan an update on the identity of the black SUV guy. She knew that he had an investigation and a case to protect, but she didn't like being fussed at. And she was annoyed that he'd been tailing her all

around town. He acted like she was going to mess up his investigation, and a thank you would have been nice for all the information
and pictures she shared with him. She hoped that was the end of her
dealings with the FBI agent.

Delanie gathered her things and headed for home and yoga. She
needed something to distract her from her encounters with the
Emerson brothers and Special Agent Ellington.

9

WITH NO AFTER-DINNER PLANS THE NEXT DAY, DELANIE DECIDED IT WAS too early to go home. She drove to Chester for one last drive-by of the Emerson property. And what would a quick pass in front of the compound hurt? She'd be in and out, and Agent Ellington would be none the wiser. She wished Duncan had a drone. Spying with a flying camera would be much better than hiding in the woods and peering around trees.

When Delanie drove past the farm, eight cars and trucks dotted the dirt driveway in front of the barn. Ignoring the FBI agent's warning, she doubled back and parked on the old fire road. She'd be careful. She knew better than to jeopardize an investigation. Plus, she didn't plan to stay too long. And she wasn't technically on the Emerson property. Delanie crept through the woods and found a spot with good cover. At times like these, she wished Duncan was more athletic like her brother, Robbie. It would be nice to have backup. But it was his video game night, so she was on her own in the dark forest.

The sun dipped below the tree line. She counted ten guys exiting the barn, each carrying at least one milk jug. The back door of the farm house flew open. She let out a gasp when the perky receptionist from RVA Recordings stormed out to talk to the Emerson boys.

Delanie let out a heavy sigh. She should have checked out the recording studio's staff further. This explained why the brothers were bootlegging bluegrass and gospel music from that particular studio. A crime of convenience.

After what looked like a heated discussion with lots of arm gestures, the brothers and the receptionist disappeared inside the old house, leaving just the chickens to scratch around in the dirt near the back door.

Delanie wanted a better look at the barn. There was more going on than music counterfeiting. She'd take a quick peek and then head home. Delanie pushed Agent Ellington's warning out of her thoughts and crept along the tree line until she found the spot to make a break for the cover of the nearest shed.

She stopped between the two sheds to catch her breath and listened for any indication that anyone had seen her. Then she eased around the corner. Before she could decide what to do next, someone grabbed her middle, and a gloved hand clamped down over her mouth. Her assailant dragged her back between the sheds.

She tried to kick and scratch, but her captor held her in a bear hug that all but eliminated any chance she had to fight back. She did get in one good stomp on his leather boot. When she paused to catch her breath, her assailant hissed in her ear, "I told you not to come back here. If you'll be quiet, I'll let you go."

Eric Ellington loosened his grip, and Delanie jerked free. Teeth clenched, she turned and asked, "What in the hell are you doing? It was a good thing I wasn't armed!"

"It wouldn't have done you any good. I caught you unaware of your surroundings. I should arrest you for trespassing – especially after I warned you."

He was dressed in black, including his boots and gloves. Her eyes lingered a few moments on an eagle tattoo that wasn't quite covered by the sleeve of his t-shirt and bullet-proof vest.

"I had a hunch. And I saw the receptionist from RVA Recordings go into the farmhouse with the Emerson boys. Something was going down in the barn. A bunch of guys left with milk jugs."

"I've got DEA staking out the property," he whispered. "The illegal alcohol and drugs are a bigger operation than the copyright violations. Stay here! And I mean stay here. I will haul your ass to jail if you screw this up. I'm gonna check the barn. I'll be back in a minute," he said as he drew his gun.

As soon as he stepped around the corner of the shed, Delanie heard three shots. She swallowed hard and stuck her head out. She watched the FBI agent stumble and grab his arm as the chickens scattered into the woods.

Delanie rushed out. By the time she got to him, he had managed to stand. She grabbed him around the waist and yanked him back between the sheds. He slid down to a seated position. "You okay?"

"I'll live." When he turned to fish out his cell phone, he gritted his teeth. He punched a few digits and said, "Move in now. They're firing from the back of the house." Before he could disconnect, a string of shots rang out and hit the shed. Debris from the siding and roof rained down on them.

Agent Ellington grabbed Delanie and forced her flat on the ground. Whoever was shooting was spraying the shed with bullets. And just like in the movies, dust rained down on everything. Ellington signaled, and she crawled behind him to the corner of the building.

It was eerily quiet. He pulled her up, and they started to run for the side of the barn. Then a boom that Delanie felt in her chest knocked them both face forward. The first shed evaporated into sticks and dust. And the fire consumed the other small building in minutes.

Delanie rolled over in the dirt and surveyed the scene. The people running and taking cover looked like they were in slow-motion. Delanie's ears rang. Men in black stormed the farmhouse.

Ellington shook her shoulder. "Move over there! Now!" he ordered as he pointed to an area in the distance. "That other shed could blow too."

|

~

IN THE SWIRLING DUST AND SMOKE, DELANIE WATCHED THE MEN IN black SWAT gear swarm the backyard. Jesse fired a few shots and then hit the ground, holding his side. Two agents rushed forward and dragged him to the side of the house. Other agents charged into the house and apprehended the receptionist and an older woman. Before Delanie could watch more of the drama, Ellington led her to the edge of the driveway where three ambulances kept company with the black SUVs, Chesterfield County police cruisers, and two fire trucks.

"You need to get checked out. Don't leave. We need to get a statement from you."

"What about you? You're still bleeding."

"I have something to do first. I'll be back." He jogged off toward the barn as more fire trucks and white evidence vehicles pulled into the driveway.

She sat in the back of an ambulance with two EMTs as they tended to scratches on her face and arms. Dust and shed shards covered her from head to toe. She looked down and noticed she had torn her jeans in several places.

Fire crews put out the blaze where the shed once stood. The hazmat crew congregated near the farmhouse. From the snippets of conversations she picked up from the first responders, Delanie gathered another ambulance had transported Jesse to the hospital. It sounded like the younger of the two Emerson brothers had sustained multiple gunshot wounds. The FBI also took Frank and two females into custody.

Ellington interrupted Delanie's eavesdropping when he leaned into the back of the ambulance.

Before he could speak, she said to the EMTs, "Excuse me. Agent Ellington was shot. He needs your attention more than I do." She jumped down out of the back of the ambulance.

Ellington glared at her, but acquiesced by climbing on the gurney that Delanie vacated.

"Ma'am, you can wait over there," said the younger EMT.

"That's okay. She can stay," he said. "I need to talk to her."

The EMT looked sideways at the FBI agent, but didn't say anything. They went to work on Agent Ellington's arm.

"What are you doing here?" Ellington demanded.

"Saving you," she said, leaning on the ambulance.

"More like the other way around. I told you to stay away."

"I didn't come looking for trouble. I did a drive-by. All the vehicles out front looked suspicious. I had to get closer to see what was going on."

"This is going to sting," the taller EMT said to Ellington.

He winced, but kept talking to Delanie. "We took Frank Emerson into custody. We also arrested the mother and the girlfriend. It seems the brothers had booby-trapped one of the sheds, and the gunfire triggered the explosion. Or they set it off – that's probably giving them too much credit. They were known for their small-time hustles. We've got enough evidence here to keep the investigators and hazmat guys busy for days."

He paused to watch the EMT tend to his arm and then continued, "The Emerson boys were opportunists. They dabbled in anything they thought they could get money for. They weren't very good at much of it. Their big money-maker was the illegal alcohol. They fiddled with a small meth lab, but it was more of a mess than anything. They probably should have paid more attention in science class. Now it's a problem for the hazmat team and the property owner. They had the CD business going along with a fencing operation at the flea market. The barn's full of stolen items. We should clear hundreds of burglaries and break-ins with this bust."

"I'm glad I could help."

Ellington cut his eyes to her. Before he could reply, the taller EMT said, "You're in luck. The bullet grazed your arm. I've stabilized it, but you're going to need to get a few stitches and a tetanus shot."

"Just bandage it. I've got some things to do here tonight. I'll go later."

As the EMT started to protest, the other, older one said, "I have something in my bag. I can put something on it to hold it closed if you'll wait a minute, but you'll still need to get that shot soon."

Ellington nodded and then said to Delanie, "I'll call you later this week."

"Okay. But there's nothing more to tell."

Before Ellington could answer, the paramedic used a glue-like substance and a large bandage to stabilize the wound. The FBI agent gritted his teeth, but remained silent.

The paramedic said, "That should hold, so you can finish here tonight. Don't lift anything, or the temporary fix won't hold. You're going to feel some pain later. Take acetaminophen and check it for infection. Make sure you get that shot."

"I'll be fine. Thanks. Are you okay?" he asked Delanie.

"Except for the bruises and scratches."

"Can you get yourself home?"

"Of course. I parked down the road."

"I'll get one of the officers to take you to your car."

"That's not necessary."

"Yes, it is. I don't want you wandering all over my crime scene. And I want to make sure you leave this time. You're lucky I don't arrest you. Someone from my office will call you."

A slightly peeved Delanie reminded herself not to alienate the FBI agent. Before she could come up with a snappy retort, Ellington hopped off the gurney and out of the ambulance.

"Officer. Excuse me. Could you do me a favor?" He yelled to a group of police near the driveway.

Ellington walked closer to them and asked, "Could you see that Ms. Fitzgerald gets to her car and leaves the scene immediately?"

"Sure," said one of the officers. He smiled as he walked toward the ambulance. A sense of dread washed over Delanie when she saw her oldest brother's approach.

Lieutenant Steve Fitzgerald escorted Delanie to his cruiser, parked next to the farm house. Once inside, he snapped, "Why does it not surprise me to find you here? Why can't you go on dates or be a homebody after work?"

"This is work. And that wouldn't be any fun," she said. The cruiser smelled like a mix of stale food and dirty socks. It never mattered how clean a police car was, that stench remained. It was the same smell she remembered in her father's police car.

"What are you doing here?" he asked.

"A client hired me to find out about some bootlegged CDs. And it seems the Emerson boys had several side businesses going on."

"Where's your car?"

"Turn right at the end of the driveway. It's a couple of hundred yards down there at the fire road."

"Can I trust you to go home?"

"Yep. I've had enough fun for tonight. And I really need a shower."

"Yes, you do. Now go home. And you're lucky I don't give you a ticket for blocking a fire road." He stopped behind Delanie's car, and she climbed out and said, "Thanks for the ride. Give my love to Liz and the kids."

"Try to stay out of trouble long enough to get home."

Delanie stuck her tongue out at him, but she wasn't sure he saw her. He gunned the cruiser's oversized engine and headed back to the Emerson compound.

Delanie cranked up the radio in the car. She had had enough of the Emerson brothers and Agent Ellington. And it topped everything off when he asked her brother to escort her from the crime scene. It would be months before Steve let her live this down.

10

AFTER HER ADVENTURE AT THE EMERSON COMPOUND WITH AGENT Ellington and her brother, Delanie was comforted at the sight of her home – her escape from the world. She loved her Sears and Roebuck catalog cottage. She checked the mail and parked the car around back. After a quick shower that made her scratches sting, she changed into her pajamas and padded down the hall to root through the refrigerator for some comfort food. Not finding any chocolate, she settled for a handful of grapes.

Someone banged on her front door and Delanie jumped. She flipped on the front lights and found Duncan and Margaret on her small porch.

He opened the screen door and stepped inside, his four-legged shadow following closely behind. "What a night!" he said.

"Come in, guys," she said, rolling her eyes. "Can I get you something to drink?"

"No, we're good. We found some stuff you've got to hear about tonight."

"I had quite an adventure too."

"What's wrong with your face?" he asked, staring at her scratches.

"I got too close to an explosion. The Emerson boys booby-trapped one of their sheds."

"What?" he asked as he sank in a barrel side chair. Margaret, bored with the conversation, curled up under the coffee table.

"I went by the property and ran into that FBI agent again. He acts like he owns the property and half the world. And then there was shooting, and one of the outbuildings blew up. A bullet grazed the FBI agent's arm. He should have been glad that I was there to help, but he didn't act that way. Oh, and I saw Steve there too."

"You okay?"

"It looks worse than it really is. Jesse was shot. They arrested Frank, his girlfriend, and an older lady, probably the guys' mother. Oh, and get this. The girlfriend is the receptionist at RVA Recordings."

"Small world. Sorry you got blown up, but listen to this. I think we're on to something. I've been looking into the Emily Menendez case. I think I've found some other similar cases in the area, but they're all in different jurisdictions. I'm not sure if anyone has connected the dots yet. And if we can prove it's the work of a serial killer, we can help Justin the boyfriend."

"What have you got? And are you sure you don't want something to drink?"

"I'm good for now. Sit down. It's like a bunch of weird puzzle pieces, but they're starting to fit together. Okay, there was Emily's murder in downtown Richmond. It happened on April 1, on a week-end. There was a murder in Petersburg a week or so ago. The victim was also a woman, but she was older than Emily. And she lived alone. Then there was another murder about a month after Emily's in Farmville. The victim there was an older white guy. Then I found another murder in Richmond, but the body was found in a car. The other cases have similarities that the one that happened in the car doesn't have."

"What makes you think the others are related? Serial killers usually stick to certain patterns. The victims' demographics aren't even close. And the locations are far from each other. Have you found any patterns at all?"

"Not yet. We've got one Latina, one African-American, and one white victim. Two were females and one was male. For now, I'm going to leave out the second Richmond case. It was a white woman found stabbed in her car. On the surface, there doesn't seem to be any similarities to the other three. I think law enforcement treated them as separate murders in three different jurisdictions. The murders happened on April first, May eighth, and September first. The one in the car occurred on July fifth."

He stood up and paced around the living room. Margaret opened one eye, but closed it again when she didn't notice any treats nearby.

Duncan continued, "The news articles didn't really detail the crime scenes. We know there were crude drawings done with Emily's blood. We saw the crime scene photos Rick Dixon had. None of the other two detailed that type of information. I want to do some more research on what could connect these three, especially before we report back. On second thought, I'm a little hungry. Do you want to order a pizza?"

"It's kinda late."

Ignoring her, he said, "They'll still deliver. I'll order one, and we can brainstorm our next steps," he said, tapping his order into his phone.

So much for her relaxing evening at home. She retreated to her bedroom to change into jeans and a t-shirt and scrunch her unruly curls into a ponytail. Duncan had seen her without makeup before, so she didn't bother with any other improvements. Delanie returned to the front room just as the pizza guy rang the bell. The scent of sausage pizza permeated the living room, and Margaret suddenly became very interested in the pizza guy.

When the food was almost gone, Duncan stood up and said, "I don't think these are three random murders. I know there's a connection. Think. Think. Think. There's got to be a common link." He tossed the dog a crust, and she wasted no time gnawing on the pizza bone.

Delanie nodded. She was too tired to go on much longer. Before she could suggest they call it a night, Duncan continued, "Okay, we know about the investigation of Emily's murder from the documents Rick gave us. Let me see what I can find on the other two." He grabbed his laptop and sat back down in the barrel chair with the last piece of pizza.

Delanie grabbed a throw pillow and shut off the TV. The last thing she remembered was Duncan clicking away on his laptop, and his dog peacefully snoring under the coffee table.

Delanie woke up to someone whistling in her kitchen. She almost reached for her gun until she remembered Duncan had stayed over, and she had fallen asleep on the couch. She found Duncan making French toast and bacon. He had coffee going, and Margaret was on food patrol in front of the stove.

"Morning, Sunshine," she said.

"We're making breakfast. I hope you don't mind."

"No, you can come over and cook any time you want. But I'm pretty sure I didn't have all those ingredients."

"You didn't. Your pantry was pretty bare. We made a run to the store this morning."

"What? You don't like beer and cereal?"

"Not today. Start with coffee. I'll have the rest of it ready in a minute. I also got fresh fruit in case you want that instead of syrup. I've been up all night, but I found some interesting stuff. Here, take this piece and get started. I'll catch you up after I make mine and Margaret's."

After Duncan made another serving and a taste for his sidekick, he plopped down in the chair across from Delanie and dug into his breakfast.

"All right. That's much better. I'll give you the highlights, so, you already know about Emily. A few months later, David Millhouse was murdered in his house outside of Farmville. He rented the property. I found a blog where someone wrote about how the crime scene had been tagged with video game references. The crude drawings weren't the same as those in the Emily Menendez's case, but there were wall drawings. The local weekly paper also ran several stories about the victim. Most of the interviews are with people who are in an uproar about the decline of western civilization and the lack of morals of the younger generation. Everyone they interviewed was shocked that something so awful could happen in their town. The articles made Farmville sound like an idyllic place," he said.

Delanie tore into her French toast. She hadn't had a homemade breakfast in months.

Duncan continued, "And then there was D'borah Styles from Petersburg. She lived alone with her cats. I picked up her story from another neighborhood newspaper. Ms. Styles' church had an exorcism of sorts in front of her house after the murder to cleanse the neighborhood of the presence of evil. It seemed her murder creeped out the neighbors, and the estate hasn't been able to sell her house. I'd be interested to see if there were blood drawings on her walls as well."

"Okay, there were three similar murders, and no law enforcement has connected them yet?" Delanie used the last few bites of French toast to sop up the remaining syrup.

"I don't know," he said. "Maybe it's on someone's radar, but I couldn't find anything about a regional task force or rumors about a serial killer. The murders are in three different jurisdictions. Petersburg's a thirty-five-minute drive south of Richmond. And Farmville's what, about forty-five minutes to the west? The police forces are different sizes with varying resources. There's a possibility they're being investigated as three unique events. The fact there aren't obvious patterns may not raise any red flags or connections. Plus, Richmond PD thinks they got their guy. Why would they continue to investigate? But the most important note is that if they were done by the same person, then Justin Martin couldn't be the killer. He was in police custody according to Rick Dixon's files by the time the Millhouse murder occurred. The fourth case with the woman in the car is different from the others. She was stabbed and left in a parking lot. Her purse was missing. I've got the details on her murder on this sheet. Do you have some time to poke around to see what you can find? We need to be able to rule it out for sure."

"I can check on it. What are your next steps?"

"I need to get all of our facts organized. I'm going to head to the office after we finish breakfast."

"Duncan, you've been up all night. You're no good to me brain-dead. You need to go home and get some sleep before you fall over from exhaustion."

"I'd hate to lose my momentum. I'm really on a roll with this one," he said.

"I know, but you can grab a couple of hours of Z's and then meet me at the office."

"Okay, okay." Margaret opened one eye and then closed it again. She didn't waste any time starting her nap.

Duncan finished his breakfast and rinsed his plate. "Leave that," Delanie said. "I'll clean up. You did enough with making breakfast. Thanks for the French toast."

"Okay. Then we'll take off now. See you later."

"Thanks, Duncan. You're terrific."

He waved as he headed back to the living room to gather his gear. Margaret sat up, stretched, and followed the love of her life to the front door. Delanie heard the storm door shut behind them.

After straightening the kitchen and a quick shower, Delanie powered up her laptop. When she retrieved her phone, she found a voicemail from Agent Ellington asking her to call him back. He needed to get her official statement.

Deleting the voicemail, she typed a statement and read it twice to make sure she sounded like a private investigator with a client rather than a crazy person. She dug the FBI agent's card out of a pile on the corner of the table. She ended her email saying that she'd received his call, and she was busy this week with clients. She hoped her statement would provide all the information he needed.

She clicked send and was pleased with herself for avoiding the interview with the boorish FBI agent.

~

To kill time while she waited for Duncan, Delanie drove to the southside of town. She parked in front of an aluminum building dating back to the 1950s. Its flaking paint hinted at its different color schemes over the decades. Six cars dotted the parking lot of the River City Rolla-rink. According to Duncan's notes, Karen Jackson, the stabbing victim found in her car, was a roller derby girl who practiced here with the Richmond River Rats.

She wandered inside the dark building. An oval track with padded sides took up most of the space in the traditional rink. Three women, in various stages of lacing up, sat on a set of rickety wooden bleachers with their backs to the private investigator.

"Excuse me," Delanie said to the woman in the pink tank top. "I'm looking for Sophia Espisito."

"I'm her most days," she said without turning around. "What can I do for you?"

"I'm Delanie Fitzgerald. I'd like to ask you a few questions about Karen Jackson."

The woman stopped what she was doing and turned around. "She doesn't skate here any longer," the tall woman said, pushing her dark bangs out of her eyes. Before Delanie could reply, the woman continued, "But you already knew that. Hey look, I'm kinda shorthanded for practice these days. If you want to stay and talk about Karen, you'll have to lace up and help me out first. Skates are over there," she said, pointing to a row of cabinets. "You can skate, right?"

"Of course," Delanie said. She hoped it was like riding a bike. It had been a long time since the days of all skate and couple's skate under the disco ball. Delanie rummaged through a pile of mismatched skates and found a two-toned blue and beige pair that had seen better days.

After lacing up and adjusting the skates, she practiced for a few minutes off to the side.

Nothing to it.

"You're gonna need these," Sophia Espisito said as she tossed her a beat up black helmet, stuffed with elbow and knee pads.

She skated over to the rink and leaned on the railing. Not that hard. I can do this, she thought. It took a little while to work the knee pads on over her jeans.

"Melody's the jammer," Sophia yelled as she pointed to the woman with the sleeve tattoos and teal curls poking out from under her helmet with the star on it. "She starts at the back and races through the pack. If she gets by her opponents, she scores points. Her teammates with the yellow jerseys will try to block you and your team, the gals not in yellow. Your job is to keep her from passing you. Most anything goes, but this isn't MMA. Do a couple of laps to get warmed up, and we'll get started. Any questions?"

Delanie shook her head, fastened the helmet, and adjusted her elbow and knee pads. She climbed over the padded barricade and followed the pack around the rink – thrilled that she didn't face plant in front of the professionals. But anything resembling Mixed Martial Arts wasn't what she planned for today. She hoped she could leave here with no broken bones and more information on Karen Jackson.

A shrill whistle pierced the din of the rubber wheels on the wooden floor. "River Rats, line up," Sophia bellowed. Delanie followed the others to the starting line. She took a deep breath and exhaled slowly.

"Ready, set, go!" Sophia yelled. Then she let loose with two more shrill whistle blasts.

The pack sped off. Delanie caught up to her team and got into a groove. On the second lap, the jammer made her way toward the pack. After a shoving battle with elbows flying, the jammer skated by a brunette who fell and took out one of her teammates.

Delanie, a quarter of a lap behind, knew that it was her turn on the next lap. She took a deep breath and steeled herself for whatever was coming her way. The jammer bumped her, and the PI leaned into her, leading with her elbow. They scuffled into the next turn, and Delanie fell when the jammer tripped her. Her wrist and shoulder throbbed. The woman with the starred helmet jeered and whistled, waving her arms on her next circuit around the track.

Picking herself up, Delanie skated hard to catch the pack. After a few laps, the jammer began to advance again. She scrapped with two of the River Rats at the back. Then the jammer managed to scoot past both of the women on her way to Delanie.

She could feel the other woman's approach. "You're going down," the jammer snarled.

"Not without a fight," she said, thrusting her hip into her. Delanie hit the other woman with enough force to cause the jammer to wobble. Regaining her balance, the woman skated closer and kneed Delanie's left leg, and a well-landed elbow sent the PI into the padded barrier.

"Pretty slick," the woman said as she skated away.

Delanie picked herself up. She was going to have a collection of bruises from this. Three sharp whistle blasts brought everyone back to the line.

"Good work," Sophia said. "Take ten, ladies. I want to talk to the newbie."

Delanie's team disappeared while the gals in yellow jerseys found seats in the bleachers.

"Not bad, not bad at all for a rookie. You held your own. With a little practice, you'd be pretty good at this. Let me know if you need a part-time job. We could always use a new rat."

Delanie smiled. "Thanks. What can you tell me about Karen Jackson?"

"She was a damn good skater for us when she showed up and had a clear head, but unfortunately for all of us, that didn't happen very often. We'll miss her. They found her out behind the rink in her car. It was sad, but probably inevitable."

"The police haven't found her killer."

"I'm not that worried. I don't think it had anything to do with us.

Plus, we can take care of ourselves. Karen caused most of her own problems."

"Husband or boyfriend troubles?"

"Nah, I don't think so. She liked drama. She bounced from guy to guy and carried her own baggage along for the ride. The police were all over this place asking questions about her friends and business contacts. They questioned all of us. This was her steady job – if you could call it that. Most of us skate on the weekends for fun. We have a nurse, computer programmer, and an elementary school teacher on our team. But Karen had trouble keeping a day job. She wasn't what you would call reliable. This place was the only stable thing in her life. We were her family."

"What's your hunch?"

"My guess is that she owed somebody money, and she'd reached the end of that someone's patience. Karen was the type who preyed on the good nature of others. She always needed something or wanted a loan, but she was full of excuses about why she never repaid anything. She latched on to anyone who was nice to her or paid her any attention."

"Gambling?"

"No. The rumor was drugs. She called in sick a lot, and there were times she looked like something the cat drug in. They said she just couldn't conquer it. She always succumbed to her demons. She'd disappear for weeks at a time. And then she'd show back up looking for us to help her put the pieces back together."

"The police report said she was found in the car with no purse or belongings. You'd suspect something drug-related over a general robbery?"

"Yep. Unfortunately, she had a history. It's not really that much of a surprise to anybody who knew her. It was just a matter of time."

"Thanks for the information and the interesting afternoon."

"You've got a knack for derby. Come back any time. But you'll need a cool name to be a River Rat – something like the Red Raven or Miss Fortune."

Delanie laughed as she found her shoes and returned the gear.

"Thanks, I'll think about it if the PI work doesn't pan out." On her way out, the jammer nodded at her and saluted with two fingers.

It was time to update Duncan – after a hot shower. She hoped the steamy water would soothe the aches from the tumbles she took this afternoon that were on top of her scratches and bruises from the Emerson explosion.

11

LATER THAT AFTERNOON, DELANIE HEARD THE OFFICE BACK DOOR SLAM and Duncan yelled, "Delanie, you here?"

"Back here. Paying bills."

"We're going to make coffee, and we'll meet you in the conference room in a few."

Interrupted by her phone's beep, she glanced at an email from the annoying FBI agent. He told her he would call her later for follow up questions. She quickly typed, "OK," and deleted his message. Persistent fellow. She wished he'd find someone else to annoy.

"You feeling better?" she asked when Duncan joined her with two mugs of steaming coffee.

"Yep. All rested and ready to get back on this thing. Why don't you work up what we know so far, and I'll look into who these people were? Maybe we'll find a connection." Delanie took Duncan's notes and started writing each case in a different color on the whiteboard.

"I went to the roller rink where July murder victim was found," she said as she wrote. "I talked to Sophia Espisito. She said that Karen Jackson was found behind the rink in her car – her purse was missing. She was a good skater with some demons that eventually caught up with her. She suspected that Karen owed a dealer money."

"The MO wasn't like the other cases. I think we can cross that one off the list for now."

"Good. I'm done with roller derby for a while – but I picked up a new moniker I'm thinking about keeping – Miss Fortune. They said I could come back and skate with them again."

Duncan raised an eyebrow but didn't have a retort. He retreated to the file folder in front of him.

Two cups of coffee later, Duncan broke the silence when he yelled, "Shazam!" Delanie jumped, and Margaret lifted her head.

"Look at this," he said. "I'm not sure if it matters or not, but D'borah Styles was a community activist. She worked with a nonprofit in downtown Petersburg that helped the homeless and underprivileged. She had a blog, and her last post was the day of her murder. She went after government agencies who treated people unfairly, and she talked about the disparities in the school systems. She railed about the lottery, road projects, and the lack of grocery stores in inner cities – stirring up some controversy all over the Internet. She was passionate about her causes. I'm sure the police have seen this, but we'll add it to our notes just in case. There are tons of comments to her posts from lots of people – some for and against what she wrote."

"Any of the commenters have real names?"

"A couple, but most are screen names. It wouldn't be that hard to track them down. Ms. Styles used to attend a boatload of public meetings. She got arrested a couple of times. Once was at a Petersburg City Council meeting when she made a comment that was construed as a threat to a councilwoman. She also got arrested a couple of years earlier for a protest she organized outside of a bank she felt had unfair lending practices. She and her group stopped traffic, so the police showed up." He paused to look at his notes. "And she got arrested another time for trespassing at an insurance firm. It seems it was owned by a city councilwoman she had a disagreement with. Ms. Styles made a scene in the woman's office, and the councilwoman had her arrested for stalking. A judge reduced the charges, and D'borah did some community service. Ms. Styles was fifty-two, twice divorced, and she lived alone in Petersburg with her two cats. She paid her taxes and drove an old blue Buick."

"The police won't have to look very hard to find a long line of people she ticked off."

"Or threatened or sued," he said. "She was active in her church, too. Go through that box over there. It has Emily Menendez's bio in it. No, not that one. The one closest to Margaret. See if you can find anything similar or something that might be a connection between the two cases."

She added the new information about D'borah Styles to the whiteboard. Then she pulled the box closer to her chair and rummaged through the folders that reduced Emily's life to facts on random pieces of paper.

Delanie interrupted Duncan's research when she asked, "When you get to a stopping point, could you see what you can find on a Douglas Black. His name came up when I interviewed Emily's room-mate Zoey. I don't see any reference to him in any of Rick's files. He was the only person Zoey mentioned who Emily didn't like."

"Sure," he said, writing the name down on his legal pad. "Anything on Emily?"

She slid back in her chair and looked at her notes. "Well, she wasn't any kind of activist. She had some causes she liked on Face-book, but she favorited a lot of things on the social media site. Her social media footprint is fairly large, and she was also an amateur photographer. She seemed like a normal twenty something who had her first job, own apartment, and a steady boyfriend. Her life appeared to be harmonious. I can't find any evidence anyone ever said anything negative about her. That's odd. There's got to be a snarky comment somewhere."

Duncan shook his head and Delanie continued, "Zoey said Emily was passionate about things. She described her as often animated. Zoey said she and Justin fought at a party the night of the murder because he thought there was another guy. Usually people who are emotional ruffle feathers. There is testimony after testimony in the file about how wonderful, friendly, and kind she was. She looks like she was a popular, All-American girl. And nothing looks even remotely like anything in the Styles case. Emily worked for a growing accounting firm. She was excited to land a job after college, and she traveled a lot to their three locations. We should look through her online pictures to see if we can find anything."

"I did earlier, and they're all benign. They're all of her friends or selfies with Justin at a variety of places around RVA. She also liked flowers a lot."

"Nothing else jumps out?" she asked.

"Does D'borah Styles have any links to Farmville or Norfolk?"

"Not that I can see. Her focus was mainly in the Petersburg area. She was a regular at City Council and committee meetings," he said.

"What about the guy from Farmville?"

"David Millhouse. He rented a house in town and worked as a veterinary assistant at a small practice that caters to house pets and barn animals. He traveled some for his job, but it was mainly to farms in the surrounding counties. He didn't have a social media presence like the two females. I can't find much on him. He was thirty-two, five-foot-six, and single. He drove a Chevy truck. He grew up in Farmville, and his mother still lives there. He has two older sisters and a cat...."

"So far, two of the victims had cats, but I don't think that's the connection. I'm going to text Rick Dixon. If we make a case for him, maybe he can get copies of the police files. Dunc, you may be on to something with these three cases," she said as she reached for her phone and tapped out a message for Chaz's lawyer.

"I'm willing to bet money that these three cases are related, but, right now, I'm hungry. You wanna grab dinner? I need a break. Let's go to the Golden Panda and see what our fortune cookies say. Margaret can take a nap and guard the office while we're gone. Can't you, Sweetie?" he said as he rubbed behind the bulldog's ears. Margaret snorted and rolled over for a tummy rub.

Delanie's phone buzzed when the wonton soup arrived. After taking the call, she said, "That's Rick Dixon. He's got some fundraiser to go to tonight, but he wants to meet around seven-thirty at our office for an update."

"That's fine," Duncan said, stuffing half an eggroll into his mouth. "I knew he'd be interested in what we uncovered." Delanie texted back their address.

"Where's a good place for dinner that girls like?" he asked after he swallowed the rest of the eggroll and wiped duck sauce off his face.

"What's the occasion?"

"I want a nice place. Evie and I have been going out for three months now. It's kind of an anniversary," he said, between bites of rice and vegetables.

Duncan met Evie Hachey last summer when his team won a superhero costume contest at RVACon, the same event where he conned Delanie into appearing as Batgirl. "What about Sylvester's? It's nice."

"How dressy is it?"

"Dressier than jeans and a t-shirt. What about the Italian place at Short Pump? Everybody likes Italian. It's an anniversary-type place."

"I dunno. We're not into the fancy stuff. We do a lot of take out."

"Why don't you ask her where she'd like to go?"

Duncan nodded and finished off his meal with orange sherbet and both fortune cookies.

~

"COMPANY'S HERE," DUNCAN SAID, SPOTTING A CLASSIC BLACK Corvette pull into a parking space in front of Falcon Investigations. Rick Dixon, dressed in a tuxedo, slid out of the car. Duncan opened the front door and turned on the lobby lights in the empty reception area.

"Delanie, it's good to see you again," the tall lawyer said.

"Hi, Mr. Dixon. Thanks for coming over on such short notice. This is my partner, Duncan Reynolds."

"It's Rick. Nice to meet you," he said, shaking Duncan's extended hand.

"The conference room is this way." The two men followed her down the hall. She cleared a chair for the attorney, but he didn't sit. He shifted from foot to foot as he read the notes on the whiteboard.

"What have you found?" he asked. Margaret waddled in and sniffed the lawyer's shoes. He leaned down and patted her head. Margaret took up residence under the conference table to keep an eye on things.

Duncan cleared his throat and said, "I discovered two murders in other parts of Virginia similar to the Menendez case. And both occurred after Emily Menendez's murder."

"Which means," Rick interrupted, "that if we can prove they were done by the same killer, Justin can't be their guy. Tell me more," Rick said as he settled into one of the conference room chairs. He kicked his legs under the table, barely missing the snoring bulldog on the other side.

Duncan recited what they had found on the three cases. Delanie was surprised. He didn't usually like to talk to people he didn't know. But he was enjoying being the center of attention tonight. First Evie and now this. Maybe Duncan was coming out of his geeky shell.

After Duncan and Delanie tag teamed to report their findings, Rick Dixon stood and stretched. "I think there's enough here to start with the different jurisdictions. I'll draft papers to get a subpoena for the Farmville and Petersburg police departments. I'll call you when I get access to the case files. In the meantime, do a report, and I may need you for additional meetings this week. Are you available?"

"I can make myself available to keep the case moving," she said. "We'll send over the update tomorrow, and I look forward to hearing from you."

"Great work," Rick said. "Thanks for all you've done." Delanie escorted him to the front door, and they stepped out on the sidewalk in the cool evening.

"Sorry you had to miss your event," she said as he climbed into his Corvette.

"No big deal. This was definitely worth it. It was one of those chichi charity things. There will be more next month. I'll let you know what I hear about the other two cases," he said as his car's engine roared to life.

The three cases had to be related. A closer look into each revealed similarities – even if the wall drawings weren't identical. But why didn't someone in law enforcement connect the dots? she wondered.

12

D ELANIE'S PHONE BUZZED AS SHE STOOD IN A LONG LINE AT THE DRY cleaner. "Hey, this is Rick. Thanks for the report. I filed a petition with the courts. We're able to subpoena the police for their investigative files on the other two cases. When I get them, I'll send copies over by courier. Thanks for the good work. Talk to you soon," he said.

"Good news," she said as he clicked off.

When she opened the Mustang's door, a blast of warm air hit her in the face. She tried not to fuss about the unusually warm autumn weather. She knew winter, her least favorite season, was around the corner. Delanie texted Duncan to give him Rick's update as she waited for the black interior to cool off.

I'm at the office, Duncan texted. *R U coming in?*

Be there in a minute. Lunch?

Yes. Bring some, and don't forget Miss M.

After a quick stop for tacos, Delanie parked in the back next to the Civic and let herself in the office.

"Hey, I'm here with lunch."

"Hey, we're here and hungry," Duncan said, walking toward the kitchen. Margaret trailed her favorite guy and plopped down under the table.

"So what's new?" she asked as they dug into the bag.

"I looked up your Douglas Black."

"And?"

"He still lives in the area. He's an odd bird. He lives in Henrico County in a middle-class neighborhood with his parents. Douglas drives a three-year old Kia, and he works at a hardware store. Oh, and he larps."

"He does what?"

"LARPs – You know, Live Action Role Playing."

"Nope. That's a new one. Good to know, I guess. What is it?"

"It's popular with the SciFi and fantasy fans. They have guilds and groups. There are themed meet ups across the area. They show up in costume at parks and...."

"Play dress up?"

"No. It's more than that. It borders on improv. There are all kinds of groups based on books, movies, and video games. Our Douglas Black is part of a medieval group that reenacts feudal life in the shires of Richmond. His character name is Sir Arthur Black. He's got a whole bio, and he's looking for a princess or rowdy wench to share the experience with. That could be your way in. You could chat him up online and go to a meet up. It's the perfect cover."

"Oh, that sounds like me, but my henin and cointoise are at the cleaners."

"Huh?"

"Pointy princess hat with a fashionable veil. But alas, I, like Cinderella, have nothing to wear. Plus, I'm about ten years older than our Sir Black. Won't he be suspicious?"

"I think he'd be happy to have anyone pay attention to him. And he's already interested in you."

"No, Duncan. You didn't!"

"You've been messaging him all morning. He answered the first one in about eight seconds. He's hooked. It'll be the perfect cover for you to talk to him and ask lots of questions."

"Duncan! What did you promise?"

"Relax. I used your picture, but the profile, Facebook, and Pinterest accounts I created are for Libby Jenkins, but you're Lady Elizabeth Locksley in medieval circles. I made you twenty-eight. You can pass."

"Thanks. And am I kin to Robin Hood and his Locksley family?"

Duncan smiled and said, "You're single and fairly new to the area. You moved here from Greensboro, North Carolina. And if you want to go, you'll have to get a costume."

"Duncan!"

"What? You volunteer me for things all the time. You'll be a lovely princess. You should be happy I didn't make you a rowdy wench."

"I already had to be Batgirl at the RVACon thing."

"That was for fun," he said.

She rolled her eyes and sighed. "I guess this means a trip to Carytown to rent a costume. Here, let me see what I've been saying to this guy. You better not have promised anything, or you're going with me."

It didn't take Delanie long to get bored with Douglas. His messages were overly sentimental and drowning with bad attempts at period allusions. And his Medieval English needed some work. Before signing off, Delanie/Libby said she might consider meeting him Sunday afternoon at Maymont, an estate from the Gilded Age, repurposed as an urban park and museum. His guild was reenacting a battle on the grassy area near the front gate. He told her to be prompt if she wanted to catch all the action. Delanie had visions of cruising down the interstate in a Glinda the Good Witch gown. She shuddered at the thought and was glad that her phone buzzed. She grabbed it and said, "Hey, Robin. How are you?"

"Great! I'm almost between projects, and I was wondering if you wanted to go to another storage unit auction on Friday. This one's in town."

"Sounds like fun. I'd love to go. What time?"

"How about if you meet at my house about eleven, and then we can drive over together?"

"Sounds good. You're still in the condo in Brandermill?"

"Yep. See you then," she said, clicking off.

"Hey," yelled Duncan. "Your guy keeps messaging you. He wants to know if you want to meet for dinner or coffee before the thing at Maymont. He wants to give you the lay of the land and background on all the participants. He said that you need the inside scoop before joining."

"Tell him coffee's okay, but he has to do it today. I can't take much more of him. I want to get this over with. He can meet me at the Starbucks near Courthouse and Beach Roads."

"Why there?"

"It's not in my neighborhood. And I don't have the energy to drive to the other side of town to meet him. If he wants to chat, he can do it on my terms."

"Be nice, princess."

"I will. And tell him to be there in an hour. And mention that her highness doesn't like to be kept waiting."

DELANIE ARRIVED AT THE STARBUCKS ABOUT TWENTY MINUTES BEFORE she expected Douglas Black to make his entrance. She ordered an iced chocolate latte and a peanut butter cookie and settled in at a table near the back where she could see the front door. She was dreading this interview.

Halfway into her cookie, a doughy guy with black glasses came in the front door. He looked from table to table until he spotted her. Without waiting for an invitation, he plopped in the chair opposite of her and said, "Libby? I'm Douglas. It's so nice to finally meet you. I feel like I know you already. I recognized you from your pictures."

"Hi, Douglas. It's nice to meet you too. Do you want to order something?"

"Nah. Well, I guess so. I'll be back in a minute. Don't go anywhere."

She watched him on his smartphone while he stood in line. When it was his turn, he ordered a caramel macchiato and a sandwich and played with his phone until his order was ready. She hoped he wasn't taking pictures of her.

Douglas landed in the chair and dove into his sandwich. Between bites, he said, "Uh, it's really nice to meet you. How did you get into role playing?"

"In college. I had a double major in English and theatre. It seemed to fit. And it was something to do on weekends."

"Oh, it's a lifestyle with my guys. There aren't too many girls in our guild. You'll be really popular. Hey, we could build an alliance. Let's keep it quiet for now, and we could spring it on them at the right time. They won't know what hit them."

"Okay," she said. "What kind of an alliance?"

"We could join forces and rule the kingdom. Will you, Lady Elizabeth of Locksley join forces with me your humble knight, Sir Arthur Black? Our kingdoms could unite and stretch across a wide swath of the Richmond shire. I have some replica swords. I could let you borrow one. I only bring them out for special occasions because they're expensive. And I rarely let anyone handle them. Oh, and guess what a few of us from our guild did? We went to the site of the old Renaissance Fair near Fredericksburg."

"Central Virginia has a Renaissance Fair?"

"This one closed in the nineties. The property is abandoned these days. The buildings and the ship are still there, but the weeds and vegetation have taken over. It's like this lost, forgotten world. We parked about a mile away and hiked over. It was really cool traipsing around the property. One of the guys even took aerial shots with his drone. It's a thing on the Internet. People go to abandoned sites to see what they can find. You know like old amusement parks and empty properties – even old sports stadiums."

"Isn't that dangerous?" She hoped he didn't catch the sarcasm. "I mean it's trespassing."

"Probably, but we were on a quest. And nobody was around. It was our own private adventure. Sir Arthur and his band of knights fought off the flora and fauna to hike to the land of our people. The only problems we had were the ticks and poison ivy. The gates and the food booths are still there. There were still signs from the last festival. We got into an office, and some of the cabinets and shelves still had paper files. It was like everyone vanished and left it as it was on the last day of the festival. Chen took pictures and video. It's out on YouTube if you want to see it. We explored all the buildings and what's left of the ship. It was like exploring a town after an apocalypse without the zombies and mutants. It was awesome!" he said, leaning forward. "And you know what? We might go back and film a zombie video there. I bet it would go viral."

"Okay, bring Douglas back," she said. After a couple of sips of her coffee, she continued with, "When did you get into reenactments?"

"I did Dungeons and Dragons and other role-playing games in high school. I continued in college and beyond. It's just what I do. My guild has detailed costumes and props. We've made a commitment to this. We're all in."

"Interesting. Where did you go to school?"

"VCU. I majored in English and business. Oh, and I ran a guild there too and played D&D."

"Virginia Commonwealth University. Did you know Emily Menendez or Duncan Reynolds?"

"Huh?"

"I'm kinda new to Central Virginia. Those are the only people who I've met who went to VCU."

"If you're in the business world in Richmond like me, you'll find that lots of locals went to school there."

"And what do you do in the business world?"

"I'm in sales. And I knew Emily in school, but not the guy. She and I, uh, dated a while back."

"You did? I thought she had a boyfriend named Justin, and it was pretty serious?"

"I don't know a Justin. She and I must have hooked up before him," he said, stuffing a hunk of sandwich in his mouth.

"Douglas, I thought I liked you," she said quietly. "But I don't think you're telling me the truth. And I'm not sure I can trust you. And if I can't trust you, then I'm wasting my time here." Delanie leaned forward across the table into Douglas' space.

He slid back and almost knocked over his drink. He sighed heavily and shifted in his chair.

"Douglas, if you don't tell me the truth, I'm outta here," she said as she rose.

"No, no don't go. Sit down. What do you want to know?"

"Tell me what you know about Emily Menendez," she said, returning to her seat.

He let out another heavy sigh. "She's a girl from school. I asked her out once, but she shot me down. She said she had a boyfriend. She wasn't very friendly after I asked her to the movies."

"When did you see her last?"

"I was in a class with her junior year. After graduation, I didn't see her again."

"You sure?"

"Well, I saw her on social media sites if that counts. I saw her in a couple of bars, but we didn't speak."

"Douglas, were you stalking her?"

"No, no. It was nothing like that. I saw her pictures on Instagram once in a while. I liked her, but she was only interested in that Justin guy."

"That sounds like stalking. When was the very last time you saw her?"

"In person?" Delanie nodded as she popped the last bite of cookie in her mouth.

He continued, "I dunno. Probably last year at the Folk Festival. She was with her friends. She didn't even notice me. I saw her dancing with a bunch of girls in front of one of the stages near the river. She was wearing a yellow dress and hanging out with friends. She didn't know I was there."

"When was the last time you talked with her?"

"It's been a long time. Probably when we were in school. Why are you so interested in Emily? It was a long time ago. You a cop or something?"

"No." Delanie put her napkin on her plate and finished her drink. "I've got to be going soon."

"Do you have to? We got off on the wrong foot here. We should start over," he whined.

"I have some errands to run." She picked up her purse and scooted her chair backwards.

When she stood, Douglas asked, "So this means you won't be into forming an alliance this weekend?"

"No, I don't think so," she said, gathering her trash.

"Are you sure? We'd make a great team. The other guys will be so jealous. We could spring it on them and watch 'em scramble. Plus, you'll get to see my swords, and we have the biggest guild in the area."

She nodded and exited through the front door. "Bye, Douglas." He didn't answer.

Out in the parking lot, she climbed into the Mustang and locked the doors. Douglas left the parking lot and turned right on Iron Bridge Road. Delanie gunned the engine and turned left. When she was sure she wasn't followed, she told the radio to call Duncan's cell.

After three rings, she heard, "Hey, what's up. How was Sir Black?"

"Creepy and sad."

"Not even demented and sad, but social?"

"No. I know why Emily was uncomfortable. I think he cyber-stalked her after she told him to leave her alone."

"Do you think he was involved in the murder?"

"No. He's all about his fantasy world. He doesn't function well in this world with real people. I think he watched her postings and showed up from time to time where she was."

"You need to see him again?"

"Definitely not. We know where he lives and works. He's not that hard to find. I don't think we need to spend any more time with Douglas Black. We can move on to the next lead."

"So I should make Libby's cyber presence disappear?"

"Good idea. I've had enough fantasy and larping to last me a lifetime. I can mark those off the old bucket list."

Delanie crossed Douglas Black off the list too. The Sir Black angle amounted to a dead-end. She had had enough roller derbying and larping to last a while. She headed to the gym to clear her head and burn off the latest round of junk food.

13

On the way into the office the next day, Delanie's phone rang. She clicked the button on the steering wheel and said, "Hello, Duncan. What's up?"

"Douglas is still checking out Libby's Facebook page after your date yesterday. He wants to know if you've changed your mind about this weekend. He thinks you should give him another chance. He's willing to share his swords. He really wants you to give him a do-over. He promises that it'll be different this time."

"Duncan. You said you were going to take my fake profile down. I don't need to talk to him again."

"I will. I will. Right after this call. I thought you'd want to know how much you impressed him. He even posted a picture of you at Starbucks. You're going to break his heart."

"Lovely. So that's what you called me for on this beautiful morning?"

"Rick's office sent over the files. You nearby?"

"Yep."

"Pick up some doughnuts. We're going to need sustenance for this."

"Gotcha. See you in a few."

After going through the drive-thru window at the combination doughnut/ice cream store, Delanie balanced a box and a cardboard tray with two coffees as she locked the car and then unlocked the office's front door.

She took breakfast to the conference room. She set the box and coffees next to a pile of files and plopped in a nearby chair.

"Oh good," Duncan said. "It's been a long morning already. Thanks for the food."

"So where do you want me to start?"

"Take this file. It's on the Millhouse case. I'm going through the one about the D'borah Styles' case in Petersburg now. We'll switch in a little while."

Delanie settled in and plowed through the folders about the murder in Farmville. About an hour and Duncan's three doughnuts later, they switched cases.

Near lunch time, Delanie stood and stretched. She did some yoga stretches, and Margaret yawned.

"I'm tired," Duncan said. "What have we found? Let's start with the Millhouse case."

Delanie picked up her notes and said, "There was a lot of graffiti in blood on his living room and entrance way walls. I see a triple six, but there's a lot of other stuff that doesn't make sense to me."

"It's from video games. From these pictures, I see stuff from Halo, World of Warcraft, and Grand Theft Auto. And that one over there, looks like a lopsided Pac Man. It looks kind of juvenile."

"The police noted there wasn't a break-in. So either David Millhouse left the door unlocked, or he let the person in."

"It must have been someone he knew or felt comfortable letting in. Was he into video games?"

"Don't know yet. I'll add that to my list. The coroner put the time of death at between seven and midnight on a Friday night. Emily died about two in the morning on a Saturday, so it was someone they'd let in during the evening," he said.

"And D'borah Styles died between seven and eleven on a Friday evening," Delanie added.

"There's not a particular day of the week. And the times vary too."

"The killer probably has a day job. They're all evenings or weekends."

"Good point," he said. "Let's lay out all pages with the crime scene photos and see if they're similar. I didn't see anything about how the person got access to D'borah's house."

"Uh, there was something," Delanie said. "There was a note. Let me see. Here, the front door was unlocked, and the back door was open. The cops mentioned that her cats weren't in the house. Another note states that a neighbor found one of the cats wandering around with what looked like blood on its paws."

"Okay. Check out these pictures," he said. "It's hard to say on all of these, but there are definitely some similarities. In the Styles' pictures, there are words on the wall."

"It looks like poetry," she said.

"No, look here. It's song lyrics. I knew I recognized it. It's from Ozzy Osbourne's 'Crazy Train.'"

"Good work, dude. So, one had demonic symbols, one had images from gaming, and the third had song lyrics. I'll start typing. I want to get our report out to Rick tonight."

An hour later, she proofread their update for the attorney with Duncan reading over her shoulder. After a couple of changes, she said, "There. That looks good. I'm going to send this, and I think we could call it a day. Did you find a place for your special dinner with Evie?"

"I asked her where she wanted to go, and she said Uptown Alley. We're going for dinner and video games this weekend. Hey, Margaret and I are going to hang out here for a while. I have some design work I need to do on a website."

"Enjoy. I've got to catch up on some errands. I'll see you all later. I'm not sure if I'll be in tomorrow. I'm going with Robin to another storage auction."

Duncan nodded and said, "Have fun looking at others' junk and leave the leftover doughnuts. Margaret and I will take care of them."

∼

HER PHONE RANG AS SHE CLIMBED IN THE CAR. "DELANIE. THIS IS ERIC Ellington. I received the statement you sent. And I'd like to set up some time to talk with you tomorrow. I have some additional questions."

"Okay. But I've got plans in the morning." She let out a sigh.

"How about three? I'll meet you at your office. It won't take long."

"There's not much more that I can tell you that I didn't already put in my written statement."

"I have some questions and would really appreciate a few minutes of your time. I'll see you at three tomorrow," he said before the phone disconnected.

Delanie wondered what more he could want that he couldn't ask on the phone. He grated on her nerves. Right now, she had to go to the post office, gas station, and grocery store. And she had several loads of laundry waiting at home for her. The life of a private investigator. She would worry about what Agent Ellington wanted tomorrow.

After putting the groceries away, she skipped the laundry in favor of driving by two of the other murder scenes. She zigzagged down one-way streets to Main Street, following the GPS instructions to the Poe Museum and down the hill to an apartment building that had popped up within the last few years. According to Rick Dixon's files, Emily Menendez used to live in one of the units that faced the back of the complex on Franklin Street.

She circled the block twice. Parking required a code to get past the gate, so she found on-street parking around the corner. The street level of Emily's building had a glass front with the access-controlled doors. Emily or someone inside would have had to let the killer in, or it had to be someone who had access. The apartment's security features would have deterred the average criminal. She snapped a few pictures and returned to her car.

An hour later, she found D'borah Styles' small house in an older neighborhood in Petersburg. An uneven aluminum fence outlined the perimeter of the property and a rusty front gate hung askew near the sidewalk in the front. The gray house, with what was once white gingerbread work, looked like it could use a good coat of paint. There was no sign of life at this end of the block.

On a whim, Delanie called the number on the small real estate sign in the front yard. She punched in the house number and listened to the recording about the house's cozy amenities.

She drove around the block to see the back of the property. Delanie peeked past the house on the next street to see the Styles' backyard where an aluminum shed sat alone next to some overgrown bushes and a rusty grill. A screened-in porch, painted a faded green, sagged on one side.

On her second circuit around the Styles' property, her phone rang with a number she didn't recognize.

"Hello."

"Hi. This is Lavinia Harper, realtor. I saw that you called about my listing on North Bush Street. Do you have any questions about the property?"

"It seems like an interesting property. It's reasonably priced."

"Would you like to see the house? I can be there in a few minutes if you're interested."

"That would be really nice if it's no trouble."

"It's no problem at all. See you in a few."

Delanie parked in front of the gray two story to watch for the realtor. She flipped through photos of Emily Menendez's building and then snapped some of this property. A black Escalade pulled in behind her while she was checking her Facebook updates. A tall woman slid out of the behemoth SUV and flipped a large designer bag over her shoulder.

"Delanie?" the realtor called as she extended a perfectly manicured hand with lots of gold rings. "I'm Lavinia Harper. I hope I didn't keep you waiting long."

"No. I appreciate you showing me the property on such short notice. I'm Delanie Fitzgerald." She felt a twinge of guilt for wasting the realtor's time showing a house she wasn't a prospective buyer for.

"Come this way," the realtor said as she punched her code in her phone to access the lockbox. Delanie stepped over the threshold, and Lavinia Harper began her spiel on all the positives of D'borah Styles' former house. "This is a traditional city row house, built in 1946. It has a roof that's about five years old. This is the formal living room. In the old days, this would have been the parlor."

Delanie shivered. Except for the new paint, it was the room in the murder scene pictures. She shook off the feeling of dread and caught up to the realtor, who had moved on to the kitchen.

"The home has an oil furnace and central AC. This is what was called a shotgun house. You know you could shoot a gun from the front door and the bullet could travel all the way through the house to the back door. The houses were long and narrow because back in the day, taxes were levied on the width of the house that faced the street. In here, the main foyer leads to all the downstairs rooms and to the back door off the kitchen. The appliances were all replaced recently. There's a screened-in porch out back and a small sitting room on that side as well." The realtor's voice tapered off as she moved through the downstairs rooms.

When she returned to where Delanie was standing in the foyer, Lavinia Harper said, "Let's go upstairs. It has wooden steps and three good sized bedrooms with a fully tiled bath." The realtor's voice drifted off again as she flitted from room to room. Delanie snapped a few pictures and caught up with the other woman at the top of the stairs.

"I'd like to get a picture of the downstairs rooms, if you don't mind."

"Help yourself."

When Lavinia Harper joined her again in the dining room, Delanie asked, "This home is nice. Why are the current owners selling?"

"The previous owner passed away and the estate is selling the property."

Delanie sighed and said, "I'm so sorry to hear that." She was wondering if the realtor would divulge anything about the murder. After a long silence and no mention of Ms. Styles' demise, Delanie continued with, "Well, Ms. Harper, thank you so much for showing me this property. I have all the information I need, and I'll talk it over with my boyfriend tonight." She shook the realtor's hand and pocketed the card she offered.

"My pleasure. I look forward to hearing from you. This house would be a great investment property. Do you and your boyfriend have a realtor?"

"Not yet. We're still in the looking stage of our search."

"Well, consider me. I could help you all put together a deal for this house that would be a great investment for a young couple."

"I'll talk to my boyfriend and give you a call." She smiled and held the door for Delanie.

Delanie stood in the front yard trying to imagine the murder scene. She snapped a couple of pictures of the weathered stoop and bent storm door with the "S" on the front.

"Thanks again," she said to the realtor who shut off the lights and replaced the key in the lockbox.

Delanie didn't pick up anything new from her visits, but it was good to see the actual scenes. They always looked different in person than they did in the crime scene photographs.

14

Delanie parked the Mustang next to the white truck in front of Robin's condo. It was odd that the house looked dark. Delanie rang the doorbell twice with no response. Leaning on the porch's wooden railing, she texted her friend and then rang the bell again. When there was no answer to either, she called Robin's cell and left a message.

After a few minutes' wait, Delanie called Robin's landline. She could hear the ringing through the door. When the voicemail answered, she disconnected.

Flipping through her contacts, she found the number for Robin's store and dialed.

"Butterfly Blue. How can I help you?"

"Hi, this is Delanie Fitzgerald. I was supposed to meet Robin this morning to go to a storage auction. I'm at her house and there's no answer. I was calling to see if she's there."

"Oh, hi, Delanie. This is Trish, her sister. No, she's not here. She was looking forward to the auction, so I don't think her plans changed. Maybe she's in the shower or something. That's not like her.

She's usually on time for things. If I hear from her, I'll have her call you."

"Okay. Thanks. I'll hang out here for a while longer. Bye."

Delanie pocketed her phone and walked down to the end of the block where the row of townhomes ended. She hiked around the back. Robin's was the third one from the end. All of the backyards had a fence with a gate in the rear. Robin's open back gate swayed slightly in the breeze.

Delanie's sixth sense tingled. This really wasn't like Robin, who was usually prompt and meticulous. Robin lived alone after her divorce. She wouldn't have left the gate open when her truck was in the driveway.

Delanie walked along the edge of the fence to the patio, surrounded by all kinds of plants in colorful pots and a metal table and chairs under the pergola. She froze when she saw the open sliding glass door. The interior view of the condo was blocked by the hanging vertical blinds that were pulled shut in front of the open door.

Pressing herself against the wall, Delanie listened for any kind of noise. She fished out her phone and dialed Robin's home number again. The phone rang six times and stopped. Delanie could hear the voicemail message on her cell. She hung up and listened for any movement inside the house. She heard only cicadas and an occasional bird.

Rummaging through her purse for her pepper spray, Delanie found it and uncapped the canister. She pushed the vertical slats of the blinds to the side and peeked into the dark room.

An overturned end table was next to a broken lamp. A shelf had been knocked over and books and small statues were strewn across the floor. Debating about whether or not to go in, Delanie heard a faint cry and then a muffled groan. When she didn't hear any other noises, she pushed the blinds aside and stepped inside.

Delanie tiptoed through the living room to the hallway, stopping every few minutes to listen for any other noises. She froze when she saw the blood trail from the hallway to the dining room. It looked like another bloody trail snaked in the opposite direction to the kitchen.

Delanie glanced around the room. Even more blood had spattered on the carpet and walls. Robin lay on her side in the tiny room. She leaned over to check for a pulse, and Robin moaned again. Delanie dialed 911.

"Virginia State Police, what's your emergency?"

"I'm Delanie Fitzgerald. I went to my friend's condo. Her house has been ransacked, and she's bleeding. She's in the dining room, and her breathing is shallow. Her address is 11328 Timber Creek Ridge. It's in Brandermill in Midlothian."

"Are you in any danger?"

"No, I don't think so. The back door was open when I walked inside, and I found blood trails in the hall and the dining room."

"Is there a pulse?"

"A faint one. She groaned several times."

"Okay. Stay with her. I'm transferring your call to Chesterfield, but I'll stay on the line. We'll have police and rescue there soon. Where was she injured?"

"In the abdomen. There's a lot of blood, and it's starting to gel."

"So there's no bleeding right now?"

"Not that I can see. There's a lot of blood on the carpet around her. And she's really pale."

"Okay. An ambulance is en route. They should be there in about three minutes. Can you open a door or stand on the porch, so they can see you quickly?"

When she walked to the front door of the condo, Delanie noticed the jumble in the kitchen. Two of the chairs were on their sides, and things that should have been on top of the countertop were scattered on the floor. Her heart pounded in her ears. She stepped gingerly into the foyer, trying not to disturb anything. Blood droplets dotted the cabinets and formed a trail across the linoleum.

"Okay," said the emergency dispatcher. "Are you still there? Delanie, are you with me?"

"I'm here. I opened the front door. The kitchen is a mess too. It looks like Robin tried to fight off her attacker."

Returning to the dining room, Delanie knelt next to her friend who was in the fetal position on her side. She heard a siren in the distance and felt a wave of relief.

"Delanie," said the dispatcher. They're in front of the house now. I'm going to hang up. They'll be inside in a minute."

"Thanks for all of your help." Delanie clicked off the phone and slid it in her pocket.

"Robin, can you hear me? Robin. It's going to be okay. The ambulance is here."

Robin moaned and tried to turn her head. Delanie turned her over on her back. There was a lot of blood around her abdomen and scratches on her arms and face.

She squeezed Robin's hand. "It's going to be all right. Help is coming. We'll find out who did this. Hang on for me. We're going to get you help."

Robin moved her lips and faintly said, "Tulip Shirt. I don't know who it was. It was a Tulip Shirt this morning."

Delanie squeezed her hand again, but by then the first two paramedics arrived with a gurney.

"Chesterfield EMS," the first one shouted.

Delanie stood, and yelled, "In here. In the dining room. I think she's been stabbed. I found her on the floor. She moaned a couple of times, and she spoke once."

The two men, followed by a woman and another male, entered the house and triaged Robin. Delanie wiped the congealed blood from her hands onto her jeans and pulled out her phone. She texted her brother Steve while she watched the first responders help her friend.

Delanie's phone rang, and she wiped the screen on her jeans again and said, "Hello."

"Delanie. This is Steve. I got your message. Where are you now?"

"I'm still at Robin's condo in Brandermill – off Millridge Parkway. The EMTs are with her now."

"Police there yet?"

"No, but I hear sirens."

"Stay put. I'll be there in ten or fifteen minutes."

"Thanks," she said as she disconnected.

Delanie waited in the hallway while the EMTs tended to Robin. A bloody pentagram and what looked like a goat's head covered part of one wall in the dining room. Delanie shivered when she realized what she was seeing. This one didn't have as many markings as the other crime scenes she'd seen in the file photos. Several Chesterfield County police officers stormed through the front door and interrupted her thoughts.

The tall one in the green uniform took off his Smokey Bear hat and said, "Ma'am, did you call nine-one-one? I'm Sergeant Hunter Cox."

"Yes. I'm Delanie Fitzgerald. I'm Lieutenant Fitzgerald's sister. This is my friend Robin's house. I was supposed to meet her here this morning."

"Let's step into the living room. Where have you been in the residence?" Pulling out a small black notebook from his pocket, he flipped to a blank page and jotted notes as Delanie talked.

"I came in through the open back door. I walked through the living room and this hall. I saw the kitchen when I opened the front door for the paramedics."

"Johnson," he yelled. "The rest of the house needs to be secured."

The officer drew his gun, and the female officer followed him upstairs. Two other officers came through the front door, and Sergeant Cox yelled, "Johnson and Whitehurst are upstairs. Lock down the rest of the bottom floor."

"Gotcha," said another officer who headed down the hallway to the half-bath and laundry room. The other officer drew his gun and lumbered toward the living room.

Sergeant Cox turned back to Delanie. "You got here when? Then what happened?"

"There was no answer when I rang the bell a little before eleven. I called her and texted her. When I called her landline, I could hear it ringing from the porch. I called her sister at their store. She said she didn't know where Robin was. It's not like her to miss appointments. Then I walked around back. The gate and the back door were open. The patio door blinds were pulled, but the glass door was open. I looked inside. The room was a mess," she said, catching her breath.

"Then you called the police?" he asked, frowning.

"No. I heard a noise. It sounded like a groan coming from inside the house. I went in when I didn't hear any other noises."

"Unarmed?"

"I had my pepper spray."

Frowning again, he asked, "Did you see or hear anyone else?"

"No. I heard several groans, and I found Robin in the dining room."

"Does she live alone?"

"Yes. She moved in here after her divorce."

"Do you know if she had issues with the ex-husband?"

"They ended up divorced, so I'm sure there was something, but I think it was amicable. They were on friendly terms. He shows up at parties and holidays from time to time. His name is Joseph Birdsong."

"How long have you known her?"

"I don't know – about twelve years. We met in college. She married Joseph a couple of years after graduation. I'm guessing they were together for six or seven years."

"Any boyfriends right now?"

"Not that I know of. She didn't talk about anything but work."

"Do you have contact information for her?"

"Yes," Delanie said, tapping on her phone. "The store she owns is called Butterfly Blue. And her sister's name is Trish Jenkins. This is the number," she said as she held her phone for him to see.

"Thanks," he said, jotting down the information.

Before Sergeant Cox could continue his questioning, Delanie's brother stepped through the door and looked around Robin's kitchen and dining room. Lieutenant Fitzgerald nodded to the sergeant and said, "Hey, D. You okay?"

"Hi, Steve. Yeah, but I didn't expect to find this today."

Before they could continue their conversation, the EMTs raised the gurney and started for the front door.

"Where are you taking her?" Delanie asked.

"Johnston-Willis Hospital," said one of the EMTs as they wheeled Robin out and lifted the gurney down the wooden steps.

"Do you know of anything else that would help our investigation?" Sergeant Cox asked. She watched Steve head toward the dining room.

"Robin whispered to me. She said, 'Tulip Shirt. I don't know who did it.' She also said something about it being this morning."

"What's a Tulip Shirt?" asked Sergeant Cox.

"I have no idea. Do you need me for anything else? I want to get cleaned up and go to the hospital."

"No. We'll call if we have any more questions. We may need to get your fingerprints since you've been all through the crime scene."

"I'm a PI. My prints are on file with my license."

"Hey, Steve," she yelled. "I'm going to the hospital."

"Okay. I'll call you later today," he said from the other room.

Delanie jogged to her car. After sliding into the front seat, she texted Duncan to meet her at the office. She put a nine-one-one at the beginning and ending of her message.

Delanie drove with a purpose to the office. Her jeans and shirt felt crunchy from the dried blood. She wanted to update Duncan, but her first goal was to get out of these clothes.

Parking in the back, she let herself in. Not stopping to lock the door, she ran to her office and grabbed a golf shirt and a pair of jeans. After a birdbath in the sink, she changed clothes and put the old ones in a trash bag. She would throw them out after she confirmed with Steve that the police didn't need them.

By the time she was back in her office checking email, she heard Duncan and Margaret moving around the suite.

"Delanie. You here? We got here as soon as we could. What's going on? You left the door unlocked."

She met Duncan in the hallway. "Oh, Dunc. This just got personal. I went over to Robin's. We were supposed to go to a storage auction this morning. When she didn't answer the door, I called and texted her. I went around to the back of her condo, and the door was open. I heard groaning, so I went in." Delanie paused. Then the tears came flooding. "Duncan, she was stabbed in the stomach. I found her lying in the dining room. And there was stuff on the walls similar to the other murder scenes."

"Oh, Delanie. I'm so sorry."

"She was in and out of consciousness, but she spoke before they took her to the hospital. Robin said, 'Tulip Shirt' and that she didn't know the attacker."

"You're pale as a ghost. I think you should sit down. Let's go to the kitchen, and I'll get you something to drink."

Following him down the hallway, she sniffed, "I'm always this color. But okay. I could use a drink."

She dropped into one of the chairs while Duncan found her a Coke. Margaret walked over and put her head in Delanie's lap. Stroking the bulldog's brown and white head, she listened to Duncan. "This is horrible for you and Robin. I'm sorry. But we'll find out who did this. Think of it this way. It's great news for Justin and Rick Dixon."

"It just doesn't feel that good right now."

"I know. We've got to keep going on this. What are you doing this afternoon?" he asked.

"I'm going to the hospital to see how she's doing. Then, I've got to call Steve to get him updated. Can you email or call Rick Dixon and give him the latest? I'm not sure who the lead detective is in Chesterfield."

"Sure. Do you need anything else?"

"I'm good," she said, wiping her eyes on the back of her hand. "Thanks, Margaret. You're such a sweetie. And thanks, Duncan. I appreciate you. I'll check in later this afternoon when I know more." She hugged the bulldog, who gave her a sloppy kiss.

"I'll call Chaz's lawyer and start researching Tulip Shirts. I'm not sure what they are. I don't think I've ever heard anyone refer to one?"

"I have no idea what it is either. I'm heading out," she said, reaching for her purse. "I need to find out how Robin's doing."

15

D ELANIE ALMOST BROKE THE SOUND BARRIER ON HER DRIVE TO THE hospital. She jammed the car into a parking space near the Emergency Room sign and jogged through the lot to the lobby. A nice lady at the circular desk told her Robin was a patient. But that's all she would say since Delanie wasn't family.

Delanie called Butterfly Blue and got a closed recording with a number that she could call. She left a message for Robin's sister Trish to call her.

Delanie's phone binged with a text from Trish while she was pacing the lobby. *Robin's in surgery. We're waiting near the ICU.*

"Excuse me," Delanie said to the same woman in pink with a variety of pins dotting her lanyard. "Could you tell me where the family waiting room is for ICU?"

"Go down to the second nurses' station. The waiting area's on the left with yellow walls."

Delanie's sneakers squeaked on the shiny floor, reminding her of a gym. She had flashbacks to eighth grade P.E. class. Then her thoughts shifted to her friendship with Robin and college. Why was Robin attacked? There had to be a connection to the other killings. At first blush, she couldn't think of any similarities to the Styles, Mill-house, and Menendez killings.

Trish and an older woman sat in overstuffed chairs in the waiting area at the end of the hallway. Trish stood and hugged her.

"I'm so sorry," Delanie said. "Any news?"

"She's in surgery. We should know something soon. I hope. She was semiconscious when they brought her in. They said she's lucky you found her when you did. We're waiting for an update. Delanie, this is my mom, Patricia Kirby."

"It's so nice to meet you," Delanie said as the woman dabbed her eyes with a tissue. Robin and Trish's mother nodded and shook Delanie's hand with both of hers. Delanie got a vision of what Robin would look like in her sixties. They sat in the stiff waiting room chairs, and Delanie flipped through outdated magazines to pass the time.

After what felt like hours, a doctor came out to see Robin's family. The man in blue scrubs and disposable hat dropped down in the seat next to Robin's mother and said, "Mrs. Kirby, I'm Dr. Bergan. I did Robin's surgery. She was stabbed six times. Three were in the abdomen. The wounds damaged her spleen, which we removed. One penetration punctured her left lung. The other two didn't hit anything vital. She also has wounds in both arms and one in her right thigh. She fought back and fought hard. We were able to get some tissue samples from under her nails for the police. She's on a ventilator right now – Also, she lost a lot of blood."

He cleared his throat and continued, "She's in recovery now, and we will monitor her today and tonight. I'm cautiously optimistic. If she's doing well, we'll move to the step-down unit maybe as early as tomorrow. We'll have to wait and see. She's a fighter – that's evident from the struggle she put up against her attacker. She should pull through this."

"Oh, hallelujah. Thank you so much, Doctor," Mrs. Kirby said, wringing her hands.

"One of the nurses will let you know when she is out of post-op."

"Thank you. Thank you," Mrs. Kirby said as she clutched her tissue.

After Mrs. Kirby hugged Trish, she stepped out to find a restroom. Delanie broke the silence with, "Is there anything I can do for you all?"

"Robin doesn't have any of her things here. Would you mind contacting the police to see if you can go in and get an overnight bag together? I have a key to her condo. I don't think we could go in her house right now."

"Sure, that's no problem. My brother is on the police force. He'll be able to find out for me. I'll pack a couple of days' worth of stuff. Anything in particular she would want?"

"Just the basics, and could you put out food for the cat? He wasn't at the store, so I'm sure he went home with her."

Delanie picked up her purse and rose. "I'm going to head out. Text me if anything changes. I'll be back later with her stuff," she said as she waved and headed back down the long hallway. She didn't have the heart to tell Trish the back door was open, and she didn't see any sign of Penguin when she was at the condo.

On the way out of the hospital, Delanie tapped her older brother's contact on her phone. After a couple of rings, she heard, "Fitzgerald here."

"Hi, Steve. It's Delanie."

"We're still at Robin's house. Forensics should be wrapping up soon. Where are you?"

"I'm leaving the hospital now. When you all are done with her house, is it okay for me to pick up some clothes for Robin?"

"How 'bout you meet me for lunch."

"You can leave the scene?"

"I'm not officially on duty today. Firehouse Subs?"

"Okay. See you in a few minutes," she said.

Delanie cranked up the radio and rolled down the windows. She hoped the unseasonably warm weather and the loud music would block out thoughts of Robin's attack for a little while.

When she pulled into the sub shop's parking lot, she saw a white

Chesterfield County cruiser in front of the mattress shop. Steve sat next to the window in the sub shop with a soft drink.

"Been here long?" she asked.

"No, just a few minutes. How are you doing?"

"It's been a long day already. I'm pretty well wiped out. I think Robin's going to be okay. She was in post-op when I left. The doctor said if she did well tonight, they'd put her in the step- down unit tomorrow."

She followed Steve to the cash register. She set her purse on the counter that had a Dalmatian pattern that matched the firehouse décor.

"That's good news," her brother said after he asked for a turkey sub. After she ordered, they returned to Steve's table to wait for their sandwiches.

"Okay, what were you doing at Robin's?"

"We were supposed to meet for a storage auction this morning. She opened a furniture store recently with her sister. She repurposes and restores old things. Most of her stuff comes from auctions and estate sales. I was supposed to help her today at a storage auction."

"Does she have a boyfriend?"

"Not that I know of. She's been single since her divorce."

"Problems with the ex?"

"I don't think so. It was amicable. He's still friendly with the family. You're asking me the same types of questions Sergeant Cox did."

"Goes with the territory. Was there anyone there when you arrived besides Robin?"

"I didn't see anybody, but I didn't go through the rest of the condo."

"The detectives think the person was only on the ground level. There was no evidence of a disturbance upstairs."

"Did you all find the cat? The back door was open when I got there. The gate was open too. Her sister asked about him."

"No cat. Why Robin?"

"I can't come up with anything. She didn't do much outside of work. She went to a lot of yard sales and auctions. She doesn't post much on social media except to advertise things for her store. She stays busy with her work projects."

"When was the last time you saw her?"

Before she could reply, the counter clerk arrived with their sandwiches.

Taking a bite of her ham and Swiss, she said, "Paisley and I went with her to a storage auction a while back. Then I had lunch with her after that. I was working on a case where the guys fenced stuff at local swap meets. Robin gave me a quick rundown on the flea markets in the area where she used to sell. Then she called me earlier this week to invite me to another storage auction."

"The Emerson brothers?" Delanie nodded and sipped her drink. "Snooping and peeking at people's abandoned junk? I guess it goes with your PI habits." She smirked at her older brother. "Your friend's life sounds pretty normal."

"She didn't barhop or party. Her circle of friends is pretty tight."

Steve nodded again and took another bite of his sandwich. "Anything else?"

"She said today she didn't know the suspect. But she did say, 'Tulip Shirt.' I have no idea what that is. Do you?"

"Nope," he said.

"I'm not sure if it's a color or a brand. Duncan's looking into it. If it is something, he can usually find it. He's amazing with online research." Steve harrumphed, and she continued, "My clothes from this morning were ruined. Do the police need them for anything, or can I toss them?"

"You can get rid of them. There's enough forensic evidence at the scene. Anything else I need to know about?"

Delanie looked down at her lunch.

"Delanie..."

"Okay. But I want to be an anonymous source if this gets to the point it gets out."

"I'm not promising anything. Speak. What do you know?"

"I was hired to find some information on a murder in Richmond from several months ago. A young woman was attacked and killed in her apartment while her roommate was away. There were some pentagrams and other satanic symbols painted on the wall in blood. When Duncan started digging around, he found two other cases with similar crime scenes, but the victims don't have any connections that we've found yet. The wall drawings are different in each case, but they are all done in the victims' blood."

"And Robin makes number four."

"Yes. And they're all in different jurisdictions across a timespan of several months."

"Okay, you've got my attention."

"It doesn't seem like any of the police forces in the area or the news outlets are investigating these as related. We think it's the same killer even though they've been spaced out over time and geography. We can't find commonality with ethnicity or gender. There aren't a lot of patterns, but Duncan and I still think they're related."

"What have you done with the information?"

"An interested party hired Duncan and me. The first victim, Emily Menendez, was the granddaughter of a friend. Her boyfriend has been arrested, but the client and the grandmother don't think he did it. That one happened in downtown Richmond. Duncan found another case, a David Millhouse who lived in Farmville. And then there was another victim, D'borah Styles, in Petersburg. We turned over what we found to the boyfriend's lawyer. He's subpoenaed the other jurisdictions for their files. He thinks what we found is enough to prove that the boyfriend didn't kill Emily if the other murders are linked."

"Because he was in police custody."

"Exactly."

"Who's the attorney?"

"Rick Dixon."

"I've heard of him. Who's your client?" he asked, scooping up several chips and shoving them in his mouth.

When she didn't answer, he said, "Delanie, you can tell me now, or if you don't, you'll have to tell me later."

"Chaz. Chaz Smith."

"I thought you were done with him last summer," he said, frowning.

"What can I say? He's a paying client, and he grows on you after a while. Emily Menendez was the granddaughter of his family's housekeeper."

"You know you give me more to worry about than my kids."

"And how are they? You should invite me over to see your little cuties and your lovely wife."

"Delanie, you're something else. Don't change the subject. I'll call you later this week. A CCPD detective will probably call you too. I'm going to let them know about the other cases and the lawyer. I'm pretty sure one of the jurisdictions will pull together a task force. Richmond thinks they have their guy, so it might be Chesterfield County."

She nodded. "When can I go to Robin's condo and get her some clothes? Her sister asked me to pack an overnight bag for her."

Picking up his smartphone, he punched in a number. "Hey, this is Lieutenant Fitzgerald. The family wants to know when they can send someone over to Robin Kirby's condo to pick up some things. The victim is in the hospital. Can I get one of the officers there to let her in?"

Then he continued, "Yep, the attempted murder this morning in Brandermill. On Timber Creek Ridge. They took the vic to Johnston-Willis. Okay," he said after a pause. "I'll let them know. Thanks."

He disconnected and looked at Delanie. "Forensics has finished, and they've secured the property. They should be gone by now. Robin's sister is going to want to get someone in there to clean up the mess before too long. The detectives will be contacting her soon, but if you talk to her, mention it. The detectives may still be canvassing the area. You have a key?"

"Yes, Robin's sister gave me one."

"If anyone stops you, explain what you're doing. You shouldn't have any trouble. What am I worried about? You've been able to talk yourself in and out of situations since you were a bossy little thing."

"Not bossy. I have leadership skills."

Steve snickered and bit into his pickle. Delanie gathered her trash and put it on the red tray. "You done?"

When he nodded, she picked up his tray too and dumped it in the trash by the door. She turned and said, "Thanks for having lunch with me. It's good to see you. And thanks for your help today."

"Be careful. And please stay out of trouble. Thanks for the info. We'll see what else we can find. If you're right, we've got something big on our hands."

~

DELANIE PULLED INTO ROBIN'S NEIGHBORHOOD. EVERYTHING SEEMED normal in the planned community. The block looked empty without all the emergency vehicles. She parked in the same spot behind Robin's truck. From the outside, it looked like nothing had happened there that morning.

She grabbed Robin's mail out of the large box at the curb and walked to the porch. Using the key that Trish gave her, Delanie unlocked the front door. Before she could go in, she was interrupted by a, "Hey, you there. What are you doing? Where do you think you're going?"

"Excuse me," Delanie said, turning to see an elderly man approaching from the front porch of the wooden house next door.

"The police were here. Somebody hurt Robin. They said to call them if I saw anything suspicious," he said, raising the cane in his hand.

"I'm Delanie Fitzgerald. I'm Robin's friend. Actually, I'm the one who found her this morning. Her sister gave me a key and asked me to pick up some clothes for her and feed the cat."

"I'm Roy. Roy Thompkins. My wife and I live next door. Do you have some ID?"

Delanie sighed and fished her wallet out of her purse. After seeing her driver's license, Roy continued, "You can't be too careful these days, especially with crazed maniacs running around. My wife

Sarah is scared to death. She won't come out now since the police have been here. She said that we should think about moving."

"Did you see or hear anything this morning?"

"No, I didn't. I already told that police lady. I don't hear too good, and I don't sleep with my hearing aids. By the time I got up for breakfast, the street was full of police cars."

"I need to get some things for Robin. I won't be here long."

"Okay. Goodbye, young lady. Tell Robin we're thinking about her. And make sure to lock up when you're done. And turn off all the lights. I told the police I'd keep an eye on the place."

"Will do. It was nice to meet you. And Robin will be happy that you're looking after things while she's in the hospital." He smiled.

Delanie stepped into the condo's dark foyer and locked the door behind her. She avoided looking at the dining room walls as she walked toward the hallway to the stairs. She knew no one was lurking in the house, but the memories of Robin and the creepy blood drawings gave her an eerie feeling. She turned on every light on her way upstairs.

In Robin's bedroom, she found a beach bag in the closet. She went through her dresser and pulled out pajamas, socks, and undergarments. After stuffing them in the bag, she wandered into the bathroom where she grabbed a brush, toiletries, and makeup kit from the bathroom counter.

Delanie turned on the light in Robin's walk-in closet. She grabbed two pair of yoga pants, two t-shirts, and a pair of tennis shoes. Folding the clothes, Delanie managed to get it all to fit in the canvas bag. Looking around the room, she didn't see anything else to add, so turned off all the second floor lights and went to check on the cat.

She found a box of cat treats and dry food under the kitchen sink. She shook the box. When no cat appeared, she assumed he ran out when the door was open.

Balancing full bowls of food and water in one arm, she opened the back blinds and sliding glass door. There was no sign of the tuxedo cat on the patio. She put both bowls on the cement slab in hopes Penguin would come back.

After locking the back door, Delanie turned off all the downstairs lights. She glanced at the dining room on her way out and gave herself chills when she saw the crude partial pentagram and what looked like some sort of animal head. She snapped a couple of pictures with her phone and hurried to the front door.

Delanie had a bad feeling about this case. She and Duncan had to uncover something soon before the killer found another victim.

16

DELANIE VEERED INTO THE LEFT LANE TO AVOID A CARDBOARD BOX AT the same time her phone rang.

"What's up, Duncan?"

"Hey. What are you doing?"

"Robin is in post-op. The doctor is cautiously optimistic. Hopefully, we'll hear some good news soon."

"That's good. Where are you now?"

"Heading back to the hospital. Her sister asked me to pack an overnight bag and check on the cat. I took some pictures of the crime scene while I was there. It gave me the willies."

"Any trouble?"

"There was no sign of the cat. He's either hiding or he ran out the open door. And the elderly neighbor gave me the third degree on the front porch. I think he and his wife are nervous about living next door to a crime scene. Robin's house is creepy. I don't know if they'll be able to get all that blood cleaned up. And there are smudge marks everywhere they checked for fingerprints."

"The reason I called is that I've hit a brick wall on the Tulip Shirt thing. When I Google it, there is a brand named Tulip, but they sell all kinds of clothes, and none of it's distinct to a particular type of clothing. There is no one style or color called 'tulip.' And it doesn't show up on any fashion or pop culture sites. This one has me stymied. It's rare that I hit a dead-end. I've got some feelers out to some fellow researchers. We'll see what materializes. It's going to drive me nuts until I find something."

"I don't know what it is either. What about fashion trends from other generations? You know, like a Nehru or a Members Only jacket. Maybe it's a throwback from another era?"

"I guess it could be. I'll keep looking."

"Okay, I'm pulling into the hospital's visitor's lot now. I'll be here a little while, and then I'm coming in to check emails and send Chaz an update."

"See ya," he said as she disconnected.

Delanie found Trish alone on a couch in the same waiting room. She twisted the hem of her blouse and stared down the hallway. She looked like she had aged ten years in the last twenty-four hours.

"Hi," Delanie said as she approached. "Any word?"

"Hey," Trish said as she stood and hugged her. "No, not much. She's still in recovery. They're watching her. Eventually, she'll move to a room in the ICU."

"I brought her some stuff and two changes of clothing. Oh, here's your key back," she said as she handed the bag to Robin's sister.

"Thanks. Are the police still there?"

"No. They're done. The house is a wreck. You can tell where they dusted for prints, and the police and paramedics tramped in and out of the house."

"The detective gave me the names of several industrial cleaning companies that specialize in crime scenes. I need to set something up with them. How's the cat? I bet he's traumatized," Trish said as she picked at her fingernails.

"I couldn't find Penguin. I shook the treat box in the house. He didn't show himself. I put food and water out on the patio in case he comes back."

"Oh, Robin is going to be so upset. She's had him for quite a while. I'll go by there later tonight to see if he comes home."

"I met the next door neighbor, Roy Thompkins. Maybe he can keep a lookout for Penguin for you."

"Thanks, we appreciate all you've done for us," she said, hugging Delanie again.

~

AS SHE STARTED THE CAR AND OPENED BOTH WINDOWS, DELANIE'S cell rang.

"Hi, Dunc. What's up?"

"Your FBI agent's been banging on our front and back doors."

"Oh, crap. I forgot all about meeting him," she said as she checked her phone. She had a text, two missed calls, and a voicemail from Special Agent Eric Ellington.

"I didn't find out what he wanted. Margaret and I hunkered down and waited for him to go away. You better call him. He was pretty fierce with all the knocking."

"Did he leave?"

"Yep. My car's the only one in the front lot."

"I'll call him. Thanks, Duncan," she said as she clicked the button on the steering wheel. She listened to the FBI agent's voicemail messages. She could hear the annoyance in his voice. He wanted her to call him immediately.

Delanie took a deep breath and dialed his cell. When the voicemail answered, she let out a deep breath and at the beep said, "Agent Ellington, this is Delanie Fitzgerald. I'm sorry to have missed our appointment. I had an emergency this morning. Please call me at your earliest convenience. I'm heading back to the office now."

Relieved she didn't have to have a long conversation with the FBI agent, she drove to her office to catch up on paperwork.

~

WHEN SHE PULLED INTO THE FRONT LOT ABOUT TWENTY MINUTES later, there was a black Suburban parked near her building. She climbed out and clicked the door lock. When the passenger window of the Suburban descended, she heard, "'Bout time."

"I'm sorry I missed our appointment. Something unexpected came up this morning."

He pressed the button, and the window of the large SUV closed.

Delanie, offended at the abrupt ending to the conversation, headed toward the suite's front door. She opened the front door, and the FBI agent climbed out and locked his vehicle.

"I missed lunch," he said. "Mind walking over to that pizza joint?"

"Uh, no. I guess not," she said. "Is this how you ask a girl on a date?"

"It's not a date. I have a few questions about the investigation, and I'm hungry."

"Glad we cleared that up," she said, rolling her eyes. "What do you need to know?" as she locked the office door.

"Why did you stand me up this afternoon?"

"Sounds like a date to me." He cut his dark eyes at her, and she continued, "I had every intention of keeping our business appointment. But a crime got in the way. I went to my friend's house, and she didn't answer the door. I found the back door open. She had been stabbed. I spent the afternoon with the police and her family at the hospital. You can check the trashcan for the bloody clothes I had to discard if you need proof."

"That won't be necessary." He stepped in front of her and held open the glass door to the pizzeria.

He ordered two slices of pepperoni pizza and an iced tea at the red walk-up counter. "Do you want anything?"

"Iced tea, please – unsweetened," she said. She found a table in the back of the restaurant away from the handful of other customers.

When he finished at the counter, he handed her the drink and slid in the red plastic booth across from her.

"How did RVA Recordings contact you?"

"They saw our website and called us."

"No prior contact?"

"No, why?"

"Just curious. You were right. The receptionist was Frank Emerson's girlfriend. It explains why they were bootlegging those particular CDs. There was about three hundred grand in stolen goods in the barn. It'll keep the local boys busy for weeks closing B and E's."

"Glad I could help. How's your arm?"

"It's nothing," he said, finishing off the first slice of pizza. "Did you get paid?"

"And what does that have to do with anything?"

"It doesn't. Never mind."

He stuffed most of the second slice in his mouth, and she continued with, "Yes, I got paid. We always collect our fee. Did you get your tetanus shot?"

He nodded and finished off the slice. "I may need you to testify when this goes to trial."

"Not a problem. Let me know when. It's part of the job. You need anything else? If not, I have to go to the office and do paperwork. It's been a long day."

"No. I'm good for now. I'll walk you back." He wiped his hands and dumped his trash in the receptacle by the exit.

They strolled across the parking lot in silence. He watched her unlock the suite's front door. "Thanks for your help," he said. "I'll be in touch about the trial."

"Thanks for the tea," she said, letting herself in and locking the door behind her.

His questions didn't seem that important to warrant two trips to her office in one day. He could have had that conversation over the phone. And why was he concerned about whether or not she got paid?

Dismissing thoughts of the FBI agent, she retreated to her office. On her way past the empty foyer, she heard a tap, tap, tap. She heard it again as she wandered into the reception area. An older woman, stooped slightly, knocked on the glass with her ring.

"Hello, may I help you?" Delanie asked as she unlocked the door and held it for the woman who shuffled her feet as she moved inside.

"I'm Mildred Mimms," she said, looking around the lobby. Dressed in a pale gray sweater over a flowered blouse and elastic jeans, the woman sported white Sketchers. Delanie guessed she was in her seventies. "I'd like to talk to your boss. Is he in? I need a private eye."

"I'm Delanie Fitzgerald. This is my company. I'm a PI. How can I help you? Would you like to sit down in my office?"

"Oh, a girl detective. How cute. I'm good here. My son will be back in a little while. He thinks I'm at the pet store. We need to talk fast."

"What can I do for you?'

"I need you to stake out my place. I live alone. And every time I come back from church or the beauty parlor, stuff has been moved around inside my house. Someone's breaking into my home or it's something freaky. Either way, I can't explain it."

"It's happened more than once?"

"Of course. That's what I just said. Stuff is moved – and it's not where I left it. So far, nothing's missing. I told my son and daughter about it. They think it's my imagination. I may be old, but I know when someone has moved my stuff. I want you to stake out the place like Jim Rockford and find the SOB who's poking around my house. I will not be terrorized. And I will not be scared into moving to one of those places where my son wants to put me."

"I can do that. I charge by the hour. When are you going out this week?"

"I have a church meeting and lunch out tomorrow. I leave about eleven. And I don't usually get back until the afternoon. Can you come then? I can write you a check."

Delanie said, "I can do a stakeout for seventy-five dollars."

"That's reasonable, I guess. I want some results for my money," she said as she rummaged through her vintage handbag. She pulled out a checkbook and her glasses.

Delanie didn't want to overcharge the woman who reminded her of her grandmother. If she couldn't help her after the stakeout, she'd have to figure out plan B. She wondered if one stakeout would make a difference.

"My company name is Falcon Investigations," Delanie added as Mrs. Mimms rooted through her purse for a pen.

"Here" she said a few minutes later as she ripped the check from the book. "My address and phone number are on the top. I hope you can help me. Call me as soon as you know something. This whole situation is infuriating."

"I will, Thank you, Mrs. Mimms. I'll be there tomorrow."

"Good. I need to get back to the car before Alfred finishes at the cell phone store. I don't want him to know I've hired a PI. He'll think I'm a silly old woman who wastes money. But I'll have the last laugh when you find out who's doing this. Thank you, Delanie," she said as she pulled on the glass door.

Delanie smiled and looked at Mrs. Mimms' check. Her house was nearby off Bailey Bridge Road.

~

THE NEXT DAY, DELANIE PARKED THE CIVIC AROUND THE CORNER FROM Mrs. Mimms' rancher. From her spot, she could see the front door and the side door at the carport. The brick one-story sat catty-cornered on a corner lot. The manicured lawn boasted small flowerbeds about every five feet. Mrs. Mimms liked flowers.

Promptly at eleven, a gold Buick pulled in the driveway, and Mrs. Mimms appeared at the front door. She paused to lock the door before she gingerly descended the stairs. Mrs. Mimms climbed in the passenger seat, and the elderly driver backed leisurely out of the black-topped driveway. The gold car disappeared around the corner, and Delanie settled in for a day-time stakeout.

She counted Mrs. Mimms' flowerbeds and the rocks that edged the neighbor's driveway to keep from dosing off. She decided to watch the house until Mrs. Mimms returned. If nothing happened, she'd try another day. She didn't want to take her money if it was just the older woman's imagination.

Delanie stretched and checked her email. A black Mercedes drove by and stopped in Mrs. Mimms' driveway. She grabbed her camera and snapped pictures as the guy in the black suit exited the car and strode to the cement porch. He climbed the four steps and let himself in the front door.

The PI had no cover in the front yard to spy through the front picture window, so she remained in the car. She also didn't want to cause any of the neighbors alarm if they spotted her sneaking around Mrs. Mimms' yard.

About twenty minutes later, the man with a manila folder under his arm locked the front door and returned to his car. Seconds later, he sped around the corner. Delanie texted Duncan the license plate number.

Delanie checked her email. When she put the car in drive, a white Volvo zoomed around the corner and stopped suddenly in Mrs. Mimms' driveway. Delanie pushed the gear shift in park and grabbed her camera. A smallish woman slammed the car door and made a beeline for the front porch and let herself in.

By the time she texted Duncan the second plate number, the woman stepped out, looked up and down the street, and hurried to her car. When the Volvo disappeared, Delanie drove to the office to print copies of the pictures.

After an hour or so of emails and client reports, Delanie packed up. She detoured from her regular route home to do a quick stop at Robin's condo. Delanie parked behind Robin's truck. The only noise in the neighborhood were faint sounds of a radio or TV in the distance. It looked like a normal evening in suburbia. There was no sign of Roy Thompkins, the self-appointed neighborhood watch. She walked around the back of the dwelling and let herself in the postage-stamp sized backyard. The gate squeaked when she closed it.

Something rustled in the plants on the patio, and Delanie jumped. She reached in her purse for her pepper spray. Exhaling loudly, she saw a flash of black and white by the patio door.

"Penguin!" He stopped to sniff the two empty bowls.

He answered with a loud mew. She rushed over and scooped him up. "Where have you been, fella? Robin is going to be so happy," she said, scratching him behind the ears. She straightened his collar and blue name tag. He nuzzled her neck and purred.

"Okay. I don't have a key, so you're going to have to go home with me. You'll like riding in the car. At least, I hope you will. I don't have a box for you, so I need you to be a good passenger and ride shotgun."

At home, she texted Trish that she had found Penguin in Robin's backyard, and that he's visiting her place.

Trish answered back almost immediately. *Send me your address. I'll pick him up tonight if that's okay.* Her message ended with three "thank yous" and a string of exclamation points.

Penguin padded around the living room and kitchen in search of an adventure. He ran up the steps and returned a few minutes later. He curled up in one of her barrel chairs for a nap. Delanie was content for the moment to plop on the couch and relax, but thoughts of Robin and her attacker kept tickling her subconscious. Why Robin? What did she have in common with the other victims?

AFTER TRISH AND HER HUSBAND PICKED UP PENGUIN, DELANIE wandered to the kitchen to see if she had anything on hand to eat. Deciding on tomato soup and a grilled cheese, she worked on assembling dinner when her cell rang.

"Hey, Delanie. How do you feel about a road trip?'

"When and where? Are you and Margaret going with me?"

"Unhuh. I need more information on David Millhouse, and you're the best at getting info from people. He didn't have much of a web presence. How about going to Farmville and poking around?"

"I can do that. Tomorrow would probably be good. Find anything else on the others?"

"I'm still looking for similarities. Right now, Emily and D'borah are the only ones who were big into social media. D'borah was on her soapbox a lot about her favorite causes."

"Okay. I can see what his neighbors and coworkers say. I may even stop by the police station. Could you pull the detective's info from the folder and email it to me?"

"Sure and I'll send you what I know about the families too."

"And where did you all hightail it to? I was expecting to see you."

"Margaret and I had some errands to run. And we didn't feel like talking to that agent. What did the FBI agent want anyway?"

"He wanted to tell me I'll probably be called to testify in the Emerson case."

"All that banging on the front door for that? Then he came around and knocked on the back door. When he finally drove off, Margaret and I went home. I didn't feel like dealing with him."

"I didn't really want to talk to him either. He was in the parking lot when I got here. I'm not sure why he came by the office twice. What he had to tell me wasn't all that important. Enough of him. I'll head to Farmville tomorrow to see what I can find out about our case. There have to be some common threads among the three murders and Robin."

"I've emailed you the detective's contacts. And info on Millhouse's family."

"Did you get a chance to check on those two license plates I sent you from Mrs. Mimms' house?"

Duncan clicked a series of keys and said, "Here they are. The first plate belongs to an Alfred R. Mimms, Jr."

"That was my hunch. And the lady?"

"Carolyn Dalton...I did some checking because I know that you'd ask. Her maiden name is Mimms."

"Interesting. The son and daughter pop in when their mother isn't home. Even if it was done for her care and well being, they're making her worry when she finds things moved. She thinks someone is breaking into her house. Thanks, Duncan. I need to go see her and drop off the pictures. She deserves to know. I'll call you tomorrow." She flipped her grilled cheese sandwich and turned the stove down on her simmering soup when the phone rang again.

"Hello, Chaz. How are you?"

"Good. Rick's been sending me updates. Alma's thrilled at what you've found so far."

"I'm sorry I haven't called you sooner. We're making progress. There are four similar attacks. Three were murders, and in the most recent one, the victim survived. I'm hoping she'll be able to tell the police a lot when she's conscious."

"That's great news for Justin."

"It is. If they're linked, Justin isn't their guy. Rick Dixon subpoenaed all the police records on the other cases. Duncan and I are still trying to find connections."

"Rick told me he's still using you guys. That's good. I told him to keep you as long as he needed you. I know you're worth it."

"Thanks. I appreciate the business. You're a good client."

"Don't spread that around. I don't want to damage my villainous reputation. I've worked too hard to be infamous around this town. What are you doing tonight? We've got a band at the club if you want to come on down. We'll make sure that you're treated like the VIP that you are."

"I appreciate the invitation, but it really has been a stressful week. I think I'm going to wind down here."

"Suit yourself. If you change your mind, you're always welcome. Hey, I want to get together soon to have you do some research for me. I'll call you next week. See ya," he said as he clicked off.

"Yep, see ya," she said to empty air. Delanie couldn't image ever mustering enough energy to hang out at Chaz's pirate-themed strip club as a VIP.

17

AFTER PICKING UP AN ICED VANILLA COFFEE, DELANIE TURNED ON MAIN Street and followed the GPS's instructions past Longwood University's campus to the government center and police station. Parking in one of the two visitor spots, she grabbed her purse and climbed the cement steps to the front door.

At the information desk, Delanie asked the woman in the beige uniform seated behind the glass window, "May I see Chief Prince? I'm Delanie Fitzgerald. I called him this morning."

"One moment, please." She punched a button on the phone and said something into the receiver. "Have a seat over there. Someone from his office will be out in a moment." She returned to the stack of papers that she was entering into the computer.

"Thanks." Delanie hoped she wasn't getting shuffled off to an underling who wouldn't be of any help. She tried to get comfortable in a plastic chair that looked like it was in style in the 1970s.

After what seemed like an eternity, a young woman in a day-glow lemon dress opened the door. The woman stood out like a tropical bird in an all beige environment. She looked at the woman behind the glass who pointed at Delanie.

"Ms. Fitzgerald?" When Delanie nodded, she continued, "Chief Prince will see you now. Please follow me."

She trailed the woman down several more beige hallways. The building looked like it was built when disco and Pet Rocks were all the rage. Its musty smell reminded Delanie of a cross between a gym locker room and an old ashtray.

The woman stopped in front of a thick wooden door. She knocked, and after a gruff, "Enter," she said, "Chief Prince, this is Delanie Fitzgerald. She's a private investigator from Chesterfield County."

"Come in. Have a seat."

After shaking his hand that was twice the size of hers, she sat in a dark leather chair across from a massive cherry desk. Everything, including Chief Prince, was the size of Texas.

Adjusting in her chair, she sat as tall as she could. "It's nice to meet you. Thank you for fitting me into your busy schedule. I'm working on a case for attorney Rick Dixon. We've had two murders and an attack near Richmond that are similar to the Millhouse case. I was hoping to talk to you about the investigation."

"There's not much to tell. It's still an open case," said the police chief, whose piercing glance and stiff look made Delanie set her jaw, determined to pry some information out of him. She wouldn't let him intimidate her.

Photos of Chief Prince shaking hands with all kinds of politicians blanketed every inch of his wall space. His "I love me" wall extended to the other three walls.

"I'm working for an attorney involved with the case. And I've seen copies of the files and the pictures," she said.

"It was gruesome. This is a quiet little college town. We have drunk students and every once in a while, someone gets killed during hunting season. This thing stunned people around here. He was a quiet vet's assistant who stayed to himself. David went away to college, but other than that, he spent most of his time about ten miles from the house he grew up in. His mother and sisters still live nearby. It was tragic. The community is still reeling."

"Did you know him well?"

"His mother goes to my church. And he used to."

"Any enemies, threats, or previous trouble?"

"Nope. He was a good kid. He kept his nose clean. He didn't have too many friends, and he never married."

"Anything unusual about his lifestyle?"

"Nope. He kept to himself. He traveled a lot in the area. He and old Doc Brewster, the vet, did a lot of house and farm calls."

"Anything out of the ordinary at his residence?"

"We didn't find anything unusual at his place. He was squeaky clean, and there were no surprises. It's sad. His momma's taking it pretty hard. If you're going to root around town and ask questions, leave her alone. She's suffered enough. There's nothing she can help you with."

"Is there anything else I need to know?" He glared at her and didn't reply.

"Well, Chief," Delanie said, flashing her best smile. "Thank you for your time and the information. I appreciate it. If you think of anything else, please give me a call." She handed him her Falcon Investigations card.

"Yep," he said, leaving her card on the edge of his desk and returning to a stack of manila folders. He picked up the phone receiver, and Delanie stepped out in the hall.

The lady in yellow swooped in. "I'll show you out," she said. Her heels clicked on the floor as they walked to the lobby. The woman waved Delanie toward the lobby with one hand and opened the door with the other. As soon as Delanie stepped across the threshold, the woman closed the door behind her. Not impressed with the information she gained from the chief of police, Delanie decided to do a drive-by of the place David Millhouse rented.

She started the Mustang and put the windows down to catch the morning breeze. After punching in his address into the GPS, she followed its instructions through town to Park Avenue. The neighborhood boasted cottage-style houses sprinkled along the main road. All had long driveways and lots of mature trees. Finding a match for the address on a black rural mailbox with a white post, she snapped a few pictures of the lonely house at the end of the empty driveway.

She climbed the wooden steps and rang the bell. Duncan's email said the victim had rented this house for over two years. After no answer, she got back in the car and drove to the nearest neighbor's house.

The white clapboard house had a wrap-around porch bordered by flowerbeds that spilled blossoms over the borders. Lots of potted plants lined the perimeter of the porch. Delanie parked on the street and followed the path to the front steps. Before she could get to the porch to ring the bell, an elderly woman came out in jeans with a large sun hat. It looked like she was wearing a man's dress shirt that flowed behind her as she moved.

"May I help you?" she asked, tilting the brow of her hat.

"Hi, I'm Delanie Fitzgerald. I'm a private investigator from Chesterfield County. I'm working on a case, and it's similar to David Millhouse's murder. Could I bother you to answer a few questions?"

"Tragic. So tragic. His life was cut short before he really had a chance to do anything. He was a nice man, but he kept to himself. He worked too much. Phillip and I would invite him over, but he usually declined. Oh, where are my manners? I'm Elsie Fanning. I've got something on the stove, so I can't linger too long, but what did you want to know?"

"Was he involved in politics or volunteer work?"

"I don't think so. David preferred animals to people. I think animals were his one true love. Only his mother and sisters came by to see him. He kept to himself. He was an old soul."

"Did he anger people or have any enemies?"

"Not David. He didn't like conflict, and he wasn't one to step on any toes. I never knew him to have trouble with anyone. He had a routine. He went to work, the Food Lion on Friday nights, and church on Sundays. There wasn't much deviation. David cut his grass, kept the house neat, and never bothered anybody. He was a great neighbor. Sorry. There's not much to say. I need to go check on what's on the stove."

"Has anyone moved into his house yet?"

"No. His sisters moved his stuff. I don't think Lester, the owner, has found a new tenant yet. He had a lot of clean up to do. I wouldn't want to live there after what happened. Is there anything else you need?"

"No, thank you so much. I appreciate the information. Your flowers are lovely."

She smiled and stepped in. When the screen shut, she closed the big wooden door. On the way down the steps, Delanie heard the front lock click.

She drove up and down the street, but it didn't look like any of the other neighbors were home. She punched the address for the town vet into her GPS. Maybe David's coworkers could help her get a better picture of him.

The GPS guided Delanie back to Route 460 and the Big and Little Animal Hospital. She parked in front of a wooden building with a long front porch and a low roofline. A tiny bell chimed when Delanie opened the glass door.

"May I help you?" the middle-aged woman in pastel medical scrubs with rainbow paw prints asked.

"Hi, I'm Delanie Fitzgerald. I'm a private investigator from Chesterfield County," she said, showing her identification. "I'm working for an attorney who has a case similar to David Millhouse's, and I wanted to know if I could ask you a few questions."

"I guess. The doctor's out. He won't be back until later this afternoon. He's vaccinating a herd in the next county," she said, reaching for a large bottle of Mt. Dew next to her telephone. She took a swig and slumped slightly forward in the office chair.

"Did you know David Millhouse?"

"Oh, yes. We all did. I'm Becca Richardson. He worked here for about eight years. He helped Doc Brewster a lot. He's going to be lost without him. He's still shook up over this whole thing like we all are. This is such a quiet town. Stuff like this doesn't happen here."

"I'm so sorry for your loss. Did he have any enemies or people who he had arguments with?"

She snorted. Then she continued with, "David was conflict averse. He would drive ten miles out of his way to avoid something. He was always calm. He did his job. He worked hard. There was nothing special about him. He was just David."

"Any girlfriends, friends?"

"Nope. He worked a lot. He didn't socialize much with the rest of us. He was very quiet. Kept to himself."

"Any causes that he was passionate about?"

"He loved animals – all of them. He joined PETA a while back. But he wasn't really a big cause person. He never called in sick. He rarely took a vacation. I would be surprised if he ever ventured out of the state. College was his big time away from home."

"Was he into computers or social media?"

"No. I don't think so. He had an iPad he used for research, but he didn't bother with that Facebook and Twitter stuff. He didn't like to answer emails. If I needed him, I had to call him."

"He grew up here, right? Did he have close friends in town?"

"He went to the high school like most of us around here. He was in my cousin's class. David was always kind of a loner. His dad died when he was a teenager. He was close with his momma. He didn't really hang out much."

"Can you think of anyone who would want to hurt him?"

"No. We were all stunned. I still can't imagine this happening to anyone around here. It had to be a crazy person from out of town. Stuff like that happens in big cities. Not here," she said as tears welled up in her eyes.

"Thank you so much for your time. I appreciate your help. If you think or hear of anything, please give me a call," Delanie said, handing her a business card.

Becca nodded, and sobbed quietly.

"Can I get you anything?" Delanie asked.

"No, I'm fine. I need to check on the critters in the back," she said as she dabbed her eyes with her sleeve.

∽

Delanie sat in the car with the air conditioning blasting. Everyone said pretty much the same thing about David Millhouse. He was as nondescript as anyone could be. She didn't think talking to the family would provide any new information. Before leaving, she took a couple of pictures of the vet's office.

She checked her email for the mother's address and typed it in the GPS. She'd do a drive-by and take a few pictures.

After a short country drive, she pulled in a gravel driveway of a little bungalow near town. Red geraniums overflowed their pots, and all the flowerbeds were neatly tended. Delanie took a couple of pictures of the empty driveway and house. When she started to back out of the driveway, an older gentleman from next door crossed the yard and yelled, "Hey."

Rolling down the window, she said, "Yes."

"You a reporter? If so, don't go bothering Missus Millhouse."

"No, sir. My name is Delanie Fitzgerald. I am a private investigator. I'm working for a lawyer who has a case similar to the Millhouse murder," she said, showing him her identification.

"Missus Millhouse is out, probably at the doctor's. Don't bother her. She's always been sickly, and her son's death is probably going to put her over the edge. She's not coping well. Poor woman's been through enough."

"Thank you, Mr. uh."

"Perkins, James Perkins."

"Have you lived next to the Millhouse family long?"

"Over thirty years. It was hard on the family when the father died. My wife and I tried to help where we could."

"Could you tell me about David?"

"He was really quiet. He only spoke if you spoke first."

"Any enemies?"

"No. Like I said. He stayed to himself. He helped his momma by cutting her grass every week and doing chores around here."

"Thank you, Mr. Perkins. I appreciate the information. Please give me a call if you think of anything that might help the investigation," she said, handing him her business card.

He nodded and pocketed her card. She drove through town and found a parking spot next to a college bar. Christmas lights snaked around the deck's railing and the two columns that supported the roof. White and green plastic tables and chairs stood next to several Tiki lamps on the worn deck that leaned on one side.

She punched Duncan's number in her phone. After a couple of rings, she heard, "Hey, Delanie. How's Farmville?"

"I didn't learn anything new. Everybody said David was quiet and a loner. I talked to the police, his neighbor, his coworker, and his mother's neighbor. His coworker said he was a member of PETA. That's pretty much all the new information I found. It was a bust. I'm heading back. I'll add my notes to the report. There's not much going on in this college town today."

"Any plans for tonight?"

"Nope. What about you?"

"It's Halo night. Evie and I are going to dinner before that."

"Have fun. See you sometime tomorrow."

About the time Delanie made it to Route 460, her phone rang again. "Hello, Chaz."

"Hey, Delanie. What're up to on this fine day?"

"I'm driving back from Farmville. I did some interviews this afternoon of people who knew the male victim. His case was similar to Emily's."

"Anything good?"

"No earth-shattering discoveries. I confirmed some of our suspicions. And I saw where he lived and worked. What's up with you?"

"I had an idea I wanted to bounce off you." Delanie rolled her eyes, but didn't comment. He continued, "I'm looking at some property in the Far West End. I have an idea for a new venture."

"What?" She wondered why he was asking her opinion. She didn't have much experience in his world.

"I'm thinking of an upscale restaurant and bar with an all-male revue. You know, like a Richmond version of Chippendales. We could host birthdays and bridal showers. There's no competition in the area, and it would probably be received better than my other line of business. Plus, there are a lot of women between twenty and fifty in the area. I think this kind of establishment would do great."

"Well," she said, trying to collect her thoughts. "I don't think there's anything like it in Central Virginia. You'd be a pioneer."

"It won't be a strip club, so the neighbors can't get their panties in a bunch."

A few objections popped in Delanie's head, but she decided not to voice them. After a pause, she asked, "Where are you thinking about putting this new venture?

"There are a couple of places in Richmond and Henrico, and there's some property on the Goochland side of the county line. I need to do a better job on the business planning this time. I'd like you to do some recon work for me in the next few weeks. I want to make sure we're good with the community this time before I invest. I'll talk with you later this week and give you the details. If you get bored, stop in and see us. Marco said to tell you hi."

"Thanks. Tell him hi back for me. Take care. I'll have an update for you and Rick Dixon soon on Emily's case."

"You do great work. See ya."

A restaurant and bar with waiters in G-strings. It might be a money maker. It was hard to picture Chaz as the proprietor of an all-male revue. He'd have to change the graphics on his Hummer. Delanie still wondered how she became Chaz's confidante and adviser.

BEFORE HEADING HOME, DELANIE SWUNG BY MRS. MIMMS' HOUSE. SHE rang the doorbell and heard movement inside. Delanie rang the bell again. The noise inside sounded closer. The door cracked, and then she spotted Mrs. Mimms in a tin foil hat. She had a tin foil cuff on each wrist.

"Hello, Mrs. Mimms."

"Oh, hi, Delanie. How are you?"

"I'm good. I have some photos to show you."

"Come on in," she said, as she waved Delanie in.

The private investigator stepped into the front room with wall-to-wall bookshelves and retro furniture. The room was a mixture of olive and mustard colors. Her velveteen love seats sported plastic covers.

"Please sit down," the woman said. "Would you like some tea?"

"No thanks. I did the stakeout after you left for your church meeting." Mrs. Mimms eased next to Delanie. "You were right. After you left, two people entered your house at different times."

The older woman blanched and looked at the photos Delanie spread out on her lap. "That's Alfred and Carolyn," she gasped. "What are they doing?"

"I don't know. Your son left with a manila folder. Your daughter didn't leave with anything that I could see."

"Well, that confirms my suspicions," the older woman said as she removed her tin foil hat. "At least I know I'm not going crazy. I thought space aliens or ghosts were tormenting me. At least now, I know who the real culprits are. I was afraid other beings were reading my thoughts of when I planned to go out. Thank you for your help. It looks like I need to call a family meeting."

"I'm glad I could help. Please call me if I can assist with anything else," she said as she stood.

"Oh yes. You're my favorite girl PI. I'll tell all my friends about you. You've been very helpful."

"Thank you. You can keep these," she said, handing the folder of photos to Mrs. Mimms. "I'll let myself out."

"Bye, dear. I'm glad that we got to the bottom of this. My children have a lot of explaining to do."

~

ON THE WAY TO THE OFFICE THE NEXT MORNING, DELANIE'S CELL interrupted a Vibes' song on the radio. The music transported her for a few moments to the investigation she did last summer on the band's lead singer, Johnny Velvet. She shook off the melancholic feeling and memories and pushed the button on the steering wheel to answer the incoming call. She wondered where John Bailey ended up.

"Hey, Delanie. This is Kathy Meyers from Lion Insurance. How are you?"

"Fine. It's good to hear from you."

"I got your email. I do have an assignment for you if you have some availability. It's a workman's comp case. His name is Chris Barbour. He's out on his second injury claim case in three years. This time, he sustained a back injury in a fall at a cookie plant in Henrico. He lives on Frederick Farms Road in Chesterfield. I need your usual report and pictures."

"I'll be glad to. I'll swing by and pay him a visit. Do you have a picture of what he looks like?"

"I'll send you the file. Let me know if you need anything else."

"Will do. Thanks for thinking of Falcon Investigations. I'll have a report for you this week."

"Appreciate it," Kathy said.

The line disconnected and Delanie headed to the nearest fast food place. She ordered a vanilla iced coffee and perused Mr. Barbour's file on her phone. He was in his mid-forties and had been out of work for eight weeks because of his latest injury, similar in description to his first accident at the plant.

She checked her spy box in the trunk. Pulling out a clipboard, some paper, and a ballcap with a camera, she returned to the car. She added her sunglasses to round out her disguise.

Plugging his address into the GPS, she decided to drive-by to see what Mr. Barbour was up to this fine morning. When she found the house, it looked like most of the neighbors had already left for work. A large red truck sat in the Barbour driveway. The insurance company's file said he had a wife and two kids. She parked two houses down where she had a good view of his front yard – and waited.

She fished her burner phone out of her purse and called the Barbour's landline. After a few rings, a male voice answered. "I'm trying to reach Chris Barbour. This is Tracey Johnson, and I'm calling on behalf of the Lawyers' Aid Society."

"We're not interested. We've already got enough lawyers around here," he said as he hung up. Not much of a conversationalist, she thought.

She watched the house. Eventually, a fireplug of a man with short gray hair came out of the side door of the garage carrying tools and a bucket. His stocky build reminded her of a wrestler. She watched him disappear around the corner to his backyard.

Pulling on Duncan's magic hat, she grabbed her clipboard and keys. She locked the door and pushed the button on the hat's brim to start recording her walk around the house.

When she rounded the corner of the garage, she saw the man working on his deck. She turned her head slowly to capture the entire scene with her hidden camera. He stooped over the framing, putting large boards in metal fittings – his drill poised for the next step.

"Excuse, me. Hi. I'm Kat Rogers. I'm with the Clover Hill High School Band Boosters. We're looking for volunteers to help staff the concession stand at the school during football games. We're also looking for adult volunteers to help with our band activities. How are you?"

He looked up from what he was doing and smiled. "Could I count on you to help the kids?" she asked.

"Uh, I guess so. My wife usually handles that kind of stuff. You can call her. Her cell number is 459-9033. Here, but you can add this to the fundraising," he said, handing her a twenty dollar bill from his pocket. Delanie wrote the number on the paper on her clipboard.

"Thanks, Mr. Uh?"

"Barbour, Chris Barbour. Put Missy Barbour on your list. She loves doing stuff with the kids."

"Well, thank you so much, Mr. Barbour," she said, jotting fake notes on the clipboard. She took more video of him working on the deck. "We'll definitely give her a call. This is a nice deck you have here."

"I designed and built it all by myself in just a few weeks. I should be done and grilling on it by the weekend. My next project is a

Jacuzzi and maybe a fire pit over there," he said, waving his arm toward the rest of the backyard.

"It's lovely. You've worked really hard on it. Thanks again, Mr. Barbour. We appreciate your support."

He nodded, and she retreated to the car. Her plans were to craft a report for Kathy's company and mail the twenty dollars to the high school.

On the way back to the office, her phone buzzed. Trish texted, *Robin came down with an infection. She almost died last night. They're putting her back in ICU. I'll let you know as soon as I hear something.*

Thinking about you all. Sending good thoughts your way. Delanie took a deep breath to fight back the tears.

18

D<small>ELANIE'S</small> <small>QUIET OFFICE TIME WAS INTERRUPTED WHEN</small>, "D<small>E-LAY-NEE</small>! De-lay-neeeeee!" echoed through the office suite.

"What, Duncan?" She responded as she ran out into the hallway. "What's going on?"

"I found some stuff. I'm not sure how key it is, but it's something. It may be what we've been looking for."

"Okay, okay. Catch your breath. Let me get my laptop, and I'll meet you in the conference room. Where's Margaret? Oh, never mind," she said as she noticed the bulldog ambling slowly down the hall. She stopped to check out the kitchen before she moseyed after Duncan.

Delanie plopped down in the conference room chair. "What'd you find?"

He sat in the chair across from her. "Just a rounder picture of our Petersburg victim, D'borah Styles. We already knew she was big on causes. But she was definitely an advocate for the downtrodden and underprivileged. She wrote a blog that took on anything she deemed as unfair. Ms. Styles didn't mince words, and most of her posts are scathing. She showed up at public hearings and had some shouting matches with officials. I've already told you about her police record as a protester. She made comments on Twitter, Facebook, and her blog. Lately, she's been ranting about urban food deserts in cities where residents don't have access to healthy foods."

"Definitely an activist who knows how to get her opinions out there in the blogosphere."

"She's also been going after road improvement projects that aren't helping the elderly and disabled. According to her, the state and localities are putting big money into a lot of road projects in affluent areas, but they're not looking at the basic infrastructure in urban neighborhoods. She's also been posting a lot about the lack of public transportation."

"My trip to Farmville didn't yield anything new. David Millhouse was off the social media grid, and he kept to himself. It was pretty much a bust. The only new fact was his PETA membership."

"Which is a cause, but not similar to D'borah's. He's also the only guy in the bunch. He's the odd man out in more ways than the obvious."

"And that stands out if we're dealing with a serial killer. We've got to find the pattern. I know it's there somewhere. It's not race, age, or gender. They all don't seem to have any common behaviors."

"Right. Emily was big on social media, but she didn't seem to have any pet causes. What about Robin?"

"She's got an online presence for the store, but she's closer to Millhouse in that she worked all the time. She has friends and family, but she didn't put herself out there like Emily and D'borah did. What else do they have in common? I don't care how dumb it sounds, let's see what we can come up with," she said.

"Okay," he replied as he stood up and faced the whiteboard. He stared at the random facts for a few minutes. "D'borah and Robin had cats. David worked for a vet. Emily traveled to the Tidewater area and Farmville a lot. David lived in Farmville. He also traveled for his job. Three were female. There were two Caucasians, one African-American, and one Hispanic. They all lived alone."

"They all had something on the walls in blood. And they all had jobs. Emily was the youngest, and D'borah was in her early fifties. Emily was an accountant and David was a vet tech. D'borah was an activist. I'm not sure where her money came from. And we know about Robin's store."

"Well, we've been able to eliminate a lot of things that aren't common among all of them. What about religion, clubs, political affiliations, or shopping habits?"

"Dunno. I'll keep digging. There's got to be something," he said as he clicked away on his laptop. "Hey, this is interesting. D'borah was injured in a car accident about fifteen years ago. And she inherited her parents' house when her father died. She was the sole heir. It looks like she had a brother, but he died before the parents did. Maybe she lived on the inheritance and settlement money. I can't find any record that she had a job."

"Maybe disability payments?"

"Not sure yet."

"Hmmm. Any luck on the Tulip Shirt?"

"Nope. I haven't found anything new. The Tulip Company doesn't put a logo on their shirts. I even put it out on some forums. Nobody had any ideas."

"That one has me stumped too. It doesn't mean anything to me. When Robin's able to talk, that's going to be the first thing I ask her. She said she didn't know the attacker. But she didn't say anything about the guy's looks. The police haven't been able to question her yet. Her sister texted me that she is back in ICU with a serious infection. They've got her drugged up, and she hasn't really regained consciousness. It doesn't look like she'll be talking any time soon."

"I'm sorry to hear that. I had hoped she was improving. Well, she's our biggest chance for info on the attacker, so we'll have to keep looking elsewhere in the meantime."

"For the shirt, did you try any gardening sites? Maybe it has something to do with the flower?"

"Hmmm," he said, pecking on the keys of his laptop. "When you first said tulip, I heard 'two lips,' and I immediately thought of concert shirts with either Mick Jagger or Steven Tyler."

She smiled for a second and then sobered when she said, "I'm still thinking about the four victims. Was there anything significant with their home lives? Emily had a steady boyfriend. Robin was divorced. I don't think she was seeing anybody. I didn't find much of anything about Millhouse's private life except he was close with his mother."

"And D'borah was twice divorced," Duncan added.

"Robin is also divorced. What about the bloody graffiti? Any luck on the contents?"

"Nope. All my searches come back with satanic symbols or references to gaming. There doesn't seem to be a connection there either."

"We aren't getting anywhere. What should we do?"

"Play paintball?"

"I was thinking more like going through all the police reports again to see what we missed."

Duncan let out a heavy sigh. "Okay. I'll take the Styles' file. You start with the Millhouse one," he said, stretching out on the conference room floor next to Margaret. "But paintball would have been more fun."

Around seven-thirty, Delanie put down her legal pad and returned her files to two neat piles on the table. "I'm beat. It's all blurring together. Wanna get dinner?"

"I guess. I feel like there's a missing piece, and I'm about to find it. Why don't you get takeout or drive-thru somewhere?"

"Burgers okay?"

"Yep. I'll buy. You fly. Get a plain cheeseburger for Margaret," he said, handing her a crumpled twenty.

"Will do," Delanie said, picking up her phone and purse.

The alert from her phone stopped her. Trish texted, *Robin is still sedated in ICU. But the doctor is cautiously optimistic.*

Good news, Delanie tapped into her phone. *Can I stop by to talk to you tomorrow?*

I'll be at the shop after 10.

"Robin's doing better. Be back soon," she said.

He nodded, but didn't look up from his current pile of folders – he was engrossed in one of the police reports.

~

DELANIE PARKED IN THE BACK OF THE OFFICE NEXT TO THE EMPTY SPACE where the gray Honda used to be when she returned from the food run. Grabbing the bags, cups, and her purse, she bumped the car door shut with her hip. She wondered what Duncan did with the Civic?

"Dunc, hey, Dunc. I'm back." Duncan, followed by Margaret, wandered into the kitchen by the time she dropped everything on the table.

"Here's the food. Hey, where's the Honda?"

"I dunno. I thought you took it home. I haven't seen it for a while. I figured you used it for something."

"No. I thought you had it."

"I'll be back," he said, grabbing his cheeseburger. He returned with his laptop. "Okay, let's see what the cameras show us," he said, taking a huge bite.

Delanie stood behind him as he zoomed through the footage of the empty alley.

"There! There," he said, pointing to the screen. "The car was there yesterday."

"I've been driving the Mustang lately. I haven't driven the Honda in a while," she said, eating her salad out of the plastic carton.

"Watch. Here it is," he said, pushing buttons on his laptop.

At two-thirty this morning, a dark car pulled into the alley, and a guy in a light-colored hoodie slid out of the passenger side. He fiddled with the Civic's door, and two frames later, he opened the door and climbed in. A few minutes later, he started the car and signaled the person in the other car. Both cars backed out of the frame, and the rest was footage of the empty alley.

"What the hell. This is the second issue we've had with cars behind our building. I'm gonna stop parking back there," she said.

"On the bright side, I got the license plate number of the dark car."

"Can you make me a copy of the video? I'm gonna call Steve. I can't believe this. The car was stolen, and I didn't even notice."

She returned to her office to call her eldest brother. A few rings later, she heard, "Fitzgerald."

"Hey, Steve. It's Delanie."

"How're things?

"Good..."

"Except?"

"I had an old car in the alley at the office. I use it for stakeouts. Anyway, it was stolen early this morning."

"You call it in?"

"Not yet. We just noticed that it was missing. Hey, to my credit, I thought Duncan was using it."

"Call it in." Duncan stepped toward her desk and handed her a Post-it note.

"Thanks. Steve, Duncan got the license plate of the other car from one of the cameras. It's IBS-958. It's a Virginia plate. And my car's plate is JEC-615."

"Maybe they can find either car."

"Thanks, Steve. But that didn't sound encouraging."

"Sorry. The statistics on recovering stolen cars aren't good. Call it in, and I'll make sure someone comes by to get your statement. Other than the car, you doing okay?"

"I'm okay, but I'm done leaving cars in the alley." She shuddered at a flashback to last summer and the thought of that stalker and the damage he did to her Mustang. And now, she had a missing vehicle to deal with.

19

Delanie yawned and climbed into the Mustang. She put her sunglasses on to hide the dark circles from another late-nighter. After she gave the video and her car information to the police, she and Duncan stayed in the office until one-thirty in the morning looking for any connection among the victims. They found lots of random facts, but no eureka moments.

After stopping at the Wawa for coffee, she parked in front of Robin's store to get an update on her friend. Balancing the drinks and her purse, she managed to open the glass door. Penguin raised his head, but didn't stir from his comfy chair.

"Hi, kitty cat. It's good to see you back at the store. Hey, Trish. Trish!"

"Back here. Oh, hi," she said when she entered the showroom. "How are you?"

"Good. How are you all doing? Coffee?" she asked offering the mocha.

"Thanks. Robin's fever has gone down. She's still intubated, but if she's doing better tomorrow, they may move her back to the step-down ward. She's been in and out of consciousness since her fever broke. It's been touch and go, but we're hopeful that she'll pull out of this."

"That's good news."

"She's got a long way to go. Come on back. The doctor said that it could be many months before she's anything close to normal. I'm going through some boxes of stuff. We can talk in the back."

Delanie followed Trish to the workroom. She had several projects going in different stages on the cement floor of the workroom. The PI leaned on a desk, covered with stacks of loose papers, while Trish pulled items out of cardboard boxes.

"These are things Robin found at a storage unit a while back. I was checking to see if there was something we could work on. If not, I'll be making a run to Goodwill this afternoon. Sometimes you get lucky at auctions, and then there are other times when you get some-body's trash. Thanks for the coffee. It's a nice treat."

"You're very welcome. Do you need me to do anything?"

"I think we're good right now. We're taking turns staying at the hospital. I hired a cleaning company this week. They're going over to Robin's tomorrow. I probably will have to have the room painted too. Dan, my husband, will probably do that so it's ready for her to come home. I don't even want to go over there. Who would do such a thing?"

"I don't know, but we're trying hard to find out. And hopefully, it doesn't create too many bad memories for her," Delanie said as she stretched her hands back on the desk. She landed one on a pile of papers that slid backwards. When she turned to move the stack, she noticed a crumpled piece of blue paper. The Thompson Ulrich, LLP logo on the form caused her to jump up and grab the sheet. It was the traffic survey from their trip to Farmville. Her stomach dropped to her feet, and she could feel her heart thumping in her head.

"You okay?"

"I think so. Do you think I could have this flyer about the traffic survey?"

"Uh, sure. I'm not sure why Robin saved it. Are there any notes on it? She often uses scrap paper to jot stuff down."

"No," Delanie said, flipping the page over.

"Sure. Take it then."

"Call me if I can do anything. I've got to go to work. Let me know if anything changes with Robin."

"Will do. Thanks for everything."

Delanie couldn't get to the car fast enough. She called Duncan and strummed her fingers on the steering wheel, waiting for his voicemail message to beep. "Duncan. This is an emergency. Meet me back at the office. I think I found something big – really big." Then for good measure, she texted him the same message with 911 behind it.

"I know what a Tulip Shirt is," she said as the Mustang's engine roared to life.

~

SQUEALING THE MUSTANG'S TIRES WHEN SHE SKIDDED INTO THE parking spot next to Duncan's Camaro, Delanie missed the curb by centimeters. Her phone buzzed with a text at about the same time. Glancing at the phone, she grabbed the crumpled piece of blue paper and jumped out of the car.

She didn't stop long enough to lock the office's front door. Running down the dark hallway, she yelled, "Duncan! Duncan! You've got to see this! Whoa! Crap!"

She tripped over a prone Margaret and almost did a summersault in the hall. Landing on her side in front of Margaret, the bulldog raised her head and glared at Delanie, noting her displeasure at being disturbed during her midmorning nap.

"You okay?" Duncan asked as he stuck his head out of his office.

"I'm fine. I landed in a wonky position because I tried not to squish Margaret. I didn't see her lying there in the hall in the dark." Delanie wasn't sure if he was talking to her or the dog. She hoped he was concerned about her fall. With Duncan, sometimes it was hard to tell.

She stood and handed him the paper from Robin's store.

"Okay," he said. Margaret didn't move from her spot in the middle of the floor. When the bulldog found a good napping spot, she claimed it.

"Look at the name of the engineering firm and the logo. I glanced at it and immediately had a holy cow moment. Look at the letters in the logo. It's right there in front of us."

"Oh, no way. This is what we've been looking for. The TU LLP looks like 'Tulip.' That had to be what Robin saw."

"Duncan, this was the firm that did the traffic survey the day Paisley and I went with Robin to Farmville for the storage auction. This could be the missing piece that connects all the cases. And Farmville might be the key to all four of our victims. It's plausible Emily and David were there. Now, we need to see if D'borah traveled that way recently," Delanie said, catching her breath.

"She may have. She seemed to be all over Central Virginia. Where'd you find it?"

"It was on Robin's desk at the store. Could the link be as simple as they all were involved in a traffic stop?"

"Would the killer be dumb enough to wear a company shirt or something with a logo on it when he committed these crimes?" he asked.

"Maybe. What if the killer used his work shirt and the survey to gain access to their houses?" she asked. "Maybe that's why they let him in without a struggle. You know, like a follow-up visit or something."

"None of the crime scenes had been broken into," he said. "It's possible. It's as good a theory as any." He continued with, "Ha! We weren't looking for something called a 'Tulip Shirt' after all. It was making me nuts when we couldn't find anything. And look at this survey. After the section about the driving patterns on Route 460, there are a bunch of demographic questions, including marital status. The bad guy had a ton of information on everyone who answered the survey. It's a cornucopia of data."

"He could pick and choose his victims. It looks like he targeted single people. Let's go see what else we can find out."

Delanie followed Duncan to the conference room, but she was too excited to sit. She paced behind him as he searched for information about the engineering firm.

"Hovering isn't going to make the Internet go faster. Why don't you go get us something to drink? By the time you get back, I'll have something for you to write on the board."

"Okay." Delanie made her way to the kitchen. She grabbed two waters from the fridge and a half-empty box of chocolate chip cookies.

Stepping over Margaret, the hallway speedbump, Delanie took the drinks and snacks back to the conference room. Duncan grabbed a water and said, "Thompson Ulrich, LLP is a small firm. Their headquarters is in McLean, but they have a pretty decent sized office here in River City. The local office specializes in roadwork and water and sewer projects. According to the VDOT website, they do a lot of work with the state. Ding. Ding. Ding. Their last big contract was a road improvement study for Route 460 between Amelia County and Farmville."

"Any company directories or org charts. I think if they answer Requests for Proposals for state and federal jobs, they have to supply stuff like that. Is any of that online?"

"Good thinking," he said. "Here's something. Wait a minute. There's an appendix to their road improvement RFP, and they've got resumes and a summary about their available staff. I'll print this, and it'll give us something to start with. Go get your laptop, and you can do some searching on the company while I focus on the staff."

"Okey dokey," she said. A few minutes later, she booted her laptop and grabbed a legal pad. She jotted down every name she came across on the firm's website – enough to fill two pages.

A few hours later, she stood and did several yoga stretches. Margaret walked in and sniffed Delanie's hair while she was in the downward dog. "Thanks, girl," she said, checking her hair for slobber.

"Here's a list of the people on their latest VDOT submittals. I love that the state puts them all online. What did you find?" he asked.

"These are all the names I found on their website," she said, handing him her legal pad.

"Okay, let's combine the lists in a spreadsheet with what we know, and then you can add it to the board."

"Here, I can do the consolidating. You keep looking in your secret places on the Internet."

An hour later, she entered the last row in the spreadsheet. "Duncan, I'm starving. I think we need to stop for a while. Let's go over and get Chinese food. It'll give us a little break, and maybe something will jump out at us when we get back."

"All right. Give me a minute to save everything here, and then I'll be ready to walk over. Margaret, you stay here and guard the office. I'll bring you something good back," he said, patting the bulldog's boxy head. She returned to her speedbump position again in the hallway.

Delanie and Duncan found a semicircle booth under a carved wooden mural of the Great Wall of China at the Golden Panda. The waiters in black with white cummerbunds outnumbered the customers at this time of the day – between the lunch and dinner rushes was a great time to grab some food.

After ordering wonton soup and beef in brown sauce, Delanie listened as Duncan ordered enough food for three people. When the waiter left, she asked, "So, what's next?"

"Well, we outline what we know and what we can find. Then we've got to find a way in. We need a way to put you in the office."

"Huh?"

"We'll find a plausible reason for you to make a visit. And I'll poke around on Holiday Road. If we can get you in there, we're on our way to unmasking the killer."

"Sorry," she said, giggling. "I know that's a serious thing. But every time you say it, I think of Chevy Chase in that movie."

Duncan scowled and continued, "We need more information before we make a move on this one. This is big. There's a killer or killers involved, and we have to get all our ducks in a row before you go to the police. We have to be right about this, and we have to be careful."

"But, we also have to be quick about it too. What if there's a fifth attack? We've got to call Rick Dixon or the police or somebody. We can't let that creep strike again."

"I know. I know. But we need a day or two more. We've got to make sure we're on the right path. We're close. I can feel it. We're wasting time here. Let's box the rest of this stuff and head back. There's something I thought of that I need to check," he said.

Delanie settled back in her chair in the conference room while Duncan fed Margaret some of his General Tso's chicken. After wiping his hands on his jeans, he plopped in the chair across from her. "Gimme a minute. I didn't look at the road project itself. I'm wondering if there are any clues there. Make us both copies of the list of employees at the firm. We may need the names later."

An hour or so later, Duncan stirred and yawned. "I think this links all our victims."

"What?" she asked, jumping to her feet and peering over Duncan's shoulder.

"There is a grassroots opposition to that road project on Route 460. It's even got a Facebook page with over a thousand likes. There are a lot of comments about how the money is being spent. For this one in particular, it affects a white, rural population. There are a lot of folks who feel the money could be better spent improving the infrastructure of Richmond, Petersburg, or Portsmouth. And guess who's right there in the middle of it? One D'borah Styles. I've printed everything I could find that she commented on. I'm not sure how I missed this before."

Delanie walked down the hall to Duncan's office to pick up the printouts.

"Hey, Dunc. On one of these pages she's lambasting the firm that did the traffic study for their archaic way of collecting data, so she definitely got stopped too. I read on the company website that the firm did two traffic stops, so it makes sense that D'borah, Emily, and maybe even David could have been involved in the earlier one. Robin and I stopped at the second one. I remember two guys coming up to the truck. One was older and the younger guy looked like a hipster with dark hair. They handed us the flyer and let us through the checkpoint."

"We know D'borah and Robin got stopped near Farmville. It's plausible Emily and David did too. Why don't you call Emily's company and the vet hospital and see if either traveled on what were those dates? I have them here somewhere," he said. "Here, they are. September ninth was the one you were involved with. The other one was March fifteenth."

"The Ides of March," she replied as she picked up her laptop and legal pad. I'll be back in a minute."

At her desk, she looked up the numbers.

"Big and Little Animal Hospital. This is Becca. How may I help you?"

"Hi. This is Delanie Fitzgerald of Falcon Investigations. I stopped in a little while back to talk to you about David Millhouse."

"Oh, hi, Delanie. How are you?"

"I'm good. I was wondering if you could help me with something I'm chasing down. Do you have records of when the vet and his staff travel?"

"Usually. They track their mileage. I'm a little behind in updating the spreadsheet, but I do have the information," she twanged.

"I was wondering if you could check on March fifteenth of this year. Do you have any records of David travelling for work?"

"Lemme see."

After a few minutes of humming, Becca continued with, "He was out and about on March eighth, twelfth, fourteenth, and fifteenth. He was travelling in early April. Oh, but he died in May," she said as her voice quivered.

"Thank you so much, Becca. I appreciate all of your help."

"No problem," she said, sniffing. "Call again if I can help."

"Will do. Thanks again," Delanie said, disconnecting the call. Delanie was sorry to dredge up bad memories, but she needed the information. She did a quick Internet search for Emily's accounting firm. On a whim, she called the Farmville office. She was hoping someone there would help her.

After three rings, she heard "Thank you for calling the offices of Smith and Keaton in Farmville. How may I direct your call?"

"Good afternoon. This is Delanie Fitzgerald from Falcon Investigations. I'm working with Attorney Rick Dixon on an investigation involving one of your former employees. And I have a travel date that I need to validate with your company. Is there someone there who could verify whether or not Emily Menendez traveled to your office on a specific date?"

"Maybe Theresa in payroll could help you. She has all the mileage reports. Hang on just a second," said the woman.

After a minute or two of canned music, Delanie heard, "Ms. Fitzgerald, this is Theresa in the Richmond office. Beth wanted me to check Emily's travel schedule. What dates are you interested in?"

"March fifteenth."

"She was at the Farmville office in March from the fifteenth through the eighteenth."

"Thank you so much. You've been helpful. I appreciate your time."

"No problem," she said as she hung up.

"Duncan, Duncan. We're four for four," she said, walking briskly to the conference room, watching for Margaret.

"That's good. Now we know we're on the right path. And now for our way in to the engineering firm. You're probably going to get a call this week from Thompson Ulrich, LLP."

"Okay. But why?" she asked.

"You, as Delanie Fitzgerald, applied for a part-time job there.

They're looking for someone to help with the phones and general office work."

"What makes you so sure that I'll get a call?"

"You're the top candidate."

"Good to know. But I suspect you had something to do with that."

Duncan smiled. "The Office Manager, Patsy Roberson, advertised the position online and in the newspaper last Sunday. She hasn't checked the email account this week. I deleted all the other submissions except one, and she's terribly underqualified. Plus, you have a stellar resume. You'll be an asset to their engineering firm. I was trying to figure a way in, and this will be perfect."

"Duncan, what about the other people who really applied for the job?"

"This is an emergency. You'll at least get in for the interview. If you get the job, they can advertise the position again when you quit."

"Duncan."

"You wanted in, didn't you?"

She rolled her eyes and asked, "So I applied for a part-time receptionist's position. What did you tell them that I need to know about?"

"I printed your cover letter and resume. You may want to look at it before they call. You never know what will come up in an interview."

"Thanks, I guess. We'll see what comes out of this. You are something else."

"You already know the history of the firm. But don't act like you know too much. You'll come across as way too overqualified. And if a woman is interviewing you, you want to befriend her, not make her worry about the competition." She smiled. When did Duncan become such an expert on female behavior?

"What else did you find on your journey on the dark side?"

"James Reynolds is the partner in residence in the Richmond office. He's been a civil engineer for over thirty years. Patsy Roberson is the office manager. I've been peeking at stuff on their network. For a company that contracts with government agencies, they don't really have good security. She's not organized with her electronic filing either. In the resumes they submitted for the RFP, Phillip Saunders,

Clinton Carpenter, Michael Owens, and Seth Jenkins are working on the Route 460 traffic study project for VDOT. It looks like Phillip Saunders is the head traffic engineer. They also had resumes for draftspersons, Mark Curtis and Shannon Sykes."

"We had a huge breakthrough when we traced the murders to this firm and the traffic stop in Farmville. Can you see what you can find on these people? I'll pull all this information together and add the names to our list on our whiteboard. How many people work for the firm?"

"It's hard to tell for sure. They only include resumes in the projects for people they propose to work on a job. Some of them are from other locations or are subcontractors. I'm guessing there are about twenty or so. The office suite is over in Bon Air in an office park. I'll add that to my list of stuff to look into."

Around eight-thirty that evening, Delanie said, "Duncan. I'm about ready to call it a night. Do you need me to do anything before I leave?"

"Nah. We're gonna stay here for a little while longer. I'm on a roll. I've found information on all the names we uncovered. Oh, and the office suite they rent can accommodate sixty-five, but I don't get the sense that there are that many staff there."

"I'm heading out. I'll let you know as soon as I hear from them about an interview. Oh. Do you have a small camera I can put in my purse? I have the ball cap one, but it won't work for an interview."

"I've got something even better. I'll be back in a minute. It's in my desk."

Duncan returned with a small box. "Here. Don't say I never give you anything."

Delanie opened it and found a silver brooch that looked like a fish with a long, flowery tail. He also handed her a burner phone.

"There's a wireless camera behind the head. Turn on this phone and put it in your purse. It'll transmit what you capture. Keep this phone nearby."

"How do you turn on the fish?"

"There's a slide button behind the head. The battery in it will last a couple of days before it has to be recharged."

"Thanks, Dunc. You're always good for the gadgets."

"No problem. Just get the job, so you can nose around in person. Somebody there knows something. And we've got to find whatever it is soon before there's another attack."

20

Delanie drove home and let herself in the side door. Dropping her purse on the kitchen table, she poked around the kitchen for a snack. Settling on iced tea, she sat down at the table and checked email.

She woke up the next morning to a buzzing sound and with her head on the table. Light streamed in through the kitchen window, and her purse vibrated on the table. Rummaging around for her phone, she pressed the button to answer it. The clock on the stove read nine-thirty.

"Hello," she said, shaking off the fog of a night spent at the kitchen table.

"Delanie Fitzgerald?"

"Yes."

"This is Ellen Peterson with Thompson Ulrich, LLP. We would like to schedule a time for you to come in and talk to our office manager about the part-time receptionist's position you applied for."

"Oh, good," Delanie replied. Duncan's skills worked again in their favor.

"We have a slot today and one tomorrow morning."

"Today would be fine. What time?"

"Eleven-thirty. We're in Suite 103 on Lake Village Drive."

"Thank you. I'll see you in a little while."

"Ask for Patsy Roberson when you arrive," she said before she disconnected. Short and to the point. Delanie guessed the woman didn't want to hang around to answer any questions.

Delanie stood and stretched. Her muscles objected to a night in a kitchen chair. All-nighters and late-nighters were getting old. At least the interview at the engineering firm could prove to be interesting.

After a quick shower, she dug a navy pantsuit out of the back of her closet. She pulled her hair back in a twist and did the bare minimum with the jewelry and makeup. She stole another glance in the mirror to see if she looked as nonthreatening as possible.

Pinning the fish on her lapel, she grabbed her phone and dialed Duncan.

"Hey."

"Hey, back," she said. "I got a call from someone at the firm name Ellen. Patsy Roberson is going to interview me at eleven-thirty."

"That was quick. See what you can see. And good luck with the job."

"She said they had another interview slot tomorrow."

After some clicking, Duncan replied, "You're the only one on Patsy's calendar so far. They haven't scheduled anyone else yet. Go in and knock it out of the park."

"Thanks, I think. What do you have on Ellen and Patsy?"

"Um, let me get my notes. Here it is. Patsy Roberson is fifty-five. She's divorced, and she's got an active page on a couple of online dating sites. She's been at the firm for eighteen years. She started as a secretary to the partner at that time. Now, she's the office manager. I'll email you a picture. She wears a lot of makeup. Oh, she has a Chihuahua that she sometimes carries around in a purse according to her Facebook pictures. She has a grown son named Alex who lives in Tampa."

"What about Ellen Peterson?"

"That's a new name for the list. Hang on a second." Delanie heard clicking. "There's a bunch of Ellen Petersons. Uh, oh, it's this one. She has a Facebook and LinkedIn Page. There's not much there. She hasn't updated either since last December if it's the same person. She works as a marketing specialist. This Ellen is thirty-two. She gradu- ated seven years ago from Randolph Macon with a BA in literature and two years after that from Virginia Commonwealth University with a masters in creative writing. According to her profile, she's been at the engineering firm for six years as a marketing specialist. It looks like this was her first full-time job out of college. It doesn't look like she does any writing. And she used to play the clarinet."

"You always find good stuff. I'll see what I can uncover in their office. I'll call you after my interview."

"Break a leg," he said as he clicked off.

Flipping through her email, she landed on the one he sent with Patsy's picture. She wondered if the office manager's personality matched her big helmet hair and what looked like theatre makeup.

Delanie made one more trip to the bathroom to touch up her makeup. She didn't want to look too washed out to the office manager. Grabbing a portfolio with the resume Duncan created, she picked up her purse and headed to her interview at Thompson, Ulrich, LLP.

DELANIE PARKED IN FRONT OF THE OFFICE BUILDING AND WAITED IN THE car until fifteen minutes before her interview. She turned on Duncan's magic fish pin and the cell phone receiver. Striding in with her portfolio and head up, she tried to look confident, but not cocky as she made her way to the suite.

She opened the heavy wooden door and stepped into the firm's sea foam green lobby. A woman in a magenta suit and poofy plat- inum hair occupied the larger of the two desks.

"May I help you?" the woman asked, looking Delanie up and down.

"Hello, I'm Delanie Fitzgerald, and I'm looking for Ms. Roberson.

I have an interview with her at eleven-thirty."

"I'm Ms. Roberson. Have a seat." She picked up the phone and said, "Ellen, to the front please. Ellen, please report to the front immediately." She looked at Delanie and smiled. "I need to get someone to watch the front desk. We'll go over to the conference room where we can talk in private. Some people are so nosy around here."

After a few minutes of silence, a tall woman with short dark hair lumbered into the reception area.

"Ellen, phones. I'll be back in a little while."

The younger woman scowled as Patsy Roberson vacated her chair and turned her back on her. Ellen plopped down at the smaller desk and continued to stare bullets at the woman in pink.

After shutting the conference room door, Patsy Roberson said, "Have a seat. Thank you for coming today."

Delanie walked around the long wooden table and sat with her back to the large plate-glass window, overlooking a lake that looked too round to be natural. The office manager sat in the over-sized leather chair with her back to the door.

"So, tell me about yourself. Why do you want this job?" she asked settling in the chair and adjusting her skirt.

"Thank you so much for taking the time to interview me. I'm Delanie Fitzgerald. I've been an administrative assistant since college. I want to start my own business, but I still want to work part-time to keep my skills current."

"What kind of business?"

"I'm partnering with a friend on an entrepreneurial adventure. We make one-of-a-kind jewelry and sell it on my Etsy site. It's a lot of fun, but I don't want my office skills to get rusty. Plus, it's nice to be around people."

"That's interesting. We have characters here. I don't know if all of them count as normal people. Anyway, so tell me how you deal with difficult personalities?"

"Well, I try to treat people as I want to be treated. I'm in a service role, and I need to make sure their questions get answered. I strive to be polite. If I don't know something, I take a message and get back to them with the answer."

"Can you handle multiple lines?"

"Oh, yes. At my last job, I had five incoming lines. I worked at a fitness center, and I was often the only one covering the phones."

"You met Ellen, but she's not a team player. She thinks she's too good to help out around here. It'll be refreshing to have someone polite and responsible like you."

"Why thank you."

"Do you have any word processing experience?"

"I do. I can type. I did a lot of letters and flyers at my old job. But I can update spreadsheets too."

"Do you have a preference for hours?"

"No, the ad said it was part-time."

"I'll make the schedule weekly. Sometimes, we'll need help in the morning and other times, it'll be the afternoons. It depends on what's going on. Do you have a problem with that?"

"That's fine. I'm flexible. That's actually really good for me."

"Well, do you have any questions for me?"

"When would you be looking for someone to start?"

"The sooner the better. I've got a couple of more interviews to do, and I should make a decision soon."

"That sounds great. I appreciate you taking the time to interview me. I like what I've seen, and I'd really like to work with you. I hope I hear from you soon. I could start as early as tomorrow if you needed the help."

Patsy stood and shook her hand. "Thanks for coming in. I'll let you know. But between you and me, you're at the top of my list. And when you come back, bring some of your jewelry with you. I'd like to see it," she said, winking at Delanie.

She opened the conference room door, and Delanie followed her back to the lobby. Ellen sat slumped forward with her head propped up by both hands. She stared at the phone.

Patsy sashayed to her seat. Delanie's brother Robbie would have made some comment about fries and Patsy's shake. The office manager interrupted her thoughts when she snapped, "Ellen, sit up. That's not the way we sit in chairs in the front office. It looks sloppy. When you're up here, you're the face of the firm. We have standards." The younger woman stood up and glared at the office manager.

Delanie wasn't sure what to say, so she changed the subject with, "Oh, is that your dog? It's so cute."

"That's my baby," Patsy replied. Her face softened to a smile. "Her name is Pixie, and she's four."

"She is adorable. If she were mine, I'd carry her around everywhere."

Ellen stirred and almost said something. Patsy and Delanie looked at her. She cleared her throat instead. "Uh, I left the traffic survey notes on your desk," she said, walking briskly toward the back of the suite.

"Don't mind her a bit. She's a little odd. It was nice to meet you. We'll be talking again soon. My, that's a lovely pin," Patsy said, putting her face close to Delanie's lapel.

The PI stifled a laugh. She could imagine Duncan watching the close up of Patsy Roberson's eye.

"Thanks. A good friend gave it to me."

She strode to the car and peeled off her suit jacket. Throwing it in the passenger seat, she started the car and said, "Call Duncan."

She heard, "Hey, what's up?"

"I finished with Patsy poo. She's a real piece of work. I only met her and Ellen Peterson. There's definitely some bad blood between those two. It should be interesting if I get the job. They really need a referee or a shrink," she said as she clicked the button on the pin and switched it and the receiver off.

"How did it go?"

"I think it went well. We bonded over her Chihuahua. I hope I hear from her soon."

"Well, swing by the office and bring lunch, and we can go over our notes. I feel like we're on the verge of uncovering something. I don't know quite what it is. But we have to find it before something else bad happens."

21

ON HER WAY TO THE ENGINEERING FIRM THE NEXT DAY, DELANIE CALLED Duncan at a stoplight.

"What's up? I'm going through the case files again."

"I won't be in today. I got a new job."

"Congrats. You'll be a great receptionist. Margaret and I will miss you terribly."

"I'm excited to start my new career under the tutelage of Patsy Roberson. I'm wearing your pin again. I'll give you a fish's eye view of my experience."

"Sounds good. I'll check the feed from time to time to see what you've uncovered. I don't have any new updates since yesterday. But I'm going to keep looking at the people working at the firm. My hunch is that if there's something there, we'll find it."

"Do you have anything new on any of the key players I need to know about?"

"Nothing earth shattering. How long are you there today?"

"Until one. She's going to give me a different schedule each day. Can't wait."

"Call me when you're done," he said.

"Will do. I'm off to catch a killer." Delanie grabbed her stuff. She pinned Duncan's fish on her black jacket's collar.

She was surprised to find the suite's front office empty at eight-thirty. Delanie stepped inside and sat in a guest chair. About fifteen minutes later, a tall man with salt-and-pepper hair came out of the office next to the conference room.

"Oh, hello. May I help you?" he asked.

"Hello. I'm Delanie Fitzgerald. I'm here to see Patsy Roberson. She hired me yesterday to answer phones part-time."

"Welcome to the team. I'm Jim Reynolds," he said, grasping her hand and shaking it with both of his. "I'm sure Patsy will be along in a minute. Just wait right there, and she'll get you situated when she gets in," he said as he walked back through the suite.

About twenty minutes later, Patsy sidled in through the front door with a large, designer purse that matched her stilettos. "Oh, hi," she said, dropping her bag on the desk. You can sit over there. I'll show you where the kitchen is in a minute. You're welcome to the coffee. It's free, but you'll probably want to bring your own mug. Answer the phones, 'Thompson Ulrich, LLP. How may I direct your call?' You can use this message book. Mailboxes are over there, or you can send the call through to voicemail. Push the green voicemail button and the extension. It's not hard. You'll catch on quick."

"Do you have a staff list?"

"Yep. I'll get you one in a minute. Oh, here's mine. Go back in that room and make a copy. You may have to turn the machine on if none of these clods warmed it up when they got here."

Delanie took the document, covered in scratch outs and notes, and found the copier. When she toggled the button on the machine, it buzzed and hummed until it was finally ready to copy.

Putting the original on Patsy's desk, she settled in the chair across from the office manager and scanned her copy. Except for the phone and message book, the second desk stood empty, a stark contrast to Patsy's area where every inch of space sported office supplies, picture frames, and other personal tchotchkes.

Patsy said, "They're old school here. If they're in the middle of something, they'll ignore the phone. Most of them are so weird. They don't like to talk to people. But you'll get used to it. It's so hard for social butterflies like me. I spend my day surrounded by nerds who are so boring. I'm going to get coffee. The better coffee is at the kiosk in the building's front lobby. Jim makes me order the cheap stuff for the staff here. If the phone rings, answer it. The partners, anyone from the Department of Transportation, and the partners' wives are important. Everyone else, not so much. Oh, the bathrooms are out in the lobby area too."

Delanie reread the organization chart and answered two calls. She hoped she wouldn't have to be here long. The work was mind-numbing. After what seemed like ages, Patsy finally materialized and made a big show of turning on her computer and checking on the partner. She disappeared again and returned about thirty minutes later with a pile of papers.

"Here are your human resources stuff. Read and fill these out. I need your driver's license."

Delanie nodded and spent the next hour reading through the stack of outdated forms. She put the ones she signed in a folder and handed it to Patsy. She didn't want to interrupt her Internet surfing.

"Thanks," she said, taking the folder and setting it on her desk. "It's unusually quiet this morning. I'll give you the scoop while we're waiting for the phones to ring. Okay, Jim Reynolds is our partner. He's in charge of this office. There are five other partners in McLean. When they call, they like to be put through immediately. After Jim, Phillip Saunders is in charge of the traffic area. Clint Carpenter, Michael Owens, and Seth Jenkins are his staff. Seth is a little freaky, but the rest of them are pretty nice. We call Seth our resident vampire. We have three draftsmen, Mark Curtis, Hugh Lowry, and Shannon Sykes. Shannon is a girl. She's friendly, but she usually keeps to herself. I have to start all the conversations. Then we have Dan Mayes on the water sewer side of the company. His team is Andy Phelps and Rob Williams. Then there's me and you. Our IT guy is Chuck Morrison. And then there's Ellen, Ellen Peterson. Just between you and me, she's got too much attitude. Jim's going to have to do something about her. She's got a sassy mouth, and she doesn't pull her weight. That's not what we need around here."

"What does she do?"

"She's the marketing person, but Jim doesn't think she has enough to do. He's always asking me to find her something to keep her busy. Come on, grab your list and I'll walk you around to meet everyone. This button here is the night attendant. It'll send all calls to voicemail until you turn it off."

After being paraded through the suite, Delanie tried to commit names with the faces. Nobody jumped out as suspicious. The staff either nodded or said a few words, but it felt like she and Patsy were interrupting their work. Delanie hoped she could get at least a few of them to talk to her later.

The phones lit up as soon as she settled in the chair across from Patsy. She spent the next hour fielding calls while Patsy pretended to be busy on her computer.

"Most of the calls you're getting are about a traffic survey," Patsy said when Delanie hung up. "We have a big contract with the state to do this study, but if you ask me, I think Phil and Seth screwed it up. We've had nothing but complaints. I'm surprised there haven't been a lot of calls today. They did these two traffic stops to get information, but they created traffic jams and pissed off a lot of people. But it's good for you because we had to create your job."

"I appreciate the opportunity." The phone console lit up again and interrupted their chat.

About an hour later, Delanie looked up to see a youngish guy with dark, shaggy hair leaning on her desk. "Do you know where Ellen is?" he asked as she cradled the receiver.

"I haven't seen her since early this morning," she said. "Do you want me to give her a message if I see her? And you are?"

"Uh, Seth. When you see her, tell her to get her butt in the chair and finish the updates I gave her." He turned on his heels and stalked down the hall.

"Alrighty then," Delanie said to his back.

"Don't mind Seth. He spends his time trying to boss Ellen around, and she spends hers ducking out the side door to avoid him. They are both so weird. It's too bad they hate each other. They should probably try dating, but she's too tall for him. And she needs to do something with that flat hair. Seth's the one who skateboards in the parking lot and plays those stupid games on his phone when he's supposed to be working," Patsy said, checking her lipstick in the small mirror she pulled from her desk drawer.

"Should I try to find Ellen?"

"Nah. She'll show up eventually. She goes to the bathroom a lot. I think she has issues."

"Do you have something you want me to work on while I'm waiting for the phones?"

"I like your spirit. Here, you can file these. Put them in order, and then file them in the cabinets in the room back there with the copier. Each job has a number. And all paperwork goes in that folder. The most recent stuff goes on top. I'll be back before you leave, and we'll talk about your schedule for tomorrow. See ya," she said, grabbing her purse and sliding out the front door.

Delanie fought off the boredom by putting three stacks of files in numeric order. Patsy was nowhere to be found, so she carried the first stack to the next room.

She laughed out loud when she realized Patsy's filing system wasn't in any kind of order. Each drawer had a label with a series of numbers, but the ranges looked random. It must have been too much work to put the drawers in numeric order.

Managing to file all the stacks before the phone rang again, she spotted a drawer marked, "HR." She flipped through the folders which in true Patsy fashion weren't in alphabetical order in the unlocked cabinet. She recorded the pages in the first three folders before the phone rang.

～

About an hour and a half after she left, Patsy returned. "Thanks for covering the phones. Wow. You got all the filing done? That would have taken Ellen a month. She is so lazy. I don't know why Jim keeps her around."

"It's been fairly quiet the last hour." Relieved Patsy finally returned from lunch, Delanie was ready to bolt out the door at her quitting time.

"Oh. Here's your timesheet. Fill it out each day you're here. And do it in pencil. We get paid on the fifteenth and the thirtieth."

"Thanks. I enjoyed my first day. What time would you like me tomorrow?"

"Come in at eleven. Do eleven to four. Then I won't need you any more this week until Friday. I want to take the day off, so you'll need to work the whole day."

"Okay. Thanks for all of your help. See you at eleven tomorrow," she said, collecting her things and slipping out the front door before Patsy could begin another conversation.

She started the car and blasted the air conditioning. "Call Duncan on cell," she commanded.

"Hey, working girl. Where are you going to spend all your money?"

"I worked a half-day, and I might have cleared thirty-two dollars. Patsy is going to drive me nuts. I have to work tomorrow afternoon and all day on Friday by myself. We need to solve this thing before I go brain dead. The reason they need a part-time person is because their full-time office manager spends her day avoiding work. And there are a few staff who really don't like each other."

"Makes you love Margaret and me more, now doesn't it?"

"Uh-huh. Find anything new?" she asked.

"One of the guys in the office, Mark Curtis, has a criminal past. He did some time in his twenties for embezzlement."

"And they hired him?"

"Maybe they don't know. I had to dig to find it. It seems he did deliveries after high school for a chain of surf shops in Virginia Beach. They had several locations in Hampton Roads and Nags

Head, North Carolina. He and another driver were convicted of inflating their mileage report," he said.

"That couldn't have been a huge amount of money, could it?"

"The court document stated it had been going on for a couple of years. He and the other guy had to pay restitution, and they got a couple of years behind bars. The only other issue I found with staff was parking tickets. Seth Jenkins seemed to have cornered the market on those. Anything suspicious on your end?"

"Seth is the interesting guy in the traffic group. He's kind of short and has jet black hair. Patsy called him things like 'vampire' and 'creepy.' I can't swear to it, but I think he was one of the guys we saw at the traffic stop in Farmville."

"Let me see what I can uncover. Hold on." Delanie heard clicking sounds. "Okay. He's twenty-eight. He went to Old Dominion University, and this company hired him from an internship. He's got a Facebook page. He likes eighties punk music and plays guitar. According to his profile, skateboarding floats his boat. He likes his collection of tattoos and being in the band, BadAzz."

"Tattoos, skateboards, and guitars," she said as she pulled out of the lot and drove toward Midlothian Turnpike. "Hmmmm. Sounds like it fits with some of the wall drawings from our cases. I'll keep an eye on him."

"And he has access to the traffic survey information. Definitely chat him up. Turn on your charm. You have a gift for extracting info from complete strangers."

"I'm too old for him. He only spoke to me once, and he wanted me to hunt down someone for him."

"I have faith in you. Age has never stopped you before. If anyone can worm information out of him, you can. Wanna borrow my skateboard? Too bad you're not a musician or you don't have cool ink."

"Thanks, but no. If I'm going to bond with Patsy, I need to be more girly. I'm going to do some research this afternoon."

"Research?"

"Mani pedi and maybe some shopping. I need a new outfit if I'm going to wow the boy engineer. And I probably need to get some jewelry in case Patsy asks again about my made-up side business."

"Only you would consider a spa day and shopping as research for the job. I'm glad I'm not your accountant. See ya back at the office. I'll keep digging while you're out doing your research." She heard him snicker as he disconnected.

22

DELANIE ARRIVED ABOUT TEN MINUTES EARLY FOR HER AFTERNOON shift. She smiled at Patsy and set her purse on the second desk. Before Delanie could speak, Patsy grabbed her red patent leather purse. "I'm glad you're here. The phone's been ringing off the hook, and I have an appointment. I'll be back after two. Seth and Phil are at their desks. They can take the calls about the Farmville road project. If you can't find them, call Ellen. Tell her to help you. And let me know if she gives you any sass. Bye." She waved and headed out the front door.

Delanie had time to put her things in the drawer and grab her notes before the phone jangled to life.

Forty minutes later, Delanie got a break from the onslaught of calls, mostly about the road project. She looked up to see Seth hovering over her desk.

"May I help you?" she asked.

"Phil and I are busy this afternoon. Make sure that all traffic survey calls go to Ellen's extension. She can answer them until further notice."

"Okay. Have you told her she's my point person, or do I need to let her know?"

"She knows. If she gives you any lip, let me know. It's her job to support us. The engineers are too busy to field all these calls. She needs to make herself useful."

"Okay," she said. Seth continued to lean toward her.

Delanie waited as he stood there, hunched forward with both palms on the edge of her desk.

"Is there anything else I can help you with?" she asked, leaning back.

"Uh, no," he said, straightening up and clearing his throat. "Uh, thanks for your help," he said over his shoulder. His handprints lingered on the top of the desk.

A few seconds later, he returned to her desk. "Uh, Delanie."

"Yes."

"Nothing. Just let me know if Ellen isn't available for the phone calls. I can clear her schedule."

The suite's door opened slightly. She noticed Ellen standing behind the heavy wooden door. The tall woman's face clouded. Then she turned and strode down the hall before Delanie could say anything. She wondered how long Ellen had been standing there.

When Patsy returned, Delanie said, "I'll be right back. The phones have been pretty quiet for the last hour. Seth said that all traffic study calls go to Ellen since he and Phil are busy."

Patsy nodded and harrumphed, but didn't reply.

Delanie strode through the suite toward the side exit. Her bathroom break was really a chance to talk with Mark Curtis. She rounded the corner where there were two rows of cubes near the side door.

The draftsman spoke in low tones to someone on the phone. Delanie slid in the empty cube that shared a divider with Mark's space. She ducked down on the floor and crawled closer to the cube wall to eavesdrop.

"Okay. Thursday at three-thirty is good. See you then," he said. Delanie scooted closer to hear better. He dialed another call.

"Yep. Yep. I'll pick Ella up and then get dinner. Have fun with Natalie and your girls' night out. We'll be home when you get there."

"What are you doing?" a male voice boomed behind Delanie.

She jumped and bumped her head on the desk. The Delanie stood up, rubbing her head. Seth blocked her exit from the cube. He stepped toward her and glared.

"Here it is. I lost an earring," she said, pulling on her earlobe and pretending to put it back in place. Seth stepped toward her again. She took a quick step toward him in an effort to catch him off guard. He hesitated and then retreated to the back of the suite without another word. She wondered if he'd tattle to Patsy.

Delanie straightened her dress pants and walked toward the suite's side door. Mark Curtis tapped on his computer.

Grabbing the knob, she turned and said over her shoulder, "Mark, did you go to school here? You look like someone I remember from Monacan High."

"Uh, no," he said, looking up. "I grew up in Virginia Beach. I went to Bayside."

"Shut up! No way," Delanie exclaimed, clapping her hands. "My college roommate went to Bayside. Her name is Lori Hastings. Do you know her?"

"No, that name doesn't ring a bell. What year?"

"Ninety-eight."

"Way after I left. I graduated in ninety-two."

"It's a small world though. I'll have to let Lori know I met a fellow alum. Where'd you go to college?"

"Uh, I took some time off after high school. I finished up at ODU later as an adult."

Delanie smiled and took inventory of Mark's cube. Papers littered the shelf and desk areas. Piles of document storage boxes filled every inch of the empty floor space, and his cube walls were covered in tear-outs from a variety of Disney coloring books. A family portrait with three kids and a big yellow dog sat next to Mark's monitor.

She slid out the side door and walked around to the front lobby.

When she plopped in her seat, Patsy glared at her. "Things have changed. I'm gonna need you Wednesday and Friday. Your schedule next week will be Monday twelve to five, Wednesday at one 'til closing, and all day on the following Friday."

Before Patsy could continue, Ellen lumbered to the front office and dropped several folders on the office manager's desk.

"Ellen," said the older woman as she turned her attention to the marketing specialist. "We don't sling things on people's desks. You are in the front office, and you need to represent the company. When you are at work, you are an ambassador for the firm." Before the tall woman could reply, Patsy continued, "Why aren't you wearing your company shirt? Jim said we could go casual if we wore them."

"I don't look good in orange," Ellen said. "It makes me look like a traffic cone."

"Orange? Seth gave all the women green shirts with the little logo on the front."

"No. Mine's orange, just like the ones the traffic guys have. Except Seth. His are black for some reason."

Patsy looked puzzled as she watched Ellen retreat to the back. "The orange shirts were for the guys," she muttered. "Whatever. That reminds me. Delanie, I'll get you a set of the green ones. Medium?"

Delanie nodded. "Do you have anything else you want me to work on today?"

The office manager's stern look melted into a smile.

DELANIE SLID INTO HER SEAT A FEW MINUTES BEFORE HER SHIFT THE following Wednesday. This case simply had to get solved. Delanie wasn't sure how much longer she could work here.

Patsy picked up the phone receiver and bellowed through the office intercom for Ellen to report to the front office. When Patsy barked a second round of commands for the marketing specialist to report immediately, they heard one of the engineers yell, "Ellen, go see what she wants."

"There you are!" Patsy said when Ellen slunk into the reception area. "I've been calling you. What took you so long? Oh never mind. I'm sure it's another lame excuse like your friend Seth. He called in sick this morning. He's been doing that a lot lately. He said that he got beat up in a skateboarding accident. Anyway, Jim needs the latest report of the comments from the traffic survey. Please send me the spreadsheet, and I'll make the copies he wants."

"First, Seth is not my friend. And second, you called me all the way up here to tell me to send you a spreadsheet? Next time, call me on the phone. That didn't warrant a trip to the front office." She glared at Patsy with a look that bordered on rage.

"Looky who got up on the wrong side of the bed this morning. You better watch that attitude. Jim doesn't like smart mouths. Just get me the report, and it better be right. Some bigwig at the Department of Transportation wants it. And what happened to your neck and face? That can't be a hickey."

"It's not. I gave the cat a bath, and he wasn't too thrilled about it."

"I'd stick with the hickey excuse. It's better than a sad, cat lady story," Patsy said as she stared at her computer monitor.

The tall woman turned red. Delanie didn't know what to say. After a few uncomfortable seconds, Ellen turned on her heels and strode to her desk in the back area that was once a storage closet.

AT THE END OF WHAT FELT LIKE ANOTHER LONG SHIFT, DELANIE handed Patsy her timesheet.

"Thanks. Have fun on Friday. I'll see you again on Monday. I'm taking a much-needed spa/shopping day. It's time for a Patsy day."

"Have fun," she replied. Delanie grabbed her purse and left through the side entrance. She caught a glimpse of Ellen exiting ahead of her. Delanie decided to follow the tall woman to see what she did after being a marketing specialist all day. Mark Curtis didn't strike her as a strong suspect, and he didn't have direct access to the traffic study data. She'd see what Ellen had planned for her early evening.

The other woman sped up, almost jogging through the building and out to the parking lot toward an older Toyota. Ellen climbed in and started the car. It took three tries before the engine sputtered to life. The blue car jerked and spewed a gray cloud in its wake.

Ellen blended in with the traffic on Huguenot Road. She didn't drive like she had somewhere to be. Delanie tailed her to the grocery store across from the mall where the PI parked and entered a few minutes behind the taller woman. Pretending to look at a display of cosmetics, Delanie scanned the store until she saw Ellen duck down the frozen food aisle. She shadowed her through the store, paying attention to stay at least an aisle away.

After a few minutes, Delanie decided to speed this along. She stepped around an endcap. Ellen was midway down the aisle.

"Uh, Ellen. Ellen," she said, approaching the tall woman in front of the TV dinners.

The marketing specialist jerked her head toward Delanie and let go of the freezer door.

"I thought that was you," Delanie said. "Do you live around here too?"

"Sort of," the other woman replied.

"I thought I spotted you in the front of the store. I just stopped in to pick up a few things for dinner. Work was something else. I was rather busy today."

"Yeah," Ellen replied hesitantly.

"It's been a lot of fun so far. We'll have to go to lunch one day and compare notes."

"I don't usually get lunch. It's more important to bill hours," Ellen said as she turned toward her cart.

"Oh, okay," said Delanie, scanning the tall woman in the ill-fitting pantsuit. Her wrinkled white blouse sported a blue ink stain. Ellen rounded out her look with a pair of black sensible shoes –

the kind a much older woman would wear. "Well, I'll see you around."

Ellen nodded and hurried toward the next set of freezers. "We'll see how long you can stand it," she muttered.

Lovely conversation, Delanie thought. This company had a serious morale issue. So far, her time at Thompson Ulrich, LLP hadn't turned up anything except a draftsman with a criminal past and a cube decorated by his kids' artwork and a marketing specialist's trip to the grocery store. She hadn't uncovered anything linked to the murders. The only thing she found loads of was office drama full of snarky and stabbing comments.

After wasting time watching Ellen Peterson shop, Delanie called Duncan.

"Hey, Duncan, what does Seth Jenkins drive?"

"Let's see," he said. "How's your new job working out?"

"Boring. Oh, so boring. At least there were a lot of calls today. I looked into Mark Curtis' HR file. There was nothing about his arrest. I talked with him. He told me that he had a gap between high school and college. That fits with what we know. He's one of the draftsmen, and also he's happily married with a pack of kids. I don't think he's our guy. He doesn't work with the traffic team."

"Here, I found it. Seth Jenkins drives a black Subaru. Virginia plates FLYSK8R."

"Thanks. Do you have his address? Nobody jumps out as a suspect. But everyone is a little odd. If it's too quiet on Friday, I may have to see what I can do to stir things up."

"Flash mobs or office karaoke would work."

"Not with this group. It's not a fun place to work. They are always nose down working – except for Ellen and Patsy who make avoiding work an Olympic sport."

"Headed home?"

"In a little bit. I'm gonna drive over to Seth's house to see if he's there. He called in sick today. He and Ellen Peterson are the strangest ones in the office. He has hobbies that are close to the bloody graffiti, and Ellen is an angry office worker who looks like she'll snap at any minute. I may need to talk to her again."

"I'll text you the address. Have fun. And be careful," he said before he clicked off.

Delanie typed the address in her GPS. She did a U-turn and drove past the engineering firm. She followed the GPS to a quiet street of condos. She cruised down the street until she found Seth's car with his skateboarding vanity plate. She found a parking place a few houses down with a clear view of the main door and his black car.

After an hour of waiting, she spotted Seth on his front stoop. She started her car and waited to see where he was going. Delanie tailed the young engineer to Chippenham Parkway. She followed his car across the bridge and through two toll booths. He finally exited on Second Street and zigzagged through a warren of downtown streets toward Shockoe Bottom.

She let out a heavy sigh when Seth turned into the side lot of the Treasure Chest. She had never heard of Chaz's club before last summer, and in the last few months, she'd tailed several men to the gentleman's club. Business must be good for the strip club owner.

Delanie turned around in the lot and headed for home. She decided against calling Marco to see what Seth was doing inside the club – she already had a pretty good idea. She gave up waiting longer for the engineer. And now she knew what he did on his sick day. The PI hoped Duncan had better luck with his research. The traffic study had to be the link – but who's the one with the motive?

23

DELANIE MADE AN APPEARANCE AT HER REAL OFFICE THE NEXT morning. Finding the suite empty, she fired up her laptop and settled in to pay bills when the office phone interrupted her.

"Falcon Investigations."

"Delanie Fitzgerald, please."

"This is Delanie."

"This is Sgt. Andrew Ridgeley with Richmond Police Department. I have some good news for you. Your Honda Civic has been recovered, and it's in our lot. You can come by and pick it up."

"Oh good. What kind of shape is it in?" She had visions of several piles of car parts. She hoped it was drivable.

"I'm not sure. I don't have that information on the paperwork. It's at the impound lot on the southside. They're open until six on weekdays," he said as he clicked off.

Duncan poked his head in the door, and she jumped. "When did you get here?"

"A few minutes ago. You were on the phone," he said.

"The police called. They have the Civic at the impound lot in Richmond."

"All in one piece?" he asked.

"Not sure. The guy who called didn't know anything about the condition. Do you have some time to take me over there to pick it up?"

"Yep. Give me a few minutes, and Margaret and I'll be ready. This should be interesting."

"Thanks. I'll Google the address. The guy on the phone wasn't too forthcoming with many details."

It took a while to find the lot that looked like a junk yard off Jefferson Davis Highway. In the shack of an office, she showed her paperwork and driver's license. He pointed to a map of the lot, over-laid with a color-coded grid on the wall behind him. The officer in the black uniform directed her to space 28P on the back side of the property.

Duncan creeped along in his Camaro in search of the gray car. He parked, and they walked up and down row twenty-eight.

"It's not here," she said. "I'm sure he said 28P."

"Uh, Delanie," Duncan said, pointing at a gray car with shiny new hubcaps. "He did."

"That can't be it." She tried her key and looked surprised when the door lock clicked.

"Wow. It sure looks different. What the heck happened to your car?"

"I dunno," she said. "What am I gonna do? I bought a beat up Civic for stakeouts – to be inconspicuous. This, this thing doesn't blend. It screams, 'look at me.'"

They stared at her car with oversized tires and gold spinner hubcaps. Curb feelers and overly tinted windows rounded out the car's new look. Metallic purple and teal flames highlighted the side doors. And a huge phoenix now adorned the hood and roof.

Shaking off the shock, Delanie climbed in and started her tricked out vehicle. It backfired and then roared to life.

Duncan leaned over, and she rolled down the window. "It's got a whole new exhaust on it. And the muffler makes that thumping sound. Someone put a lot of money in upgrades in your car. It's a teenaged boy's dream."

"Oh, joy. Please follow me back to the office. I want to make sure this thing doesn't blow up on me. I can't believe this. Oh, and it has a kickin' new stereo with giant speakers. How can I be so lucky?"

She rolled up the window when Duncan could no longer stifle his laughter. She left him standing on the tarmac as she thumped and popped her way back to the impound office.

Once inside, she said, "Excuse me, sir. This isn't the condition my car was in when it was stolen."

"Sorry," the guy behind the desk said when he looked up. "You'll have to take that up with your insurance company. We turn them back to the owners as is."

"No, I mean, it's souped up and decorated – tricked out. It looks nothing like my old car. I liked my beat up old Civic. It now has a new paint job, and it makes thumping noises."

Stifling a grin, he said, "Sorry. That's how we found it. Looks like you got an upgrade. Enjoy the bells and whistles and the new paint job."

She put her sunglasses on and slunk down in the seat. The car sputtered and thumped its way back to the office, and the new exhaust made noises she didn't know a car could make. She and the made-over Civic received lots of stares and catcalls at stoplights. And to top off the morning, Patsy called and asked her to cover the office phones tomorrow afternoon.

Her first task would be to put this thing back online to see if she could sell it. There was no way she could do stakeouts with this monstrosity. But it might liven things up at the engineering firm if she drove this. It would give Patsy something new to complain about.

THE NEXT DAY, DELANIE FILED PILES OF CORRESPONDENCE UNTIL HER mind was numb. She wondered what happened to the concept of the paperless office. This firm wasn't all that hip with technology or current business practices. She would be glad when her gig at the engineering firm ended. She wouldn't miss this place or the work.

She watched the clock's hands crawl all afternoon. At five o'clock, she almost knocked the chair over to get to the door. She paused long enough to say goodbye to the partner, who didn't look up from whatever he was working on at his desk.

On a whim, she decided to follow Seth Jenkins again. He had access to all the traffic data, and his interests seem to be close to the bloody graffiti at the murder sites. She waited in her car about an hour before the Goth looking engineer left the building with his black backpack. If Seth or Ellen didn't lead her to any a-ha moments soon, then she'd have to reevaluate her strategy and check out the older engineers.

He jumped in his Subaru and sped out of the lot. Delanie followed him to the Powhite Parkway. She hoped he wasn't visiting the Treasure Chest again. If he did, maybe she'd call Marco this time for backup. Staying two cars behind, she trailed Seth across the bridge and onto the downtown Expressway. She had to cut over several lanes when he sped across three lanes of traffic to the Cary Street exit.

He cruised into Carytown and darted into a spot at the curb. She slowed down and watched him jump out and enter a record store, famous for its used vinyl collection. She ducked down an alley and looped back to the main road. By the time she neared his car, Seth had returned to his car. He pulled out, and she eased a couple of car lengths behind him to blend with the traffic.

Seth slowed down and then made several quick turns. She let him get about a block ahead of her. He parked by an old oak next to a white and black townhouse on the corner. The townhouses on this street were older, but many had been revitalized as single-owner homes – not like the ones that had been converted to apartments for off-campus housing for VCU students. She circled the block and parked in front of a brick house down the street from Seth's car. She hunched down in the front seat to snoop.

He sat in his car for a while with the radio blaring. Then

suddenly, he jumped out of his vehicle after a woman and a stroller passed. The woman pushed the stroller to the front of the townhouse and stopped. Then she picked up the baby and disappeared through the front door. She returned a few minutes later to drag the stroller up the cement steps. Seth stood by his car and watched. Then he reached in and pulled out his backpack from behind the driver's seat. He walked briskly around the back of the woman's house.

Delanie's pulse quickened. She grabbed her pepper spray and crept through the backyard. A rickety wooden railing bordered several cement steps to the back door. Tall trash cans stood sentry on the other side. She lost sight of Seth. Pausing by the trash cans, she listened for footfalls. She had to stop him if he was going after another victim in broad daylight. And this time, there was a baby involved.

Delanie's heart pounded as she stood in the tiny backyard behind a camellia bush listening for Seth. The trash cans' stench made her stomach roil. She heard a scraping noise. Slipping to the side of the house, she watched Seth lift the large door on the detached garage. The woman and baby were nowhere in sight.

Seth disappeared in the garage. Delanie crept around the bush for a better view. Boxes stacked three high lined the walls. Delanie spotted a keyboard and a drum set nestled between black amps and mic stands. Seth reappeared with an electric guitar. He plugged it in and started strumming. He tweaked something and continued strumming as he paced around the small garage.

Delanie let out a deep breath. The butterflies in her stomach banged around into each other. She thought she was walking in on something sinister, but she was really spying on Seth at band practice.

She hung around a few minutes longer. Two guys joined Seth, and the noise pulsated from the garage. Delanie couldn't understand the lyrics – a sign she knew that she was moving into a different age demographic. She slipped back to her car before anyone noticed her and tuned her radio to the classic rock station that played lyrics she understood.

24

ON FRIDAY MORNING, DELANIE BATTLED MORNING TRAFFIC TO GET TO the engineering firm on time. She slid into the parking space with six minutes to spare. If today was anything like her previous work days, she'd be in for what seemed like endless phone calls and filing. So far, the sleuthing hadn't turned up anything worthwhile. She hoped today would fly by. She and Duncan were going to have to rethink this reconnaissance work. So far, they hadn't learned much of anything new about the engineering firm or its employees. And Duncan's research didn't turn up anything on the older engineers at the firm.

She grabbed her purse and hurried to the front door. No one was in the front office, so she settled in Patsy's chair. When the phone lit up, she took off the night attendant and transferred the call to Jim Reynolds. A few minutes later, he stuck his head out of his office and said, "Oh, hi. I didn't know anyone was out here. You start early."

"Yes, sir," she said. "Do you have anything you need me to do?"

"I'm good," he said, retreating to his office before she could reply.

Delanie answered call after call that she dutifully transferred to the engineering staff. Then as quickly as they appeared, the calls dried up. To keep from falling asleep, she wandered into the next room and pretended to file. She rifled through staff folders, but didn't find anything suspicious. She returned to Patsy's desk to see what she could find in the drawers or credenza.

While she was rummaging through the only desk drawer that wasn't locked, the front wooden door flew open so hard it hit the wall and bounced back. Delanie jumped. Six men in FBI jackets and two guys in suits strode in and filled the lobby.

The tall guy in a black suit flashed a badge. "I'm Special Agent Mark Moss, and I need to see Jim Reynolds right now."

Before she could reply, the partner stuck his head out and asked, "What the hell is going on?"

"Mr. Reynolds. I'm Special Agent in Charge Mark Moss. I have a warrant to search the premises and question your staff. Please tell your employees to remain where they are and wait for further instructions," he said as his team in black gear fanned out through the suite. He handed Jim Reynolds several sheets of paper.

Delanie almost cracked a smile, but she managed to keep a grim look pasted on her face as the agents spilled over into the hallway. She never imagined an FBI raid on the firm. The task force decided to move forward with its investigation of the multiple murders. Patsy would be sorry she took today off. This would have given her plenty to talk about for weeks. Plus, she'd miss the opportunity to flirt with the army of FBI agents.

Jim Reynolds stepped forward and pushed a button on Patsy's phone. "Attention all staff. We have a situation we need to deal with. Please remain at your desk until further notice."

He dropped the phone in the cradle, and the thunks echoed through the speakers. He looked at Delanie and said, "Call McLean and get Al Bright on the line. Then fax this to the legal department."

～

AFTER PUTTING THE McLEAN CALL THROUGH TO JIM REYNOLDS' office, Delanie faxed the search warrant to the lawyers in McLean on the antiquated machine crammed between the copier and the filing cabinets. Four more agents in FBI jackets passed through the hallway while she waited for the machine that belonged in the Smithsonian to suck in and scan the pages.

She read the two-page document. According to the warrant, the FBI had the right to question staff and to search the premises for evidence in the three murders and the attempted murder. Delanie had goosebumps when she thought of Robin lying in all that blood in her living room. Someone here was responsible.

After reading it twice, she texted Duncan an update and a picture of the warrant. Friday was going to be more lively than normal. This was probably the most excitement this engineering firm had ever seen.

When Delanie returned to the front office, Agent Moss stood in Jim Reynolds' doorway. The phone console lit up, and Agent Moss said, "Don't answer those lines now." Delanie nodded and pressed the night attendant button on the phone. More agents came in through the front door, toting boxes and crates.

Jim Reynolds stuck his head out of his doorway and said, "Go and give this to Dan Mayes." Delanie looked at Agent Moss, and he nodded. Taking advantage of the long walk to the water and sewer team at the back of the suite, she watched agents rifling through files and cubes. Most of the staff stood nearby looking shell-shocked except for Seth. He was doing something on his phone and didn't seem to notice what was going on around him.

She stopped in Dan's doorway and said, "Excuse me. Jim wanted me to give you this."

"Thanks. Any word when this will be over?"

"No. The agents are searching the office. Maybe we'll know something soon. We've been waiting for them to give us some direction." Dan nodded and she returned to the front to see what else was going on.

A flash of movement in the hallway near Mark Curtis' cube caught her eye. That hall, bordered by empty cubicles, deadended into a heavy wooden door to the building's lobby. She saw Seth Jenkins slip out of the side door of the suite.

Delanie ducked down the little hallway near the vacant cubes. The door closed behind Seth. Wondering if she'd find police or agents guarding the exit, she opened the door slightly and stuck her head out. She saw Seth striding out the front glass doors to the parking lot.

In the split second before Delanie decided to stay or go, someone put a hand on her shoulder, and she tried to stifle a squeal. It came out as a squeak while her heartbeat pounded in her ears.

She turned to see Special Agent Eric Ellington standing behind her.

"What are you doing here?" he hissed.

"I could ask you the same thing. Do you always have to scare the crap out of me? I didn't see you come in. I'm the new part-time receptionist, so don't blow my cover. One of the people I've been watching left through the main doors out front. His name is Seth Jenkins. He's about five eight with longish jet black hair. He's wearing all black, and he's got about a five-minute head start," she whispered.

"Okay. Stay here. Do not leave," he barked as he pulled out his phone and slid out the side door.

Delanie strode back to the front office and plopped down in Patsy's chair. Ticked that Agent Ellington got to chase behind Seth after he ordered her to stay put, she sent another text to Duncan. *Look into Seth. He played video games while Rome burned and then snuck out the side door during the raid. Our favorite FBI agent went after him.*

Duncan fired back with, *Ok. Have fun at the raid.*

"Loads," she said to herself, wondering if she'd need to come back next week.

She spent the next two hours watching law enforcement carry boxes, bins, and computers out the front door. She hoped they had better luck with Patsy's filing system than she did. It looked like a tornado hit the office. She could almost imagine Patsy's outrage at the mess in the hallway and reception area.

Ellen Peterson, leaning with both hands on the desk in front of her, startled Delanie out of her daydream. "Can I help you?"

"Any word on when we can leave? I'm going to have to go to the bathroom soon. This is too much. And what about lunch? Are they going to hold us all day? How long can they detain us? Are they planning to feed us? Has anyone said anything? I'm sure old Jim won't spring for any food." Ellen paused, taking a break from peppering Delanie with a barrage of questions.

She didn't remember Ellen being this animated before. "I'm sure if you tell one of the agents, they'll let you step out for a moment for a restroom break."

"This is crazy. What if the company gets sued? What would cause this? I need a job, and I don't want to have to go out and look for another one. Did they give you any hint of what this is about? And what are they looking for? Oh, this sucks. I bet they caught them cutting corners on jobs. This is just too much."

"I don't know. They said for me to sit here and not answer the phones."

"That's what Patsy does most days."

Delanie smiled. "If I hear anything, I'll let you know. I guess it's wait and see for now. There really isn't much we can do until they tell us something."

"They've started taking computers out of the office. That's a big deal. At first it was just boxes of paper. I hope some people around here get in big trouble. Serves them right. I hope someone interviews me. I know where a lot of the skeletons are. It's exciting, but frightening at the same time."

"I don't know much. I haven't been here that long to get to know all the staff."

"Lucky you. They're not nice people. Nobody's talked to me yet. I don't usually have too much to say, but I will today if they ask me about some people around here." Ellen threw her hands in the air and left as quickly as she appeared. Delanie wasn't sure what to make of the marketing specialist and her rant.

Agents Ellington and Moss came back through the front door.

Ellington paused and said, "I want to interview Ms. Fitzgerald here. I'll catch up to you in a few." Moss nodded, and Ellington continued, "Ms. Fitzgerald, would you mind stepping into this conference room?"

She followed him into the long room and chose a seat facing the window. He crossed the room and sat in the chair looking out the open doorway.

"Did you find Seth Jenkins?" she asked.

"No, but we're watching where he usually haunts. He'll turn up soon. What are you doing here? And start at the beginning."

"I have a client who hired us to look into his former housekeeper's granddaughter's murder. The boyfriend was accused, but the family didn't think he did it. My partner found some similar cases in different jurisdictions. And my friend Robin Kirby was the latest victim, but, thankfully, she survived. We've been poking around, and the traffic survey from this firm seemed to be the common denominator in all the cases. I thought if I worked here for a little while, I'd get some information on the staff."

"How long have you been here?"

"A few very boring weeks."

"Any revelations?"

"A lot of people spend a lot of time around here avoiding work, including the office manager, Patsy Roberson. Ellen Peterson and Seth Jenkins aren't like the others. But I don't have any definitive proof of anything nefarious yet."

"What's your hunch?"

"Seth is a creepy Goth-wannabe. He skateboards in the parking lot and listens to punk music. He's in a band, and he likes video games that seem to match some of the symbols left at the crime scenes. Patsy Roberson gave me an earful of Seth and Ellen's weirdness. Ellen is the tall one in the traffic department with brown hair. She does the marketing and other clerical jobs around here. There's bad blood between Seth and Ellen and between Ellen and the office manager. There's a lot of drama for a small office."

"Anything else?"

"One of the guys, Mark Curtis, has a criminal past. I don't think he's the guy you're looking for. He was arrested for embezzlement out of high school. He seems to have reformed and is married with kids. He's a draftsman here at the company. I'm pretty sure he doesn't have access to the traffic survey data. I guess I'll hang out and see if they need me to come back next week to work."

"If they call you to come back to work, contact me. Go to your desk and act like you don't know anything. I'll let you know when you can leave." She nodded.

Peeved again at Agent Ellington for dismissing her so quickly, she returned to Patsy's chair.

About an hour later, Agents Moss and Ellington entered the partner's office without knocking. A tired looking Jim Reynolds made a beeline for Patsy's phone. "Attention please. Everyone report to the conference room now. All staff to the conference room now for a mandatory meeting."

Delanie filed in behind Dan, Ellen, and some of the others from the traffic team. Most of the group stood around the perimeter of the room. Phil Saunders and a few of the older engineers took seats around the table.

"Who's missing?" Jim asked, scanning the room.

"Seth and Patsy," Dan said. "And Andy. He's off today."

"I've decided to close the office this afternoon. Wrap up what you're working on, and go home. Call the voicemail number on Sunday to see if we're going to open on time on Monday."

"What is the voicemail number?" someone asked from the back of the room.

"Eight oh four. Five nine eight two three eight four," Dan replied. Delanie added it to her phone contacts.

"What is going on?" asked one of the tall engineers standing next to the window.

Agent Moss interrupted with, "The firm is under investigation. More information will be forthcoming. In the meantime, you're free to go. I need to see Jim Reynolds, Phil Saunders, Chuck Morrison, Clinton Carpenter, Michael Owens, Mark Curtis, and Ellen Peterson.

Please stay behind. The rest of you can get your personal effects and leave for the day. Please exit through the front of the suite."

When Delanie filed out near the end of the line of staff, Agent Ellington grabbed her elbow. "Get your purse and come with me."

He escorted her back into the suite to the side door. "Go this way," he said, pointing to the left. They walked down a hallway to the glass exit door by the smoker's patio at the back of the building. "You parked out front?"

She nodded. "Follow this sidewalk around to the parking lot. There are camera crews and reporters in the front lobby."

"Thanks."

"Call me if you're asked to go back to work next week. And try to stay out of the fray," Agent Ellington said.

Delanie nodded again, but she had other ideas.

25

SLIDING IN THE FRONT SEAT, SHE STARTED THE ENGINE AND HEADED FOR Seth Jenkins' home. She drove about ten miles to a subdivision of condos. Wending her way through streets that looped the neighborhood, she parked down the street and watched the front door until she got restless. It felt like hours had passed.

On a whim, she pulled into Seth's empty driveway. She didn't notice any movement in the darkened house or in the neighboring houses. It was odd that there were no neighbors or traffic on side streets. She backed out slowly and punched in Ellen Peterson's address into her GPS. She planned to find a good spot for lurking. She hoped Ellen Peterson was still with the FBI.

Delanie drove down Midlothian Turnpike near the State Police Headquarters. Following the bossy lady on the GPS, she turned on a curvy road that ended in front of a brick rancher in need of some curb appeal. Finding a spot down the street where she could see the front door, she parked and waited about an hour until Ellen's beat up blue car sputtered to a stop in the driveway. Ellen slammed the car door and walked around the side of the house.

After a while, Delanie fished through her purse for her burner cell phone. Clearing her throat, she dialed Ellen's number. "Ellen Peterson?"

"Yes."

"This is Kelly Jackson. I'm calling to see if you want to take advantage of a special opportunity to refinance your mortgage."

"I rent, and I'm not interested. Check your facts. And stop calling me."

"Okay. I'll update the information in my files. Would you be interested in refinancing a car or a boat?"

"Are you freakin' kidding me? I have a 1990 Toyota that runs only on hope most days. Take me off your list and don't bother me again."

Clicking off, Delanie threw the phone in her purse. She opened the windows and decided to wait to see if Ellen materialized any time soon.

About two and a half hours later, Ellen locked her front door and headed out with an oversized backpack. Starting her car, Delanie waited until Ellen backed out of the driveway.

She followed her west and had to cut across two lanes of traffic when Ellen darted left on Courthouse Road. Eventually, the marketing specialist came to a stop next to a one story house in a neighborhood near a shopping center. Ellen parked down the street in a cul-de-sac and walked back to a house with the burgundy door and a pink and white wreath made out of netting. Delanie hoped this wasn't another waste of time. Most of her stakeouts related to the engineering firm hadn't yielded much information.

Parking next to a corner lot where she could see Ellen, she called Duncan.

"Hey, check on 3910 Oxbridge Road for me."

"Why are you whispering?"

"I dunno. Habit of stakeouts. Ellen Peterson is acting weird. She left work, went home, and then drove to this address."

"The address belongs to your new boss, Patsy Roberson. Two years ago it belonged to Patrick and Patsy Roberson. Patrick must be out of the picture now."

"Patrick and Patsy? Interesting. She's a free agent now."

"Uh huh. Do you need any other info?"

"I don't think so. I'm gonna hang out here and see what Ellen does. I'll call you later."

She disconnected and watched Ellen climb the steps to the small porch with aluminum railings. The tall woman tossed a black backpack over her shoulder. After she rang the bell, she stood there, looking toward the street. Ellen walked back to the driveway and looked up and down the block. Turning, she followed the driveway to the edge of the house. She opened the gate and let herself in the backyard.

Delanie flipped through her phone's contacts. After two rings, she heard, "Agent Ellington."

"This is Delanie Fitzgerald. I tailed Ellen Peterson to an address off of Courthouse Road. She's acting suspicious at the house of one of her co-workers. I think you need to check this out."

"How so?" he interrupted.

"She's parked down the street from the house. She's been looking over her shoulder constantly, and she's headed around to the backyard. And she's carrying a backpack."

"Gimme the address.... Stay put. And don't try to get in the middle of this. Let me know if anything changes."

"I'll text you the address. The house belongs to the receptionist at the engineering firm. I don't think she's home. There's no car in the driveway, and she didn't report to work today."

"Don't move. I'll be there soon."

Delanie needed to see what Ellen was up to. She slid the phone in her jeans' pocket and pulled her hair up in a ponytail. She locked the door and jogged in front of the neighbor's house and up Patsy's driveway. Delanie froze when she heard a crack and glass breaking.

Peeking around the open gate, she saw Ellen looking through what was left of a back window. Clicking on her phone's camera, she recorded her entering the house. It didn't take much for the tall woman to hoist herself up on the sill and swing her legs up.

Delanie stepped back around the corner. Skirting the edge of the house, she cut through the neighbor's yard to get to her car.

She scrunched down in the seat to wait for Agent Ellington to arrive. About ten minutes passed, and she didn't see any movement in the neighborhood or around Patsy's house. The deserted streets were eerily quiet.

At about the time Delanie started to get antsy, a black Lexus rocketed into the driveway. Patsy climbed out toting a huge purple purse and several shopping bags from stores at Short Pump Town Center. She balanced the bags and her large purse as she locked her car and trudged to the porch.

Delanie dialed Agent Ellington while the office manager let herself in. She swore softly to herself when the call went to voicemail. After the beep, she said, "Patsy Roberson arrived and let herself in the house. Get here now. I saw Ellen break in through a back window," she said, disconnecting and pocketing the phone.

She slammed her car door shut and ran to the house. Ringing the doorbell frantically, she started pounding on the door when Patsy didn't respond.

Patsy flung open the door and snapped, "What the hell do you want? And why are you making so much damn noise? You didn't even give me a chance to get the door open."

"You need to come with me now. I need to tell you what happened today at work."

"Whatever it is, it can wait until next week. I'm off today, and I'm not thinking about those damn people until nine o'clock Monday morning. They take up too much of my life as it is. And you have some nerve coming to my house. Who do you think you are? You need to leave now! Are you stalking me?"

"Patsy, it's not what you think."

"I don't care what it is. You are out of line for bothering me at home. When I tell Jim what you did, we will probably decide we no longer need your services. This conversation is over," she said as she started to close the door.

Before Delanie could comment, two black Suburbans zoomed

down the street and screeched to halt near Patsy's driveway. The second one missed the driveway and stopped in her front yard.

"What the hell is going on?" Patsy screeched. "He just drove on my grass. Hey, hey, you. What do you think you're doing? Your stupid car is on my grass," she yelled and waggled a finger at the guy.

Ignoring her, Delanie waved Agent Ellington and the other agent around to the back of the house. They jumped out and ran with guns drawn.

"Come with me now," she said, grabbing Patsy's arm and dragging her out onto the stoop. "I'll tell you when we get to my car. You need to hear this."

Half dragging a wriggling Patsy across the yard, Delanie led her to the Mustang in front of the neighbor's house. "Get in."

"What the hell is this about? This is nuts. You better have a good reason for all of this."

They watched Agent Ellington's partner return to the driveway. With gun drawn, he crossed the distance to the porch in a few seconds and bounded through the front door.

Delanie turned toward the office manager, who was playing with the button on her shirt. "Patsy, I'm a private investigator. There have been some murders we linked to the traffic survey your firm did. I followed Ellen Peterson from her house here. I watched her break one of your back windows and crawl in. I didn't mean to scare you, but I couldn't leave you in the house with her. I'm pretty sure she's not planning a tea party for you. And the FBI raided the office today."

Patsy let out a humpf and slid down in the passenger seat. "I knew I didn't like her. Ellen is such a freak. And what the hell is she doing in my house? Damn, I guess this means you won't be back next week to help me in the office. I knew you were too good to be true," Before Delanie could comment, Patsy continued, "Now I'll have to find someone else for the office. I cannot wait until I retire. I hate that place. Did you say FBI raid?" Delanie nodded, and the office manager continued, "What a day. This just can't get any worse. Jim and the partners will be raging about this. This will be a headache for weeks to come. I wonder who'll get fired over this. They don't like bad publicity."

Three rapid shots interrupted her rant. Patsy screamed, "Pixie," and jumped out of the car.

"Wait," Delanie yelled, but Patsy was halfway across the front yard, running at breakneck speed. She slammed the Mustang's door and followed the office manager up the driveway. Patsy flung open the door and rushed in. Delanie hoped the FBI agents heard Patsy enter the house. At about the time Delanie got to the corner of the house, she heard two more shots and a scream.

Delanie ducked around the corner. When it got quiet again, she followed the sidewalk around to the gate. Not seeing anyone nearby, she slipped around to the patio. She quickly texted the FBI agent, *Patsy's inside looking for her dog.*

When he didn't respond, she moved one of the patio chairs over to the open window. She hoisted herself up on the sill and climbed in. She landed with a thump on the laundry room floor. Delanie sat there for a minute, listening for any kind of noise.

The refrigerator hummed, and she heard a clock ticking in the dark house. She crept to the accordion doors that separated the small room with the washer, dryer, and laundry sink from the rest of the living space. She slid the door open and it provided a clear view through the house to the empty front room. Nobody seemed to be nearby in the hallway or kitchen.

Something crashed and shattered in the back of the house, and Delanie jumped. "Get away," screeched a woman. Delanie pressed her back against the kitchen wall next to the refrigerator.

A male voice said, "Put the gun down and nobody gets hurt."

"I don't trust you," Ellen said. "You shot at me!"

"You shot first. Put the gun down now. And let's let Patsy and her pup go out the front door. She doesn't need to be here. Then we can talk."

"I hate her," Ellen screeched. "She's made my life a living hell. She's not going anywhere. She needs to pay for what she did. She's evil like the rest of 'em."

Patsy said something that Delanie couldn't hear. Then the agent snapped, "That's enough. You're not helping." Then after a pause, "Come on, Ellen. We'll talk this through. It can't be that bad. Put the gun down. We can work this out."

"This is too big now to work out. This wasn't supposed to happen this way," she sobbed. "You were supposed to arrest Seth. It was clear that he was guilty. I must purge the evil from among us."

"I'm going to come toward you. Put the gun down and we'll see what we can do."

"No," she hissed. Someone fired again, and the sound reverberated in the small house. Delanie gasped. Then she heard footsteps running toward the back of the house. She heard more running and the front door slam.

Another door slammed somewhere at the other end of the house, and then it was quiet. Delanie eased around the corner and saw that the front room stood empty. From the large glass window in the living room, she could see the other agent, Patsy, and Pixie in the front yard next to the black SUVs. Three Chesterfield County police cars and an ambulance blocked traffic near Patsy's driveway.

Delanie considered an exit through the front door when she heard Eric Ellington yell, "Ellen, come out. There's no escape. We can work through this. Come on. You have family and a future to think about. Let's not do this. We can walk out the front door now."

"Ha. Some future. It wasn't supposed to be like this. You were supposed to see that it was Seth, so he'd go to jail. They're all evil. They need to be punished. It's not me. It's Seth. Seth's the one you want."

"Okay, okay. We'll talk about it out here. Come out before somebody gets hurt."

Agent Ellington stepped into one of the doorways off the main hallway. He slid his phone in his pocket, and Delanie waved to get his attention.

"What are you doing here?" he mouthed.

She made a hand gesture for a gun. Taking two steps toward her, he grabbed her elbow and guided her to the kitchen. "What the hell are you doing? You are trouble. Go out the back door now and wait at the command center," he whispered loudly. "I have enough to worry about here without you being in the middle of my crime scene. Go. Now."

Before she could comment, he grabbed both of her shoulders, kissed her, and shoved her toward the door.

26

DELANIE'S HEART POUNDED. SHE WASN'T SURE IF IT WAS ALL THE action at Patsy's house or because the FBI agent had the gall to kiss her, but there was a little tingle of excitement that she tried to suppress because she wanted to stay angry with him for the time being. She wasn't ready to date anyone now – there were too many feelings from last summer's fling with John Bailey.

By the time she returned to the front yard that looked more like a parking lot for emergency vehicles, she saw two officers in SWAT gear storm the front porch, and four more ran past her with guns drawn to the back of the house. Patsy sat on the edge of the ambulance with her white Chihuahua in her lap.

"You okay?" she asked, sitting next to the office manager.

"I guess so. What's going on inside my house?"

"Ellen barricaded herself in one of the back bedrooms. She's yelling a lot about evil people. The FBI agent is in the hallway trying to talk her out. It looks like reinforcements have arrived."

Before Patsy could answer, there was a flash of light and a loud boom. They jumped and the little dog started barking and shaking.

"There, there," Patsy said, hugging Pixie. "They'll get that terrible woman out of our house soon. And things will be back to normal. The FBI raided the office today?"

Delanie nodded. "About ten agents searched the place and questioned staff. They left with computers and files."

"Mine?"

"I don't think so."

"Good. But, damn. I missed all the action."

Everything got eerily quiet. The two women and the dog sat staring at the front porch. Delanie jumped up when Ellen climbed out the side window on the far side of the house. "Hey! She's escaping!" Delanie yelled, pointing toward the neighbor's yard.

Ellen launched herself from the window and fell face forward in the flowerbed. She rose and stumbled. Righting herself, she ran through the neighbor's yard as smoke started billowing out of the window.

"My house!" Patsy yelled. "What did she freakin' do to my house? Hey, firemen! My house is on fire! And that crazy bitch is getting away."

Delanie looked around. None of the local police were nearby. When nobody responded, Delanie took off after Ellen Peterson. She closed the gap between her and Ellen. The marketing specialist's speed surprised Delanie. Ellen tore through the neighbors' front yards toward her blue car. She barreled through a mulch bed full of small shrubs and flowers. Delanie hurdled it and landed on the taller woman's back.

They tumbled to the grass, rolling and scrapping. Delanie ended up on top of the marketing specialist. When Delanie paused to catch her breath, Ellen raised her fist and punched Delanie on the side of her head. Stars flashed in front of Delanie's eyes, and she blinked to shake off the dizziness. She swallowed hard to fight back a wave of nausea. Ellen took advantage of the moment. She shoved Delanie to the ground and kicked her in the side.

Ellen grabbed a handful of Delanie's hair and her shoulder. "Get up now," Ellen hissed. She slid a gun out of her front pocket and dragged Delanie to her feet.

Ellen looked over her shoulder and grabbed Delanie. She slung the private eye in front of her like a shield and wrapped her arm around her neck. Delanie's head throbbed. She blinked back the pain. She knew she had to be alert for an opportunity to take Ellen down.

Ellen startled her when she screeched, "Stop! Stop right there" at the two approaching police officers. She waved the gun around in the air, and Delanie waited for a chance to break free from the crazed woman's grip.

"I said, stop!" screamed Ellen, who waved her free arm around and adjusted her grip again on Delanie's neck with the other arm. "We're leaving, and you're not going to try to stop us."

Delanie noticed the officers said something quietly to each other. The officers paused with their guns still drawn.

"Wait a minute," said the officer closest to them. "Let her go, and we'll talk. Put down the weapon."

"There's nothing to talk about," Ellen yelled. "Drop your guns. I'm through with all of you. We're leaving."

"You can't do that. We need to talk first," the second officer yelled as Ellen dragged Delanie backward. She tried to slow Ellen down by going limp, but the taller woman readjusted her grip and inched them closer to the car. Delanie dragged her heels – anything to stall.

"Stay there. Right there, I said," Ellen yelled at the officers. She waved the gun around wildly with her free hand. Delanie heard more sirens in the distance. They waited for what seemed like minutes. Then Ellen let go of Delanie's neck. In that split second, Ellen jammed the handgun in the PI's side. Delanie felt the cold metal as the gun pressed into her ribs. The taller woman grabbed Delanie by the hair, making her wince.

The police officers crept forward, closer to the car. Delanie saw the FBI agents and other police approaching from the direction of Patsy's house.

"We're walking back slowly," Ellen hissed. "Get in the car and drive where I tell you," she ordered as she opened the door to the blue Toyota. "And don't try anything. I will shoot you."

Delanie tried to give the police some time by reducing her pace toward the car to a crawl. She needed a distraction in order to make her break. Delanie went limp, but the taller woman grabbed her and hauled her to her feet. "Quit stalling," she sneered. "We're leaving. Do as I say, or I'll kill you. I've had enough, and I'm done talking. I'm not playing. It's time they took me seriously," she said as she opened the driver's door.

Ellen shoved her in the driver's seat. The seat was too far back for Delanie. She fiddled with the lever to adjust the seat, so her feet would reach the pedals. The keys dangled from the ignition.

"We're leaving," Ellen repeated, swinging the gun wildly from Delanie to the police officers. "Start the car. And don't try to be a hero. I'm walking around the car, and I'll shoot you if you try anything stupid. Do you hear me?" she yelled at the officers. "If you try anything, and I mean anything, I'll shoot her."

Delanie leaned forward and turned the key. The Toyota sputtered and stalled. She cranked the key again. Delanie mashed on the gas in hopes of delaying the start. On the second try, the car jerked and jumped. She rammed it into drive, and the car shook.

Ellen ran to the passenger side and wrenched the door open. She dropped in the seat and slammed the door twice before it closed completely.

"Go. Go. Drive!"

"Where?"

"That way." Ellen pointed at the windshield with the gun.

Delanie pulled out slowly, fastening her seatbelt with her left hand. Ellen shoved her shoulder. "Faster. I wanna get the hell out of here. No delays! This is not how today was supposed to go."

Delanie slid forward and slammed her foot on the accelerator. She heard shots pepper the trunk as they sped away.

"Keep going. Faster. Faster!" Ellen yelled as she turned around in her seat to look out the back window. "They're coming," she whined. The car sputtered and jerked. The gas finally made it to where it needed to go, and the tiny car lurched forward, gaining speed.

"They're shooting at us," Ellen said.

"Well, what did you expect? They aren't going to let us drive off," Delanie hissed as she accelerated again. The small car shuttered when she hit forty miles an hour.

"Shut up!" Ellen said without turning around. "Just drive. I need to think about this."

Delanie took a hard left at the next intersection. She hoped it would knock the other woman off balance, but she steadied herself with her free hand.

Two houses ahead, Delanie spotted an opportunity. Delanie stomped on the gas pedal. The car hesitated and then lurched forward.

The speedometer twitched toward fifty. Ellen's muscles seemed to relax slightly as the car gained speed. Delanie jerked the steering wheel to the right and stood on the accelerator. Delanie had an idea that might give her time to escape. While Ellen was looking out the back window, she stomped on the brake. The wheels skidded and the back of the car fishtailed. Delanie gripped the wheel with both hands and steered toward a parked SUV.

Delanie managed to slow the car down, but she braced for the impending impact. She hoped it would be enough of a diversion for her to break free.

Ellen's car hit the back of the black sports utility vehicle, moving it forward a few feet on impact. The Toyota's radiator hissed as water splashed on the asphalt. The other vehicle's bumper hung loosely on one side. Ellen's car was headed for the junk yard.

No airbags deployed in the older Toyota. The crash jerked Ellen backward. She hit the back of her head on the dashboard and then rebounded into the headrest. Her nose started to bleed, and the gun bounced into the back seat. Not waiting to see what else happened to Ellen, Delanie flung open the door and stumbled out. She put her arms up in the air and ran across the street.

Three police cars and two black SUVs skidded to a stop by the wrecked vehicles. With guns drawn, the agents encircled Ellen's Toyota. A cop motioned for Delanie to come to his car.

He opened the back door, and she slid inside after a short sprint.

Wiping her lip, she discovered blood. Her heartbeat pounded in her ears, and her head throbbed in time.

The police jerked open the passenger door of the Toyota and dragged Ellen out onto the pavement. They cuffed her and left her face down on the asphalt. One of the officers said something in his shoulder microphone.

A forensics van pulled in behind Ellen's wrecked car. An ambulance followed the van and started what looked like a train of emergency vehicles that looped around the block.

The cop who waved Delanie over stuck his head in the door and said, "Nice driving. I'm gonna have the EMTs check you out. Your mouth is bleeding pretty good there."

"Thanks. Sorry about that guy's SUV," Delanie said. She could feel her mouth starting to swell. She ran her tongue across her teeth to see if she'd loosened or damaged any. Her mouth ached, but her teeth seemed to be intact. Plus, her head was still sore from the earlier fight with Ellen. Delanie climbed out of the police car and walked toward the ambulance. She'd feel the effects tomorrow.

Ellen remained face down in the street with her hands cuffed. An officer attached shackles to her ankles, and then two officers struggled to pull her to a standing position. They half-guided and half-dragged her back to Patsy's front yard.

TWO EMTS CHECKED DELANIE OVER AND GAVE HER AN ICEPACK FOR her lip. Nothing seemed to be broken, and she passed the concussion checks. The bruises were already forming, and her lip felt like it took up half her face.

She rode in the ambulance back to Patsy's house. After parking, the driver opened the back doors. Delanie watched firemen drag hoses across the lawns. Flames licked around the bedroom window, and the roof blackened.

Delanie took her icepack and walked to where Patsy and Pixie sat quietly on the ground, watching the fire consume their home. Patsy sobbed and stroked the little dog.

It took the fire department almost an hour to extinguish the blaze. At about the same time, an FBI agent approached Patsy and said, "Ma'am, I'm Special Agent Terry Richards. I need to get your statement. The battalion chief will let you know when you can get back into your house. It may be a day or so. Do you have someone we could call for you in the meantime?"

Patsy nodded. Delanie spotted Agent Ellington standing behind Agent Richards. "Ms. Fitzgerald, if you'll step over there, I need to get your statement too." Delanie rolled her eyes at his standard line.

Delanie followed the taller of the two agents to his Suburban. He unlocked the doors with his key fob and held the door for her. "Get in. What is it with you and not staying put? You always have to be in the middle of things."

"What is it with you always taking my statement? I had to do something. Ellen broke into the house. I saw her climb in through the back window. I couldn't let her surprise Patsy. I didn't know what she had in that backpack."

"Okay, but you didn't have to come back in the house."

"I heard shots and Patsy ran in the front looking for her dog. I had to make sure she was okay."

"You are one stubborn – Never mind, what else do you know?"

"That's it. I heard a loud bang when I was in the front yard. Then Ellen climbed out of the window and we saw smoke."

"Flash-bang. We were trying to drive her out of the bedroom. She barricaded herself in by pushing a dresser in front of the door. Then she set fire to the bed and the froufrou lacy thing on top of it. She had gone out the window by the time we got the door open and the dresser moved."

"Canopy. The thing on top of the bed is the canopy."

"Whatever. And then you decided to give chase?"

"She was getting away, and nobody else did anything. Somebody had to."

"How did you end up in her car?"

"I tackled her in the front yard of a house a few doors down, but she got the best of me when we were rolling around in the grass. She pulled a gun and dragged me to the car. But her mistake was letting me drive."

"You said it. Not me. Then what happened?"

"I turned the corner and saw a parked car. I hope the guy has insurance. Ellen was fixated on what the cops were doing. She wasn't paying attention to me. I sped up and then slammed on the brakes."

"You coulda gotten really hurt or worse."

"It's not that bad. And thanks for your concern. I was able to slow the car down, so it wasn't a horrible crash."

"She rambled on about how everybody at the engineering firm had to be punished," he said.

"I heard her call her coworkers evil a couple of times. She was agitated and not making a lot of sense. What's next for her?" Delanie asked, brushing the hair out of her face and reapplying the icepack. Her lip felt like it had swelled to three times its normal size.

"They'll take her in for questioning. Then they'll send her off for a mental eval."

Two officers in green uniforms walked toward them, and the first one said, "Excuse me. We're taking the suspect to headquarters."

"Go ahead," Ellington said. "Agent Richards and I will follow. The main building off Lori Road?"

The Chesterfield County officer nodded and jogged to his cruiser where Ellen sat slumped forward in the back seat.

"I've gotta go." Delanie climbed out of the Suburban and walked toward her car.

He yelled, "I'll call you later. Stay out of trouble."

She refrained from saying something snarky, but the FBI agent had already started the SUV's engine and closed his tinted window.

27

DELANIE, TOO ANTSY TO GO HOME, DROVE TO THE OFFICE TO WRITE HER report of today's events. She parked the Mustang out front and grabbed the mail. Letting herself in the lobby, she relocked the front door and walked down the dark corridor to her office.

"Anybody home?"

When there was no answer, she downed two aspirin, hoping they would deaden the pounding in her head. Then she changed into her last spare set of clothes. Blood had trickled down the front and onto her neck and arms. She'd have to throw out another shirt.

Where are you? she texted Duncan.

A few moments later, her phone chimed with his response, *Grabbed an early dinner with Margaret and Evie. It's movie night. What's up?*

Ellen barricaded herself in Patsy's house. The FBI got her.

Sounds like a fun afternoon. You be in tomorrow?

After lunch. I'll fill you in on our murderer. Have fun.

Glad it's over. Gotta go. Date night.

Smiling, Delanie returned to drafting her statement. After she was satisfied that it detailed the afternoon's events for the FBI agent, she emailed it to him. She'd reuse it for her final report for Rick Dixon and Chaz.

She dialed Chaz's cell.

"Hey, Delanie. What's shaking?"

"The police task force arrested a woman named Ellen Peterson this evening. She worked at an engineering firm that did a traffic study. It looks like all the victims responded to the survey. She was angry with her employer. I don't have any other details, but I'm pretty sure she's going to be charged with several murders and an attempted murder, among other things. This will clear Justin and get him released soon."

"A chick did it. Interesting. Who would have thought it would have been a woman? Does Rick know?"

"I called you first. I'll call him after we hang up. It's over. They have her in custody."

"Thanks, Delanie. You're great. Alma will be thrilled. Hey, if you want to celebrate, come on down, and I'll break out the champagne. We're due for a good party."

"Thanks, Chaz. It's been a long afternoon. I think I'm going to head home after this. I'm glad we could help you and Alma. And Justin." Delanie with her fat lip and bruises, wasn't up for a celebration. She was sure she looked lovely with her beatup face. She longed for a hot shower and a quiet evening at home.

"If you change your mind, you know where to find me. Hey, I'm gonna call you next week. I still want you to do some background research into those properties I want to develop for my restaurant and all-male revue. It's time to shake up the Richmond nightclub scene. And I have another idea I want to run by you. This one's big."

"Okay. Talk with you later." She smiled as she disconnected. Despite his eccentricities, Chaz was always a reliable, paying client, but she wondered what his next big idea would entail.

Delanie dialed Rick Dixon's cell next. At the beep, she left a voicemail about the traffic survey and Ellen Peterson's arrest in Chesterfield. Then she called Robin's sister and left a similar message.

Before she could call Duncan, her cell phone buzzed. "Hey, Delanie. This is Eric Ellington. I got your statement. Thanks."

"No problem. Did Ellen Peterson confess to the murders?"

"Sort of, in her rambling about devils and evil and punishments meted out by the righteous." He cleared his throat and continued with, "We're waiting for forensics to come back, but we're pretty sure she left DNA at several of the crime scenes. It's just a matter of time before we charge her with murder, attempted murder, kidnapping, assault on a police officer, discharging a weapon in a residential neighborhood, and arson, among other things. The DA is piling up a list of charges."

"That's great news for the boyfriend in the Menendez case. My client and his attorney will be very pleased. And I won't have to be the part-time receptionist any more."

"Yep. I'm going to be tied up here for the foreseeable future. Do you want to grab dinner tomorrow?"

Delanie's stomach fluttered. She hesitated and then said, "Uh, okay. You're asking me on a real date or you just taking my statement?"

"Funny. I'll call you later," he said, disconnecting.

It was just dinner. And he owed her for the help with the Emerson arrests and the Tulip Shirt murders.

ON SATURDAY EVENING, DELANIE ANSWERED THE DOORBELL. ERIC Ellington, sporting a fresh from the shower look, stood on her small porch. Dressed in black jeans, a dark shirt, and cowboy boots, he looked younger than he did in his work garb. A behemoth black, F Series truck sat at the end of her driveway.

"Hi," she said, grabbing her purse.

"About ready?" he asked. "I thought we could grab dinner near town. Nice house. It fits you."

"Thanks. I've had it for about five years. It's a Sears 1939 house.

The original owners ordered it from the catalog and had it shipped here by rail. I like it."

He held the door for her as she climbed up into the cab. It took her a minute to finagle her black skirt back in place.

When he started the truck, she asked, "So. How's the Ellen Peterson case going?"

"She had a psych eval this week. She's convinced that everyone at the engineering firm was evil, and she was doing the world a favor by uncovering their deeds. All she did was rant and spout twisted versions of scripture. Never mind that she killed three and almost a fourth person in the process. She's convinced herself that she's on the side of right. A lot of what she said didn't make sense."

"Do you think it'll go to court?"

"Probably, but not for murder. My guess is that a judge will make her a permanent resident of one of our state facilities until she's competent to stand trial."

"Do you think she's faking the insanity? She was fairly lucid when I talked with her at the engineering firm. But she didn't seem to be in control at Patsy's house. Actually, it bordered on unhinged."

"I dunno about faking it. You probably gave her a concussion when you wrecked her car." Delanie smirked, but didn't reply. He continued, "Her family hired a lawyer. We'll have to see what happens as this proceeds through the court system."

"Where did Seth Jenkins end up the day he left the engineering firm – the day of the raid? He wasn't home when I did a drive-by of his place."

"I lost him, but we picked him up about an hour later. We found him in a video game store near the mall. Then he went to a comic book store. It looked like he took advantage of the opportunity to skip work," he said.

After dinner with drinks and a shared slice of cheesecake, Eric walked her to her front door.

"Thanks for a lovely evening where nobody got hurt or arrested, and I didn't have to make a statement."

"Cute. Hey, are you busy next Sunday?"

"No. What do you have in mind?"

"I have two tickets to the Skins game in Washington if you want to go. They're playing the Giants."

"Sounds like fun."

"Your lip's looking better. It's not as swollen as it was," he said as he touched her face lightly. But before she could answer, he kissed her, and she forgot all about how much he had a habit of annoying her.

"I'll pick you up next Sunday about nine. The game's at one. Dress warmly."

"See you then," she said as she let herself in her bungalow. It's a good thing he invited her to a Washington game, she thought. That was the only football team her father and brothers ever watched – a fan by family tradition.

Her phone rang after she shut the front door. "Hello."

"Hey, sorry to call so late," Duncan said. "I got a call from Tod Eastman, you know Tish Taylor's assistant. Anyway, he wanted to let us know that the tell-all author's book on Johnny Velvet would be out next month. We're mentioned in it, so we may get calls for interviews or contacts about our investigation."

"Oh good, I guess," she said, settling on her couch and letting her thoughts drift to John Bailey and last summer. She felt a twinge of sadness about how their fling turned out. It was fun to know that she had dated the Johnny Velvet and that he didn't die in that fiery crash in the eighties. And if he hadn't hightailed it out of town when she uncovered his secret, she would have probably kept his real identity quiet. She wondered how he would react to the international release of the book. It would probably skyrocket to the top of the charts. She hoped he had a better alias this time.

"Delanie, are you still there?"

"Uh, yeah. Sorry. I got lost in thought for the moment. Do we want to do Johnny Velvet interviews?"

"We'll see how often we get asked. If it's a bother, we can always say, 'no comment.' We can worry about that later if it ever material izes. What else is going on?" he asked.

"Ellen Peterson made her statement to the authorities. We'll have to see if she's competent to stand trial. Agent Ellington said that she came unglued in the interrogations. When I called Chaz to give him an update, he said that he has a research project for us. He wants to know if it's viable to open an all-male revue in the area."

Duncan let out a heavy sigh. "Hopefully, he'll have better luck with this real estate venture than he did with the last one. Somehow, I have the feeling that he's in our lives for the foreseeable future. At least he always pays in cash."

Delanie smiled and said, "Good night. I'll see you and Margaret tomorrow after I stop in to see how Robin is doing. She's got a long way to go before she can get back to her normal life. See ya."

"Night night," he said as he clicked off.

~

THE NEXT DAY, DELANIE SLID IN A BOOTH BY THE FRONT WINDOW AT Gino's Pizzeria on West Broad Street. By the time her second iced tea arrived, she noticed Chaz at the front door. Today, he had a shark gray blazer over a shiny black dress shirt, unbuttoned at the collar, and his skinny jeans. He took off his sunglasses and dropped a folder on the table across from her.

After the waiter took his drink order, he said, "Delanie, it's good to see you. Thanks for all you did for Justin and Alma. They are so appreciative, and they want to meet you some time."

"My pleasure. We're glad we could help."

"And now, I want you to do some research on some properties for me. A couple are in Henrico, and one is on the Goochland side of the line," he said, pushing the folder toward her.

"What do you want to know?"

"I'd like you to research the deeds and then poke around and talk to the neighbors to see if they're amenable to the expansion of busi nesses in the area. I don't want to deal with the public outcry like last time. I'm leaning toward the one in Goochland. It's more rural, and not technically in the Short Pump area. I don't want to invest if I'm gonna have similar issues like last summer. I'd like you to get a pulse on the community opinions before I pull the trigger on this one."

Delanie flipped through the contents of the folder and then handed him a contract from her portfolio. He signed it without reading it. "Are you sure the suburban part of Central Virginia is ready for an all-male revue? Wouldn't downtown be a better fit?"

"I want to expand. Plus, most of the females are in the suburbs. Our demographics are women eighteen to fifty-five. Many of them aren't the downtown crowd. Plus, they don't like the hassles of city parking. I think a county location would be better."

"Okay, Duncan and I will get to work on this. I'll send you what I find in a week or so."

"Good," he said, handing her a bank envelope filled with cash. "I have something else I want to bounce off you." After a long pause, he continued, "I'm gonna run for mayor."

Delanie hoped her face didn't show her surprise. "Really? The last I checked there were nine others vying for the vacancy that the mayor's murder created. That's a crowded field."

"I know. It started out as a joke. We were doing shots late one night at the club, and someone thought it would be a good way to turn this town upside down. But I can run a successful business, and I know Richmond and how it operates. And it's time to shake up the politics around here. It's way too stuffy. Plus it'll be fun. I can't wait to see the looks on some of the old faces when they see I'm in the running. It's time for a change."

Delanie bit her tongue to keep from reacting to his announcement. She drew a breath and asked, "What do you need Falcon Investigations to do per se?"

"Well, I filed the papers to run this morning. I start campaigning this week. My team is gonna help. The Treasure Chest has become campaign central. I need you guys to do some research on the other nine candidates – mostly their business dealings. A couple of them are shady landlords. I want the scoop on how they conduct themselves and any blemishes on their pasts. The last page in that folder has all of the details. I'm late to the game. There's a 'meet the candidates' event in two weeks that's going to be televised, and I need some ammo. And I'm sure that there will be a debate soon. There should be enough money in that envelope for both jobs. If not, let me know."

"We can handle both requests. We'll start with the debate research. I think I can get that information back to you next week. But you do know you're probably going to get pushback on your run for mayor."

"I know. It's nothing I haven't experienced before. If I win, I think I'll be a pretty good mayor. And if I don't, it's great publicity. So it's a win-win either way. I'm glad you're in and on Team Chaz." She wondered what she had agreed to and whether it came with a t-shirt or hat. She had visions of Chaz campaigning with his dancers.

After Chaz paid for their lunch, they said their goodbyes and she headed for the Mustang.

"Dial Duncan's cell," she said.

"Hey," he said a few seconds later. "I have news. I found a guy who's interested in your tricked out Honda Civic. I'll text you his contact information. You may even make a profit on this."

"Oh good. I have news too. Chaz has two jobs for us. He wants us to research some properties for him for a new business."

"That's easy. What's the other job?" he asked.

"This is the jaw-dropping one. He's decided to run for mayor," she said.

"Seriously? That should go over like a lead balloon in polite Richmond society."

"He thinks it's good publicity for him. He wants the scoop on his opponents' business dealings. Can you help me?"

"That won't take long either. Get me the names and we'll see what I can find."

"You're okay with this?" she asked.

"Why not? He pays well. Plus, it might just be a wild ride. Can you imagine if he wins? That'll be one victory party that Richmond won't forget. I'm game. We can divide and conquer the two jobs. I'll look into the candidates, and you can cover the business research."

"Deal. See you soon," she said, heading for I-64W. She wondered what Richmond would be like under Mayor Chaz. Marco could head up his security detail. But would Chaz drive his gold Hummer to City Council meetings?

LOCALES

These are Real...

Acca Train Yard – This is now the CSX train yard located northwest of downtown Richmond.

Bon Air – This is an area of the city where Richmond residents went to escape the southern summer heat. Most of the Victorian homes in the village date back to the 1800s.

Brandermill – Awarded the "Best Planned Community in America" in 1977, this was the first community of its kind in Chesterfield, Virginia. It surrounds the Swift Creek Reservoir and has a golf course.

Carytown – This is a specialty shopping district on Cary Street in Richmond, near the museums and the Fan neighborhood. It has trendy shops and restaurants, and it opened in the 1930s. It's an eclectic place to hang out.

Chester – Originally a stop on the Richmond/Petersburg rail line, this neighborhood, part of Chesterfield County, is located near Route 1 and I-95. It's home to Henricus Historical Park and Point of Rocks.

Farmville – This is a real town in central Virginia (not just a Facebook game). It's home to Longwood University and Hampden-Sydney College. And it hosted the 2016 Vice Presidential Debate.

Goochland County – Formed in 1728, this county was named for Sir William Gooch, Royal Lieutenant Governor. It was originally part of Henrico County.

Lanexa – This is a small community in New Kent County near Williamsburg, Virginia. There is still a full-service gas station there on Route 60.

Lynchburg – This is a city in the geographic center of Virginia. It's bordered by the Blue Ridge Mountains. Wintergreen ski resort is nearby.

Maymont – This lovely park, mansion from the Gilded Age, and gardens are located in downtown Richmond near Byrd Park. Once the home to financier, James Dooley, the park has a wildlife rehabilitation area, Italian and Japanese gardens, and a petting zoo/nature center. I always visit the bears when we go to Maymont.

Mechanicsville – This is part of Hanover County and is the birth place of pop star Jason Mraz.

Midlothian – This is a town in Chesterfield County. It was originally a coal mining region and home to Virginia's first railroad.

Monroe Park – This is the city of Richmond's oldest park. Located on the Virginia Commonwealth University campus, it's a hub for city residents and college students. Over the years, the site has been the site of rallies, fairs, and a camp for Confederate soldiers.

Poe Museum – The Old Stone House in Richmond, VA houses a vast collection of Edgar Allan Poe artifacts. The house is near his boyhood home and the Southern Literary Messenger, where Poe worked. The museum also hosts "unhappy hours" in the garden.

Renaissance Fair – In the nineties, there was a Renaissance Fair near Fredericksburg, Virginia. It had buildings, a ship, and a jousting area. It has since been abandoned, and the vegetation has taken over.

Richmond Folk Festival – This is an annual fall music and cultural arts event in downtown. The event is free, and it features traditional music from all musical genres and cultures. The venue stretches from the hills of the City to the Tredegar Ironworks to the banks of the James River.

Route 1 – This part of the highway system ran north to south down the East Coast. The Virginia parts are dotted with restaurants and little roadside motels from a bygone era.

RVA – This is a brand for the Richmond, Virginia area. Designed by RVA Creates, it's a logo that creates an identity for the capital city and the nearby region.

Science Museum of Virginia – Housed in the former RF&P train station built in 1917, the Science Museum of Virginia has a planetarium and many hands-on displays.

Sears Catalog Homes – While there are several Sears Catalog homes in Hopewell, Virginia in the Crescent Hills neighborhood, I moved one to western Chesterfield County for Delanie's residence. The homes were ordered from the Sears and Roebuck catalog, and they were shipped by rail. Delanie's Yates model dates back to 1939. (My friend and long-time Chesterfield County resident let me know that there are several Sears homes in the Bon Air area. Thanks, Gerry Fuss.)

Short Pump Town Center – This is an upscale mall on west Broad Street. The area used to be home to a tavern for travelers between Richmond and points west. Legend has it that the name came from a porch installed over the pump at the tavern. When it blocked the handle, it had to be altered to fit under the new room. After it was cut off, it was a "short pump."

Undercover Colors – The nail polish that Delanie uses to detect drugs in her drink is currently a prototype. Undercover Colors is working to develop and market the product.

VCU – Virginia Commonwealth University is a public, urban research university in Richmond, VA. Its hospital and graduate art programs are renowned.

ACKNOWLEDGMENTS

Writing is often a lonely and solitary effort. I want to thank my family and friends who provided all the wonderful support for this book – Stan Weidner for letting me drag him into all my writing projects, Mickey and Sandy Baker who instilled in me a lifelong love of reading, Cortney Cain for all the sanity checks, Meagan and Jocelyn Cain for the social media advice, and Bill Cain for always keeping everyone in stitches. And I appreciate all the encouragement, love, and support from my Bethia UMC family.

I am so grateful for my talented Sisters in Crime, Guppy, Virginia is for Mysteries, Lethal Ladies, Pens, Paws, and Claws, and James River Writer friends. Your support is invaluable! Tina Glasneck, Frances Aylor, LynDee Walker, Kristin Kisska, Maggie King, and Teresa Inge, I cannot thank you ladies enough!

Thanks to my critique group: Mary Miley, Rosemary Stevens, Rod Sterling, Susan Campbell, Frances Aylor, Mary Dutta, and Sandie Warwick for all the helpful comments. And Sandie, thanks for being on "Team Chaz" and giving me the idea that he should run for mayor.

Many thanks to Lynda Bishop and Cortney Cain for all their

amazing editing skills, Joy Pfister and her wonderful crew at Studio FBJ, Tina Glasneck for her design work and wonderful advice, and Fiona Jayde Media for her incredible designs.

ALSO BY HEATHER WEIDNER

Secret Lives and Private Eyes: A Delanie Fitzgerald Mystery

Short stories in:

50 Shades of Cabernet

Virginia is for Mysteries

Virginia is for Mysteries, Volume II

ABOUT THE AUTHOR

Heather Weidner's short stories appear in the *Virginia is for Mysteries* series and *50 Shades of Cabernet*. She is a member of Sisters in Crime – Central Virginia, Guppies, and James River Writers. *The Tulip Shirt Murders* is her second novel in her Delanie Fitzgerald series.

Originally from Virginia Beach, Heather has been a mystery fan since Scooby Doo and Nancy Drew. She lives in Central Virginia with her husband and a pair of Jack Russell terriers.

Heather earned her BA in English from Virginia Wesleyan College and her MA in American literature from the University of Richmond. Through the years, she has been a technical writer, editor, college professor, software tester, and IT manager. She blogs regularly with the Pens, Paws, and Claws authors.

Connect with Heather online:
www.heatherweidner.com

www.ingramcontent.com/pod-product-compliance
Lightning Source LLC
Chambersburg PA
CBHW031236120726
47905CB00002B/614